NATASHA KARIS

The Truth Between Us

First published by Diamond Roads 2021

This novel is entirely a work of fiction. The names, characters and incidents portrayed in it are the work of the author's imagination. Any resemblance to actual persons, living or dead, events or localities is entirely coincidental.

Natasha Karis asserts the moral right to be identified as the author of this work.

Natasha Karis has no responsibility for the persistence or accuracy of URLs for external or third-party Internet Websites referred to in this publication and does not guarantee that any content on such Websites is, or will remain, accurate or appropriate.

First edition

ISBN: 978-1-8380652-3-2

Cover art by Jelly Tots Design. Photographs by Shutterstock.

This book was professionally typeset on Reedsy.
Find out more at reedsy.com

For Bryan.
My friend, my partner in crime, the love of my life.
You always know how to make me smile.

For Angela.
You are not only the best mother, but a best friend too.
Every day you inspire me with your love and support.

Check out the back of the book for your exclusive offers from the author. But not until you finish… you don't want to know the truth just yet.

Contents

Ascent

Andrew stepped on first. With me behind, as usual. We boarded the plane in silence, which was, of late, our preferred choice of conversation. We were surrounded by noise. The whirr of engines and the clatter of luggage. The excited chatter from people boarding and the sing-song hellos from the bright smiled air hostesses as I handed our tickets over. The noise was a welcome diversion from our self-imposed lack of sound. Noise can distract from unwelcome issues, I've learnt.

Most of the seats were empty, a late night, mid-week flight out of season, made sure of that. I contemplated slipping into one of them instead of sitting next to my husband, but changed my mind. That would definitely set the already fragile holiday on the wrong start. Andrew stopped without warning, then tsked when I bumped into him. Row eighteen A, B and C. He had understood then, the words I'd mouthed while he wore his headphones.

Our seats were in the middle aisle. Right on the wing, the part of the plane I hated the most. Although the back scared me on take-off and I always panicked when sat at the front, with visions of being sucked off first. Of doors being ripped open and chairs vomited from the aircraft. Of me as I surged through the hole and free fell in the sky.

I stopped myself. I couldn't go there yet. Instead, I focused on Andrew's back; on his black, unmoving hair and waited. I wedged my heavy bag between my hip and the seat beside me to take the pressure off, while he took forever to put his holdall overhead. He moved with deliberate slowness. There was always an agenda with Andrew, always some reason to annoy me. Andrew clicked the locker shut, then made his way to the window seat with no offer of help. I reached overhead, but my fingers were an inch off. Right before he sat, Andrew hesitated. A look of contemplation crossed over him. A sigh of frustration. He came back.

'Let me put that up for you,' he said.

I stood back but smiled in thank you, surprised at the act of chivalry. At the same time I wondered if it was more to do with the people stuck behind me, who would have to wait, as the small woman struggled to get her too big of a bag overhead.

He flinched when I brushed against his arm on sitting. I tried to remember the last time we sat this close to each other. Before the children came along, for sure. They usually acted as physical buffers for us, or cock blockers, as my husband used to say.

For our relationship was make or break. We were arriving at the last chance saloon. I dreaded the trip, as it would be fruitless. Doomed to fail, the pressure on us too much, to think that somehow a week away could unbreak us or reverse the disintegration of a marriage. It couldn't erase the damage. We couldn't travel back in time and play things out differently. We couldn't change what happened.

We already made our minds up. The real reason was for final proof for the kids, so in years to come if they threw at us how much the divorce hurt them, we could provide the evidence. See? We tried.

Despite going on the break, I still planned to leave him, with dreams of getting away and beginning a shiny new life somewhere, a fresh start where I could be anything, with no one holding me back. Without spitting words at me. Or gritted teeth when I asked a simple question like what he would like for dinner. The same person who walked out of a room when I walked in. That slept somewhere else. That, in secret, despised me. A secret, so secret, no one noticed. Except me. It was hisses and scowls and hunches and sneers when no one was around. It was silence and abruptness or indifference, the latter hurt more. There were no arguments. We acted in front of the children, in front of our neighbours, at the school plays and the work dinners. All very civilised, all completely false, and I hated myself for being that way. It robbed me of my soul, it destroyed my energy. No, there was no choice in it for me, I couldn't take it anymore. I would not take it anymore.

But I had no viable prospects and no income of my own and dependents we would devastate if we broke up. I wanted to be me. I *had* wanted to be with him. I wanted my life but a better form of it and was without a clue of a solution. All the other times in the past, when I reminded myself of this, I focused on being better, of making more of an effort to be nicer and everything for a while worked on the surface. Until one of us remembered and our manners declined again, and hence why we were on the flight together. For me, the holiday was about making a plan. About getting my head together and splitting amicably. That's the best I could hope for.

I tried to relax, I rummaged in my small bag for my new book, bought specially for the trip. It wasn't there. I backtracked my steps: the purchase of the book at the airport shop, the taking it away from the counter, placing it in my bag. Then I remembered, after I took it out to get to the passports for security, I placed it on the counter. Andrew picked it up and slipped it into the front pocket of my holdall. The same holdall that was above our heads. The thought of just me and Andrew on a plane for over four hours; I couldn't survive the flight without some distraction. I tapped him. He freed one ear from his headphone.

'I need to get my book.'

Andrew sighed a short puffy sigh I'd heard too many times. 'Get it then.'

I waited until the aisle was clear. Even on my tip toes my arms still only reached the plastic overhead. The handle was too far off. Andrew stared at his newspaper, his eyes bug-like in concentration. There would be no other way but to stand on the seat. How graceful. I hated how he used my height over me. My smallness contributed to the constant shift in power between us.

'Do you need help?' A guy in his twenties asked. A handsome, young guy who looked at me with a grin and a suggestion he could do more than help. I could be his mother. What did he see? A small, green-eyed brunette that tried her best to still look good? I smiled back at him. Still got it then. The shift in power moved.

'I'll help my wife, thank you,' Andrew said, the headphones on the seat. He stood too quickly, so he threw himself off balance and fell slightly backwards onto the seat. On to those headphones. I stopped myself from laughing. He steadied himself and edged out to the aisle, nudging me with his hip to move to the opposite seat. He stared down at the young man.

'Just trying to help,' the young guy said, putting his hands in the air.

'Yeah, well, if we need help, we'll call a flight attendant,' Andrew said.

He was fuming, I could tell, by the slow way he unzipped the bag, even though there was a queue of fresh arrivals that waited behind. Also, by the *wishing I would die* looks he was throwing at me now. It didn't bother me, I was used to it.

'Sorry. No matter how many times we go on trips, my wife always forgets something in her bag. Every time,' he said. With an apologetic smile to the passengers, a *look what I have to put up with* smile. Always my fault.

So, already, we were going there to the tit for tat. He knew how I would hate to inconvenience anyone. Well, I wouldn't rise to it.

That's the only way I would win.

Andrew found the book. He wouldn't make eye contact and shoved past me, even though I had moved out of his way. Once seated, he returned his headphones and turned his back on me. He stared out the window while he still held the book. I knew I'd have to ask. Another game to play. Another win for him to claw back. The idea of sitting there with him, with only our silence and failures and memories, drove me on.

'Can I have it?'

He didn't look at me but dangled the book over my head, then dropped it in my lap. It just missed my nose. He continued to stare out the window, his breathing heavy with anger.

I'd booked this holiday on a whim, for the same time as the kids' scout's trip. If we stayed, we would be alone together in that lonely house and I didn't want a repeat of last time. *That* didn't go well. So, it was a trip away or leave him. Or a trip away *by* leaving him. The night I received the confirmation dates, I worked up the courage and started the confrontation.

'Andrew, I am not staying here when the kids go camping. I have to have time to think. To decide about us. I can't keep living like this. You mustn't want to either. I'm going to go away.'

He answered, 'I'll come too,' and that was that. Decision made.

'Where do you want to go?' I asked.

He folded his paper. Stood. Spoke four words before he walked out of the room. 'I couldn't care less.'

In all the days and weeks that followed, Andrew didn't once try to give an input to where we would fly to, he asked no questions, and every time I started a conversation about flights or the trip he changed the subject or walked away or picked up his phone and ignored me. For anyone else that would be unbelievable; to go on a holiday without wanting to know. Even in our good times, Andrew was a lover of surprises. On his birthday, he would baulk at the thought of anyone hinting about what they may get him. He didn't want to know. Before the flight, as I drove us to Dublin from Cork, he said nothing. Asked nothing of where we were going. The journey seemed unproblematic when I booked, but I kicked myself for it on the drive. I could have made it easy and just selected a flight from Cork to a different location. Arrived somewhere sunny in the same time it took us to get to Dublin. Right then I could have been sipping a glass of wine on a balcony instead of sitting next to him on the plane.

At the airport, Andrew didn't check the ticket, or scan the sign at the check-in desk. He actually averted his eyes, looked at the floor or behind him. At the counter, he avoided the gaze of the hostess. It was me who handed over the tickets and passports. He wore headphones in order not to hear. Childish. A pet hate of mine. He got the surprise while I got all the work. Andrew went out of his way not to know. He reserved the same level of interest for our marriage.

I read the same line of the first page over and over, but nothing lodged. The unwinding I hoped the book would help me reach was unattainable. My annoyance was palpable. Even sitting next to the man provoked me. Reading ruined. I carried on pretending anyway because I wouldn't allow Andrew the opportunity to say I'd created a drama for nothing. So every couple of minutes I turned a page. The only chance of reprieve would be sleep. I prayed for rest, cursed myself for being foolish. For arranging an entire week with a person I no longer wanted to be with. A person who didn't want to be with me. Why contemplate an impossible possibility? Why try to fix the unfixable?

The last of the passengers filtered through. The flight was busier than I thought; there was barely any room left on the plane. I should have known it would book out. It was midterm after all; the noise from all the kids on the plane reminded me of that. Reminded me of

Sophie and Henry, the children we left behind. I shifted my thoughts away.

I hated flying. The fear was already in my throat, my eyes kept flicking to the exit door. This was a stupid idea, the bad vibes between us could only mean I plummeted to my death next to an idiot. Or was a life with him worse? Maybe. But I'd still take it, because if I stayed alive I could leave him and live too. Never seeing my kids again was the worst horror imaginable. Even the thought of it tightened my already tight chest. Andrew continued to listen to his headphones and looked out the window, or at the ceiling, or at the other passengers, or air hostesses. Anywhere but at me.

It used to be different. Andrew knew how to calm me, holding my hand, distracting me with his jokes and excitement for the holiday. He would squeeze my hand and his hold would anchor me over the shudders. His dark eyes on mine would calm and reassure me without words that the bumps or whirrs or dips were perfectly normal. I would look at this guy and wonder what I did to deserve him and his gestures of kindness. Then the years stacked up and the reasons that ripped us apart occurred. The damage eroded our relationship like rust on a boat. His jokes turned mocking if there was a patch of turbulence, a joke at my expense instead. Used against instead of for. So to shift the power, I pretended that flying didn't bother me anymore. Pretended about another thing. Another on a long list that became easier to ignore.

A man who looked like he was seven feet tall traipsed the aisle and I knew without question he would sit next to me. Still kicked myself though when he smiled and sat. Stuck in the middle with two giants. Claustrophobia clawed at me and the world closed in, the seats and people condensed my space. I tried to focus on the goings on.

The man was the last passenger. The air hostesses busied themselves with their checks, then it was time for the exit door show. They stood doing their over practised positions, tugging on deflated life jackets, pointing to the different doors. Most passengers looked away or read or pretended to pay attention. I understood their indifference, knew it was only fear deployment because if you didn't hear about needing exits then it couldn't happen. If you didn't acknowledge the possibility that the plane you were sitting in could lead you to your death, then it couldn't occur. Those same people would be the ones screaming the loudest when the plane went down.

There was only minutes before the plane would move. All I could see of Andrew was his back, no help to me. For a moment I contemplated standing and pounding on the doors until they let me run out of the aircraft, leaving a gaping Andrew in his seat. That statement, that action would say enough. It would end my marriage right then. But I was a coward. Dying on the flight was still less scary than leaving Andrew.

The plane noises got louder. The signs of panic simmered. Only thoughts of Sophie and Henry would sedate me. The thoughts of seeing them again. The plane moved. It was coming. Slow at first, any calm before left, the simmer turned to a boil, the fear bubbled in my stomach. The plane made its turn and from the lights that lit evenly on the ground outside; I saw we were on the runway. I gripped the armrests as we surged forward and made a silent prayer that I promised, swore, if there was anyone up there in charge, if he or she let me survive I would make the trip worthwhile. There would be a purpose. Either way, I would decide. I closed my eyes and repeated those silent words like a mantra, to distract from the lurch in my stomach, as we ascended. The acid turned, and the bile rose. Different degrees of temperature washed over me, burned inside, flashed in my chest and head, yet a cold clamminess sat on my skin and face in a veil of cold heat. Then we were off the runway. The wheels left the ground. I waited for the falter, the dip, the oncoming crash.

I scrutinised the facial gestures of each air hostess. Were they hiding fear? Did they know that any moment we were going to soar out of the sky? To distract from the fear of impending death, I would need to shift my thoughts to something else, something more important. I needed to decide, but to do that I would have to go over it all. It was time to bring it to the surface. If the flight forced me to sit in the one spot for over four hours, I would use the time to confront the things I hadn't been able to face. My playback began.

Adaline

I was named Adaline after a song. According to my mother, she stood in her kitchen one day eight months pregnant, her legs swollen from oedema. Unable to bend, her back burning in pain from the extra weight. Feeling bloated and unattractive when this man's voice sang from the radio pleading with this woman, this Adaline, to be with him. If she did, he would drop the woman he was with. That a woman could be that strong, that capable of doing what she pleased, astounded my mother. Adaline could have the man, just like that. My mother wished in that kitchen she could be more like her; she rubbed her stomach, hoping the boy inside would listen and learn of the possibility of a woman like that. The song was catchy and iconic. A sing-along that everyone knew, it still played regularly on the radio. After the song finished, she went straight to the local music shop and bought the record and listened to that seventies song on a loop, hoping to absorb this woman's strength, to figure out her secret.

The song spoke of a fire in the woman, but there was no fire in me.

In the delivery room after the midwife handed over her surprise daughter, my mother knew that song had been a sign, and decided that was my name. My father didn't argue, for once there was no protest or opinion from him, the disappointment of having a daughter didn't impress him enough to want to name me.

They brought me home from the hospital to Knockfarraig, a seaside town on one of the many coastal edges of Cork. A picture perfect place in the summer. Long streets that ran the length of the water with smaller interlocking alleys between, giving a glimpse of the sea at every gap. Little cafes and boutiques. Seafood restaurants and cubby hole bars happy to serve traditional meals for curious tourists.

Except for the house right next to us, we were alone on the road. We may as well have been alone, the old man Terence was rarely seen and even more rarely spoken to. The beach only a minute's walk away, just at the bottom of the steep hill and along the path. The path wasn't really a path, just an overused, worn trail.

I grew up with the sound of waves surrounding me, comforting in the day, drawing me near in the summer, scaring me in the winter, when the wind screeched and shook the windows. The silence in the evening only accentuated the sound outside. When the noise came in the night, his noise, I wished for those sounds, I prayed to still hear the wind or the waves.

Declan Flynn, my father, owned the biggest bar in the middle of town. Its wooden alcoves and dark corners made it a popular place to drink. I've heard the bar came alive at night. The private snugs made it perfect for singles to get together. The night brought the young crowd. The day brought a different type of clientele. It meant I didn't see him much. Long hours. Late nights. I loved him when I was younger. I looked forward to him picking me up, to the times he would hold me in his arms. He was tall and lean. Springy. My light brown hair came from him. I woke early in the mornings, because I knew it would be the only chance I'd see him. If I was lucky, if he was in a good mood, he would ruffle my hair or give me a kiss on the cheek. Most times he would pass me without a word, close the door with a quiet click, as if he hadn't seen me. As if by slipping out, he could ignore the fact that I was actually there.

On rare occasions he brought me with him to work and sat me on a high stool by the counter. I got to know the regulars, got to love the eccentricities of men who drank during the day. The after workers who just wanted to forget. The before dinner ones who would have their few scoops and get home for a certain time. The ones who waited in the morning were the saddest, those who stood outside before my father opened up. They were the ones that needed it most, that it had taken hold of. The sociable ones lived longer. The ones who supped alone in the dark corners until they couldn't stand all died early.

When I was very young, I would sit on that stool and feel like I was in the prime spot. I loved to watch. They spoilt me, these men, bought me snacks, always had a word of greeting. I got used to the smell of smoke, of spilt beer and men's tears. When I was older and the interest had faded, when he dragged me there for some unknown reason despite my protestations, I brought a book. One look from my father told me not to move, not to wander. I never disobeyed.

There was never any real trouble. If a raised voice drifted or a scuffle broke out, my father would swoop in. Without a word, he would pick the troublemaker up by the shirt or neck and throw him out the door as if he was tossing a bag of rubbish. I never saw what happened outside. A long time would pass before his return. When he did, he would rub at his knuckles, his cheeks bright red, bursting open the doors as he came back into the bar. His bar. There was always order there, he made sure of it. He was my hero in those moments, for that brief time at least.

The house was old but not dated. With many nooks and crannies; places you could hide in if needed. It was cold, not from lack of heat but from the ability of the old heating system to get to every room with any strength.

The stairs opened out to a large landing. The front wall was a window with a large ledge purposely built for sitting. My favourite spot of all. It was comfortable too. A multitude of cushions made by my mother invited you to sit and sink. There were shelves on either side of the window filled with books; a reader's paradise. Every time I came midway on the stairs it made me stop; the window made a perfect picture frame of the sea.

The night I discovered fear, a roar woke me. More sounds followed from a crash, then a smash. As my eyes adjusted to the dark, my fists balled the fabric of my sheet towards my face like a shield. It had to be a monster. Some indescribable horrific creature that was coming for me. I screamed for my mother and she came into my room and whispered to keep quiet, her long hair loose, her face contorted as she tried to hide her own fear. She prised my hands away from her, but I wanted to cling. To make her stay. To keep her arms around me until the noises stopped. She stroked my face and gave me a reassuring smile, then walked out to the noise. A terrifying horror gripped me that she might never come back. Then I heard a sound I didn't understand. A voice.

'Did you hear me?'

The sound came from my father. A low rumbling from my mother followed. The words indefinable but soothing. I couldn't understand his anger. When my mother came back and lay beside me in my bed, as I listened to the smashing of chairs and kicking holes in doors and throwing expensive frames that left splinters of glass everywhere, and would still pick out months later.

Even when my father was at his worst, even when I knew the damage he was capable of, I always felt somewhat protected beside my mum. Because of her. Because she would stand in front of him and block my view and answer in a monotone, with her eyes averted, displaying no urge to carry on a fight. Words that were submissive yet instructive, 'Go to bed Declan.' Most of the times he would go, walking past us like a robot being programmed, with deadened eyes from his batteries running out, the smell of alcohol wafting after him. I never felt safe in his presence while he was drunk, but I felt her protection.

When you are younger, you cannot rationalise what is happening around you as being separate, because you are the centre of your universe. You think everything comes back to you. I thought my father was angry at me, that reasoning backed up by what he would tell us. If only I could behave better, if only we didn't annoy him, if only we were perfect. As a child, I thought the man had lost his mind. That we had somehow made him lose his mind. That there was something wrong with me that caused the man to get angry. You are not meant to be that scared as a child. You are not meant to know fear so young.

You can probably tell that my mother wasn't very assertive. I learnt from a master on how to be quiet, how to pass through life causing the least fuss possible, knowing it was the only way to survive. My father was the opposite. We avoided him most of the time, but especially when we heard his voice change. A raised tone still sent shivers down me.

The way my father acted in the town hung over me like a stench. Everyone knew I was Declan Flynn's daughter. That was the title I went by. Never Gloria's daughter, never Adaline, always Declan Flynn's. Like I was only property. Like I belonged to no one but him. It filtered down to the other children in the school and Knockfarraig, whether through their parents' fear or just because there was something off with me, they stayed away.

As you can imagine, I was lonely as a child. Except for the old man Terence, there wasn't anyone else around. On one particular occasion when I followed the postman to the end of our drive, tugging at his pants leg to just stay a minute, my mother stood with her arms crossed at the open front door, waiting for me. Her eyebrows furrowed with the expression she used when she searched for the right words. She said, 'Adaline, let them come to you. If you beg, they never stay.'

After that, I would sit on the big window ledge on the second floor and wait for hours for someone to pass. If there was a glimmer or a shadow of anyone mounting the hill, I would run down the stairs two at a time and hover around the front of my house. My vision anywhere but in their direction, my focus solely on the sound of their footsteps, praying they would get closer; my outward disinterest betrayed by the pounding of my heart. The excitement compounded as they reached our door, where I would pretend to play with my dolls or skip with my threadbare rope, never acknowledging them until they spoke or approached me. Afraid that my eyes would reveal my fear of their impending passing. I'd learnt desperation repels.

I practised different tactics in the mirror in my room. Adopted ways of looking at someone without them seeing or noticing. Hours of practiced ways of not seeming so tongue hanging out like a dog eager.

There were good memories too. Of times when my father came home with arms full of gifts. Laden with new clothes, with swinging tags from the expensive shop in town and fancy cakes from the best bakery in Knockfarraig. He would turn on my mother's radio and sweep me up into his arms and whisper to me he had won big. For an hour or two, I would forget how he could be, I would forget the terror that could come at night.

Or the times he took us to the cinema. Or restaurants, although any occasion where he could drink never ended well. Mostly, when I recall the good, I remember the sea. How my mother and I would make the short walk to the beach. All summer with sand in my mouth and hair and every orifice. The strands of my hair bleached lighter by the sun. Chewing on seaweed. Digging in the sand to find the other side of the world and freaking out when I discovered water. Holding her hand as we searched for seashells. My best moment was after we came out of the water, when my mother would wrap a fluffy towel around me. There was an elegance to her, something I've always tried to emulate. She wouldn't look people in the eye. It thrilled me; it was more than aloofness, a movie star in profile always looking wistfully in the distance. The only person she made eye contact with was me. That alone made me special. On that beach, after she dried me, she would sit behind me with her arms folded around my shoulders, lost in her daydream out to sea. I would stay completely still, breathing the moment in, afraid to even move in case it woke her from her trance, and she moved on. A fragment of me left too when she took her arm away.

She was a seamstress. A good one, with people making appointments months in advance to alter and design their clothes. Her sense of fabric and cut reflected in her clothes and always suited to her shape. Silk blouses and flared wide leg trousers were her signature style; a throwback to the decade before. My mother wasn't a fan of the style of the eighties. She was quiet, reserving her words for only when necessary. But she was always there, waiting for when I needed her. My father was different.

I spent a lot of time in nature, in our garden. Listening to the waves. Or the seagulls in the distance. Our garden was my mother's masterpiece. For a child it was magical, with little alcoves and scrubs to hide behind. It was long, with flowers planted at the sides running the full length of it. Several trees dotted throughout, providing shelter on rainy days, allowing swinging and climbing too, and gave the possibility of getting lost and hiding, of exploring and investigating. My mother added many features, a fairy door to my favourite tree, a path of glass mosaic that swirled around a bird bath and feeder, a bench hidden behind a rose bush, a hammock to daydream. A saviour for an only child. I spent hours watching different birds land, scouring every inch of grass for caterpillars, or ladybirds, or various bugs. The holy grail was finding a chrysalis as it hung under a pot or on a leaf, its transparent sheath monitored hourly in order to catch the moment the butterfly broke through.

The sounds around reminded me I was never completely alone; the rattle of my mother's sewing machine coming from her open window. The bees as they passed by. The birds as they watched me and sang.

One of those days, I noticed the apples had ripened on our apple tree. I climbed the stone slab water feature, every year it had been my stepping stone to reach the apples. What I didn't factor was how much I had grown since the year before, how the weight of the ten-year-old me would be too much for the heaped stones. I reached up and grabbed for the nearest apple and the top slab moved like a seesaw with only one person sitting on it. The slab went down and flipped me off onto the glass tiles, slashing my elbow. The sight of blood sent me screaming to the house. I ran to my mother and when I reached her; I wrapped my arms around her waist. She winced. Her hand went to her stomach. I pulled up her blouse and saw a jigsaw of purple and yellow.

Even though I knew what his temper was like, I thought our clashes happened in the hall, or in the kitchen, always with me there, always where he took it out on an object. And after he'd exploded, she would calm him down. I hadn't contemplated before, about the fact she would have to go lie with him afterwards. That he may wait for her. That she may have angered him more by ordering him to bed. Or had there been a pact between them? An offering from her to take his punishment when she joined him in the bedroom. Before, I looked at her in soft focus, like through a filter on a camera. That day I saw the lip puffy on one side, camouflaged by lipstick and concealer. Heavy eye makeup spread thick across the corners of the eyes, eyeshadow in shades of blue, a colour she would never wear.

We did not cry then, although her eyes filled with tears. Instead of talking, she busied herself with stopping the blood flow. It was superficial. Its existence on the surface, like I'd just discovered, was my family. She placed a pack of cotton wool on the table and a bowl of water and after cleaning, held a dry piece of cotton wool on the cut.

I needed to do something, to address her pain, but I couldn't find the words. I forgot my pain. I took a piece of cotton wool and dabbed it in the clean bowl of water, and as careful as I could I removed her camouflage of makeup. There was a need in me to see what he'd done. To confront the truth. I also needed to show her I knew. As I unveiled her bruised face, my mother cried. I like to believe now they were cathartic tears, released because someone finally knew her secret. She never spoke, and I was afraid to question my father even when he wasn't around. Removing that layer was the only way I could think of to help, removing it with as much tenderness as I could. Standing up to my father wasn't an option. Her bruises proved there was no way he'd let anyone else win. With each stroke she relaxed more, the lines of fear decreasing, smoothing out her face. Her body softened with the truth. It felt good to know I relaxed her. For the first time, I got an inkling of what I could do with my life.

Touché

The drinks trolley stirred me from a fitful doze. My mouth was dry, with a clag in my throat from artificial air. The aircraft was gloomy; the light dulled to allow sleep, and most people had given in to their dreams. There would be no point trying to get back to slumber. It surprised me I'd even drifted as I was wedged between two men. The stranger on my left was tall and wide. One leg stuck out in the aisle, his other leg was so long he had to sit spread-legged with his thigh against mine, and still, his knee rammed the seat in front. The arm rest between us had become *his* arm rest, my arm resorted to staying in my lap. Andrew has done the same on his side. I was trapped. I checked my watch. Two hours down, less than halfway. There was only one way I would get through this. I turned to Andrew, who was awake, reading his wide paper. I touched his arm to get his attention. He moved it away on instinct.

'I'd love a drink, do you want one?' I asked.

He closed his eyes, even though he saw me mouth something. A bug bear, another one. A game he played where I would always lose. If he said nothing, if he didn't answer, he could always say afterwards I made the wrong choice. I pushed it down. The air hostess waited for my order.

'Can I get two white wines please?'

If he didn't want it, there would be another for me. Win-win.

I paid the air hostess, an Irish girl, lucky for Andrew as she wouldn't give the destination away yet. I settled back as she moved on. Andrew's eyes were open and full of contempt.

'Why did you get that?'

'Because I'm on holidays. Because I wanted to relax. I take it you don't want one?'

'No,' he said. The way he spat the words in disgust. He acted like ordering a drink was a disgrace. My cheeks flushed hot with anger. I pushed it down. The annoyance tempted me to blurt out where we were going, to gain a little win. I didn't though, I still allowed him his excitement.

'More for me then.'

I made an exaggerated point of shrugging. I undid my table, even though I couldn't lock it in place with the man's knee. Purely for theatrical effect, I placed the two bottles out in front like awards I needed to display. Then I took my time unscrewing the cap on one. Poured it nice and slow into the plastic cup. Threw my head back after the first sip, as if the slightly warm wine was the best thing I'd ever tasted. I hated myself a little for doing those things. For resorting to those actions. That there were sides, and we chose opposites. That the only thing left for us was winning and making the other a loser. I still wanted to win.

Andrew stood and nearly knocked my little table. I was quick though; I saved the goods.

'Are you all right?'

'I just want to get something,' he said.

'You can have the other wine. I got it to share.'

'I want nothing from you.'

'That's true.'

I stood, locked the little table, and let him shuffle past. The tall man slept on. Andrew and I stood in my seat space with nowhere to go. It was the closest we'd been in a very long time. Too intimate to face each other, Andrew stared at the sleeping man, while I looked out the window. Andrew coughed. The man slept on. I sensed the anger bubbling in Andrew. The eye-widened irritation. The vein in his forehead that appeared when he got annoyed. I freed myself by scooting into his window seat. Freedom. I sat and took a large sip of my wine. Andrew sat in my middle seat. I handed him the extra wine bottle. Then the other empty cup. Win to me.

'Switch seats,' he said.

'No,' I said and took another sip.

'Why not?'

'Because you wanted to go somewhere and you haven't yet and I'm not moving twice.'

The vein bulged. Andrew stood, then handed me back the wine.

'Excuse me?' He said.

A dollop of drool escaped from the tall man's mouth. I smirked, took another sip. Oh, Andrew wanted to win so bad. He tapped the man on the arm. The man startled.

'Sorry. I just want to get out,' Andrew said.

'Course,' the tall man said. He took an awkward amount of time with many attempts to stand, then hovered in the aisle until Andrew moved past. The hostess had got quite far, now five rows down. Andrew rushed to her. Tapped her on the shoulder. I saw her shake her head. Andrew's hands rested on his hips. I snorted with laughter. Andrew turned. Stormed towards us, but he didn't stop at our row. The vein and him walked past. I knew what he was doing, he'd go to the bathroom now to save face. In the attempt to convince me that going to the bathroom was the real reason he got up, to distract that there was no wine left. Tall man had gone back to sleep. I laughed and sipped. After a few minutes, Andrew walked past us. To the trolley, again. He came back to our row, grinned with a whiskey in his hand. I unscrewed the second bottle and poured.

Stew

The door opened with a smack. His eyes were shiny, with spittle already around his mouth. As an adult, that's what I remember most about my father, the spittle. How his rage would become so heightened, spit would form at the sides of his mouth and rain torrents of saliva down on whoever was the source of his anger. You could tell by that spittle how the evening would go.

This time, I was on the couch. My instinct was to get up, to run to my room, but it was too late, he was too near and any movement could trigger him. It was better to freeze. Stay impassive. Become like stone. If I stayed still he may not notice, may go straight up the stairs. I cursed myself for getting complacent. Normally as the evening grew later, I would move to my room or if there was something on the TV, I would listen for the sound of the key in the lock and scamper, but that time my book distracted me. It was one of those nights he didn't want to go straight to bed. His head turned in slow motion. He swayed, then on seeing me clenched his teeth. My father was looking for a fight.

'Look at the waster.'

I made an exaggerated point of glancing at the books beside me in answer. I wouldn't dare speak the words I'd love to say, that I was studying all those hours while he drank. Silence was the way to survive. As the years went on, my father got more brazen, louder, more violent. He drank all the time, letting others run the bar, choosing to stay on the other side of the counter. He'd never hit me. Even as I got older and slightly more defiant. Instead, it was arm grabs or twists. Sneaky jabs to the ribs. Shouting and barking orders with a raised voice and eyeball popping stares. The threat he could go further was enough.

I returned my gaze to the TV, hoping he would lose interest, hoping by not looking at him he would disappear. He drew nearer. I could feel the space between us grow narrower, reducing. I tried to keep my breathing normal. It was better not to react. As if she knew, my mother slipped in from the kitchen.

'Here she is. God forbid I may want to talk to my daughter alone.'

'Hello Declan. Are you hungry?'

She held a tea towel. Wrung it between her two hands. It was the only way she gave herself away, everything else composed.

'What? So you can poison me?' he said, then hiccupped. He slumped down on the couch beside me. 'What is it?'

'Your favourite. Stew.'

'Don't you tell me what my favourite is. You know nothing about me.'

'I'll get you some.'

My father hiccupped again. I heard my mum rummage around the kitchen, the door of the microwave open and the ping when it was ready. It was taking forever, I wanted to get away from this couch, away from him. My eyes burned from the intensity of keeping them on the TV, from his constant stare. His mouth opened, then closed, about to say something. My skin prickled in reaction to his scrutiny. My hands trembled, but my face didn't move. It was important not to react because any reaction gave him an excuse. The smell of stew wafted in with my mother. Steam swirled from the bowl. As she passed him his dinner, my father backhanded it. My mother screamed as the liquid burned her bare arms, as the upturned bowl landed on the carpet.

'Get over yourself, woman. Do you hear me?' He stood, caught her by the hair, pulled her onto the floor. I froze. 'Do you see what you made me do?' He put her nose to the stew. 'You wouldn't give that to a dog. Is that what you think I am, Gloria? A dog. You're the dog. You're the one that needs treating like a dog. Eat it. Taste the muck you make me.'

My mother whimpered, kept her face towards the congealed brown mess. My legs and mouth were unmoveable, my weakness paralyzed me.

'I said eat it.' He tugged at her hair again, then pushed her nose into the carpet stew. The spittle was out, foam bubbles splattered down and mingled with the chunks of carrots and grey beef. This was about to get worse. The foam was rising. My chest tightened. I needed to do something, but I was too afraid. My mother braved one look at me. Her eyes like steel bored into my fright. It was enough. It reminded me of the plan. I walked as quietly as possible out of the room. In the kitchen, I found the secret stash and held it like an offering as I walked back to the sitting room. With shaky hands, I made an exaggeration of twisting the cap off, more to conceal what we'd done than anything else. Then plonked the bottle on the table with a glass.

'Would you like a drink, Dad?'

He looked up at me, surprised. For the interruption. For the offer. It served its purpose. He ungripped my mother's hair and sat on the floor.

'Why don't you start in on that and I'll go down and get you fish and chips instead.'

He studied me. Minutes passed. I did not know what way this would go, I never intercepted before, never made a suggestion, never even looked in his direction when he was drunk. This stunned us both. I held my breath as he picked up the bottle and poured. He drank a full glass in one gulp.

'What are you waiting for? Tell Gerry to not be a scant with the serving. I don't want his manky fish. Get me a curry chips and a cheeseburger.'

He stood, unsteadily. 'Do you want something Gloria from the chipper?'

My mother stayed looking at the floor. 'No thanks Declan.'

She wiped her hair away from her face, wiped the stew from her nose with her sleeve. She turned away from his view while she did it because we both knew anything could provoke him. He slumped onto the sofa. His head went to rest on his hand but missed. I didn't want to leave her with him, but I needed air. I rushed to the door. Heard the chink of glass on glass, another vodka being poured.

'Adaline.'

'Yes, Dad.'

I was afraid to turn. Afraid if I did, he would transfer everything he usually lay on my mother on me.

'Get yourself a bag.'

'OK, Dad.' I closed the door to the hum of my song. Breathing freedom, I ran down the hill as fast as I could without falling, with each step, I cursed myself for being such a coward. In the chipper, I worried about what he would do to her. Of what I would find when I returned. Whether it was me, he would blame this time.

I heard his snores before I turned the key. The vodka laced with a sleeping pill had worked. My mother stood against the kitchen doorway with a suppressed smile. We sat across from each other in the kitchen and shared his curry chips, laughing between bites. We had found the secret. A sleeping man cannot continue a fight.

Now that I am the age he was then, I wonder what it must have been like to live with that anger all the time, to carry it like a backpack or a heavy chain around your neck. There must have been a weight to that anger, a responsibility to that role, a knowing once he accepted it he could not change or claw his way back to normality. How he looked at us and decided we were the perfect people to vent it on. I'm sure he probably felt trapped in the marriage and burdened down with a kid he didn't love, having to work in a job he despised. I'm sure if you delve into his childhood he had a sucky one, but I don't care, I still hate him. Because as much as he may have made himself believe all that, he wasn't the one trapped. We were. He had us the way he wanted us, scared and on tenterhooks until we heard the slam of the door or his snores. We wanted him gone and wished for it. Deep down, I think he knew. There was the real problem.

The times he came at me, my mother always stood in front of him. She took my beating; she offered herself to him as a sacrifice to keep me from getting hurt. The guilt I carried, even though I hadn't provoked him. We never did. He was angry because we existed. The fact there was breath in our lungs annoyed him. Of course he didn't say that, he always manufactured a reason. Who left the door unlatched? Why isn't my belt in the same place it always is? Why are we having mince on a Tuesday? You get the drift.

I learnt the signs. My father was an alcoholic and he used drink as an excuse to blame us for his anger.

One night, when I was thirteen, he came home earlier than usual. He shouted and roared, 'open the door.'

We both knew what was coming if we done as asked. If we didn't open it, he'd kick in that door and his wrath would be worse. We looked at each other, first in fear, but this time the fear changed to acceptance. Not of the situation. In agreement, we wouldn't take this anymore. It's funny how you can expect and pray for something for years, but still feel surprised when the moment arrived. The time was here.

I picked up the saucepan in the kitchen and walked towards the door. My mother stopped me with a hand on my chest. She never said a word, just took the pan, then pushed me gently into the other room and pulled the door closed. I opened it and left it ajar. I didn't fight her, the fear of him still overrode my want to stand up to him.

As my mother opened the door, my father gushed in like a tidal wave. The door sent her banging against the wall. Still, she held onto the pan. He wasn't looking for us, he was in a rush and on a mission. There was something unexpected from his expression, something I'd never seen before, so uncommon in him it took me a minute to decipher. There was fear in my father's eyes. He ran up the stairs. I came out of my hiding spot and stood beside my mother. We exchanged confused glances. The saucepan hung limp in my mother's hands, almost touching the ground. I removed it from her grip and put it back in its rightful spot hanging on the kitchen wall. We wouldn't need it now.

Chaotic sounds came from upstairs, from banging and pulling and removing. My father was looking for something. I didn't dare hope. I wouldn't allow myself to. We waited in silence, the only noise from us was the sound of our heaving chests. There was a bubbling inside of me, rising now with every extra bump I heard. Each noise added to the anticipation because this time was different; something else was happening. We waited for what must have only been five minutes, but it felt like I was waiting a lifetime for my father to come down those stairs. It felt like my future depended on it. I sensed my mother felt the same. There was something in her eyes I hadn't seen before either. Not fear, I had seen that many times. Too many times. What I saw in my mother's eyes was different. Hope. I took her hand in mine. Both of ours were trembling.

The crashing came closer and next he was pounding down hard on the bannister so it creaked from its hinges. My father held a suitcase in his arms, hastily closed with a gap in the zip. A pants leg and an arm of a shirt stuck out. Some loose notes fell on the stairs. He didn't speak. I made the mistake of making eye contact. In all the times he had been drunk, he still seemed in control. Even when the spittle and the rage was at his very worst it had felt he had been very aware of the choice he made. That night, he looked vulnerable. In the displaying of his fear, I realised he was once a scared child too, a child who wanted love. I smiled at him because despite it all, there was still a part of me that craved his approval. My father walked towards me until his bloodshot eyes were close to mine. Declan Flynn opened his mouth to speak, but instead of saying a word, he spat at me. A glug of green spit landed on my chin. The ultimate word. He grinned with satisfaction. I left it where it was until he slammed the door, only then wiping it away. You may not believe it didn't upset me. I'd take it again and again if it meant the same outcome. Because he was gone and our life could begin.

Sleepless

I sipped my wine and played back the earlier drive. The journey to Dublin had been a nightmare. Even though I left with plenty of extra time, it started shaky with the emotional goodbyes from the children, and got worse when we got a puncture on the M50. Convinced Andrew was going to let me deal with it alone, I ran to the boot and got my jacket and rooted around for the spare tyre, but he joined me. With a withering look, as if it was my fault, he took over. Still, I felt obligated to stand and watch in the rain, yet relegated to useless at the side of the road. Afterwards, the traffic in Dublin left no leeway to relax. Andrew, dripping until dry, relished my panic. From his hums to the radio and the taps on the window that mimicked the annoying beat, he showed he loved my discomfort. Nothing would thrill him more than to shove my failure in my face. He was getting his speech ready, I could already hear his berating monotone that missing the flight wasn't his fault. He didn't book Dublin, he didn't allow too little time, he didn't even know where he was going. His condescending silence spoke to me more.

It hadn't mattered. The weather delayed the flight by three hours, anyway. Plenty of time to sit bored with nothing to say in the airport lobby with me holding my phone, wondering if I could ring the kids already and embarrass them at camp. To pretend that I was checking up on them when really I needed to hear their voice to make sure *I* was OK. All the while, Andrew ensured he didn't pay attention to the flight screens or find out where we were going, stuck inside his stupid phone, his ear buds embedded in him. I often wondered how he could be so oblivious to his surroundings. He did that in our marriage too, zoned out so I only had one-way conversations. After a while I stopped talking, tired of hearing my own whiney voice.

Next to me on the airplane seat but nowhere near me, Andrew let out a contented sigh, he slept easily, never struck with insomnia like me. Andrew acted like he had no worries in the world. As if his conscience was clear. While I lay awake night after night, contemplating our worries. Wishing a million things could be different. Or just one, I would settle on changing one. All those thoughts and wishes got me nowhere.

His face looked peaceful. The whiskey had relaxed him. As we sipped, both of us curved, became less hard edged. The tension between us softened a little, enough for him to sleep and me to sit here.

It wasn't complete silence. The tall man wheezed on the intake and made a funny whistle on expulsion. Andrew's breathing was shallow in comparison. In our early days, when I woke before Andrew, I would watch him as he slept and wonder how I became so lucky. As we lay there, I would place my hand on his chest just to feel it move, full sure death would take him from me because it felt obscene to be that happy. How can life twist the truth? Twenty-something me would want to shake old me for ruining our relationship. Young Adaline would never comprehend how things could go wrong. I don't want to ruin it yet for her by saying.

There had been too much pain. Pain I couldn't deal with. Pain I had tried to deal with, but still it lingered. Because if I let go of it, I had to let go of him.

I hated the smells of an aircraft, of mingled, stale breath. Or the underarm clamminess. I also hated the artificial air that caught at the back of your throat bringing the taste of dehydration, no matter how much water you swallowed. I hated that nagging in the head that made you want to sleep. The tight, claustrophobic spaces.

What I hated most of all was the loss of control. For someone who lived a perfectly ordered life, that was the most derailing. There is nothing I could control about that flight. A slave to the pilot. To gravity. To machine parts and speed.

A child cried in the next row. From the gap in the chair, the mother's strained face tried to shush the child. I remembered her pain. The eagerness not to disrupt the peaceful journey of the strangers around. The red-cheeked child cloyed at her ear. Her gesture gave me an idea. I rummaged in my bag and only hesitated when I found what I looked for. I spoke through the gap.

'Sorry, hi.'

The woman jerked in my direction, expecting an attack.

'I have little gummies,' I whispered. 'They can help pop the ears. My little ones used to get fierce pain on flights. They used to scream the place down, not like your gorgeous girl here.'

There were so many things I would have loved to say to that woman. How she was doing a brilliant job. How it was the hardest job in the world but also the most rewarding. How she shouldn't worry what any fool on this plane thought, because the only person who mattered was in her arms. I wanted to remind her to enjoy her child's need for her because that dependence was fleeting. Of course, I didn't say any of that. It would only embarrass her and she wouldn't listen. Or it would come across as condescending or as a lecture.

I handed her the pack, and she smiled as she took it. 'Thank you,' she said.

'My pleasure,' I said, and meant it.

Distracted by the offer of sweets, the child's sobs softened. As she sucked, the sobs couldn't continue. The woman shifted in her seat, purposely so she wouldn't stay in view. It didn't offend me, it's uncomfortable when someone else fixes your problem. To busy myself, I picked up my book again, turning unread pages for the second time.

33

The Teenager

The day after my father left, we woke in my mother's bed. Afraid in case he came back during the night, we had clung to each other as we slept. Through sleep crusted eyes we looked at each other in disbelief. Could it really be only us? My mother smiled that beautiful rare smile that became her normal and she moved a strand of my hair away.

'Things are going to be different,' she said, more to convince herself I think rather than me. 'I want to show you something. If.'

She didn't finish the sentence, but I knew what she meant. If he came back. If he came back in such a rage and done something to my mother that couldn't be undone. We took every glorious second of his absence, knowing what it was, a reprieve that at any second could be taken away.

She took my hand and led me out of the bed to her sewing room with her desk and the pair of sewing machines. My mother took a screwdriver from the drawer and twisted a panel open on the larger one. Inside was full to the brim with notes.

'The sewing machine was the only thing I could be sure he wouldn't take away from me. He wouldn't destroy anything he made a profit from.' She screwed the panel back on and, once finished, took my hands in hers. 'If anything happens, use this. I waited for this day, Adaline. Every chance I got, I skimmed some. I upped my charges some years ago and took the extra and hid it. There's more in a bank account in Crookstown. I saved since the very first day he hit me.'

It turned out my fearless father did fear something. He left over an argument. A bet gone wrong. The bar was the barter and when my father lost he flipped. Only it was with a guy with a much worse reputation than him. A guy who my father beat enough to put him in hospital. A guy whose own father was the biggest dealer in Cork. The father was fair. He gave him a chance; if he handed over the bar and left, he would survive, but if he didn't get out of Ireland within the day, he would slice him from ear to ear and kill him slowly. Normally my father would have braved it out, but the man had already taken two of his fingers as a warning.

A few days after, there was a gentle rap on the front door. My mother and I answered together, terrified in case my father had come back, or worse, was about to happen. A potbellied man that my father would have floored in two seconds stood in front of us, I understood straight away who he was. It surprised me that such a normal, unassuming man could be capable of taking my inheritance. Until I saw his eyes. Emotionless. Impassive enough to tell you he was immune to all empathy or care. They said he was a man capable of doing anything to get his way.

'Your father there?' he said to me.

'No, he's gone,' I said, looking at the floor. I didn't want him to see anything but fear from me. My mother taught me well, being subservient could work here.

'I've taken Flynns. Is that going to be a problem?'

'Not for me.'

'Right so,' he said as he backed away. 'You make sure you let me know if your father comes back now, you understand?'

'Will do,' I said as I pulled my mother inside and closed the door.

There were other knocks to the door too. The whole of Knockfarraig seemed to sigh in relief when my father left the town and us. The pies and donations of clothes and anonymous envelopes of cash proved that they all knew what we thought he'd hidden, that my father was a tyrant. With his money and influence and attitude.

Declan Flynn's running away also brought unknown blessings. Two weeks after he fled, there was another knock at the door. A grey-haired woman stood outside. I didn't even get to ask who she was before she wrapped herself around me, smoothing back my hair to get a good look.

'Oh, Adaline, look at you. Aren't you a beauty?'

There was a softness to her. A vague resemblance. Under her scrutiny, in her embrace, with the way she looked at me, I melted into her. As this woman drunk me in, I cried at a stranger's touch. I didn't even ask who she was. Strangers never scared me, it was the people closest to me I've feared.

The woman wiped away her own tears, then nodded expectantly at the open door.

'My mother is asleep. I can call her for you.'

'No, leave her. Let's speak first, get to know each other. Maybe not out here though?'

'Sorry. Come in,'

I made her some tea. She patted the seat next to her when I came back into the sitting room. I went without question. She waited until I settled before she spoke.

'Do you know who I am?'

I shook my head, embarrassed.

'Oh Adaline, what has he told you? I'm your nana. I heard your father got run out.' She fiddled with the lining in her dress. 'You're very like your mother when she was your age. You're beautiful.'

My nana, who I thought was dead, who I'd only seen a younger version of, in a single photograph. A woman with a smile that didn't meet her eyes. Stood behind my beaming mother at her wedding. A woman they never mentioned in the house.

Her hair was long enough to tie into a low bun, a few blonde-grey loose strands framed her face. She held her body with grace. It was easy to tell she belonged to my mother.

'Why haven't I seen you, was it because of my father?'

She nodded. 'I stayed away to make it better for you.'

'I don't think it could have been worse.'

'It could.'

'Did he do something to you?'

She nodded. Fiddled with the lining some more. 'Maybe we should wait for your mother. She might want to tell you herself.'

'All my life has been full of the unsaid. Please tell me,' I whispered.

She patted my hand. 'I never liked your father, and he knew it. Your mother was only a teen when they met, just a few years older than you are now. Gloria was innocent and sweet and so beautiful, I worried about her because she was a dreamer. In her own world. It was my fault, I sheltered her. Made her naïve. Because we made her think love was easy, that all she had to do was choose her prince. He was handsome, your father, I'll give him that. With long brown hair and a cocky walk the young girls love. Clever too, he always treated her well in front of people, but I saw him when he thought no one was looking. He let the pretence drop. After seeing, I couldn't let it go. I saw a hatred in him, for her. There was a falseness in the way he acted. A flashy way about him, like he thought he was better than everyone else. It caused friction between me and Gloria. She was besotted. That man didn't have one redemptive quality, I knew the day would come when he'd show his true colours.' She looked around the room, stroked the arm of the couch. 'Did you know this house was mine?'

I shook my head. I knew nothing.

'This was my childhood home. My parents built the house next door when I married, so I'd moved in there. They'd both passed away by the time your mother met Declan. My sister died in a horse riding accident when she was twenty. Gloria's father, my Tim, dropped dead when she was only two from a massive aneurysm. We had money, you see? Gloria was a catch. I knew it. Your father knew it. The only person who didn't seem to know was her. As my only child, she was always going to get this house, no matter who she married. But when I signed it over to her, I made sure there was a clause. He could live in it but would need to give up all rights. He signed the agreement, it was just before their marriage, you see?'

I nodded.

'He never looked at me again, though. He'd be all smiles around everyone, but he would make a point of not speaking to me. He would look at anyone but me. Gloria didn't even notice. She thought the sun shone up his behind. Everyone did back then. Gloria was adamant he treated her well. Strangers told me the same. I hoped I was wrong. After they married, I saw a change in her. She shrunk into herself. She started calling to me less and less. They would pass my house with him holding on to her, almost pulling her down the hill, her with her head bent, without even a wave. Not my Gloria at all. One day I waited until he drove off and I called to this house but she didn't answer the door. Well, I'd had enough, so I let myself in with a spare key I'd kept. Adaline I took no pleasure when I saw the bruises, and I knew by the way she acted it hadn't been the first time. I insisted she leave him right then and even helped her pack her bags. She never said a word, but she didn't stop me either. We got to the door when he walked in. I dropped the bags in fright. Declan just picked them up, brought them upstairs. I'll never forget your mam's look. She turned ashen. I pleaded with her to go before he came back down. She just kept shaking her head. Then in a whisper she said, "Where am I going to go?" The only place we could go was next door. He came down as calm as you like and said real quiet. "Go upstairs Gloria." And she went, without so much as a backward glance at me. He stepped towards me and said, "Get out of my house." "No," I said, "it's Gloria's house." What he said next sent chills down me. "Ah, but I've checked it out. If she dies, it becomes mine." He told me if I came anywhere near her again, he would kill her. That he would make my life hell until I moved. And by god, he did.'

'What did he do?'

'For a start, he smashed my windows. I would get them replaced and would find later that day he'd smashed them again. Then he doused the house with red paint. All things that were obviously him, but impossible to prove. He would ring the house phone constantly. One night I heard a noise downstairs. Something smashed. I sat up in bed and on the pillow next to me was a knife. Declan left dead animals in my house. More things I couldn't prove, of course. A rotting rat on my kitchen counter. A smashed up bird under my cushion by an open window. A cat with a twisted neck on my doorstep. All random. All plausible as accidents. He terrorised me to the point I thought I was losing my mind. I went to the guards, but it was different in those days. By then he had used Gloria's inheritance to buy the bar and he had pull in the town. He had them on side, giving them free drinks whenever they popped in. He had already laid it out to them I was the disgruntled mother-in-law who didn't want him making something of himself. They wouldn't even take my statement. Then one day I had a call from an estate agent telling me a couple wanted to view the house. I didn't even have it on the market. Your father's doing. I knew it wouldn't end. Your mother wouldn't talk to me. By that stage, he had already broke her down, conditioned her to believe she was his, that this was her lot in life. I noticed the growing bump. Times were different then for a pregnant, single woman. I called to her house every day and faced a never opening door. It got to the stage I felt I was going mad. I'm ashamed to say I left. The day I was moving, I waited until he left the house again and I knocked on the door. Your mother wouldn't answer. The spare key didn't work, he'd changed the locks. I shouted through the letterbox I was leaving and would she come with me. I knew she was there, I could hear movement. I waited and waited but in the end I had to accept she made her choice, so I told her I was putting a scrap of paper through the letterbox with my new address and if she ever needed somewhere to go or changed her mind, she would be welcome to join me. I convinced myself that her life would be better if I wasn't around. That he wouldn't treat her that way if I left. Or if he still did, she would have my address and would follow me. I was at my wits' end by then. Declan had me wound up so tight, it terrified me to look over my shoulder. Even standing there scared me, until I couldn't stay any longer outside the house. I was afraid of him coming back and finding me but I waited as long as I could. She never answered.'

'I couldn't,' my mother said. She leaned against the doorway, her cheeks wet from tears. 'I wanted to. I woke up to your voice. I'd passed out and when I came to I was lying on the floor and couldn't move. He squeezed my throat so hard, my voice was a croak. I tried to call out, but I was too far away for you to hear. My back had locked from the angle I fell after he threw me. I couldn't get up, couldn't walk. But when I heard you shout you were leaving something clicked inside me. It finally made sense. Declan would never get better. It wasn't my fault like he said it was. I didn't deserve the things he did to me. You loved me, the way you treated me was love, the way Dad did too. Declan didn't treat me with love. I knew I had to go, for my baby. I couldn't sit or roll, but I figured out a way if I kept my back straight I could push with my legs and move. It took me a long time to get out of the bedroom. The stairs were like a mountain. I had to pull myself up and if my voice was there, the whole of Knockfarraig would have heard me. You were gone at this stage, but that scrap of paper was my signal for a new life. All I had to do was reach it. I'd saved money. It wouldn't matter if you left, I could follow you once I had the address. Step by step, I got braver. As I reached the end of the stairs, I cried with happiness. Then I heard a car pull up. I tried to be faster. The scrap of paper was near enough I could almost touch it. Declan opened the door. Straight away he saw it, the white paper on the dark floor. He picked it up and laughed and watched my reaction as he lit the piece of paper with his lighter. As it burned down, he threw it at me, its ashes sprayed to the ground. I asked around when I could, but I had to be careful. You both know how manipulative he was. Declan warned people to tell him if I asked about you, Valerie in the shop told me that, mum. No one I asked knew where you went. Or would admit they knew, anyway. That was the way he was, and everyone complied. Everyone wanted Declan on their side. I gave up fighting back after that. The only way to survive was to become compliant, and I would do anything I could to keep both of us alive. You don't know how sorry I was for not getting down that stairs quicker, for not leaving with you.'

My new grandmother stood, and the two women met in the middle of the room. 'That man,' she said, 'he didn't win, we got there in the end.'

They embraced and through their sobs, broke their hug for me. I walked into their arms and the three of us stayed that way for a long time.

Later, as I went to sleep, my mother slipped into my room to say goodnight. She sat on my bed and stroked my hair.

'He did, you know?'

'He did what?' I asked.

'He had some good in him. He was handsome, the best-looking man I ever saw. I would have looked at him forever.'

I sat up, ready to butt in.

'Please,' she said. 'Just listen, it's important to know the truth. Your father wasn't evil. He did many nasty things, but you need to know the whole of him because his blood runs through you too. He was a beautiful singer, people came from all over to hear him. A great hurler. What's most important for you to know is that he loved you. The day after you were born, after he got over the shock of not having a son, he grinned from ear to ear. Every night when you cried, he'd take you in his arms and sing your song to you. He just didn't know how to love Adaline. I couldn't teach him, I thought I could. His own childhood was traumatic. He lashed out all his life, especially to the one's he loved the most. I just thought you should know that.'

She kissed me and left the room and I went to sleep with questions: after all he did to her, how could my mother still think it important that I saw good in him? How could anyone label their actions as love while they hurt you?

Gloria Flynn went back to being Gloria O'Connell. I dropped all association with my father with glee. Nana sold her house and moved in with us and used the money on the sale to set up a shopfront in town for my mother, a proper tailoring business with other employees. Nana took over my mother's role of being there when I returned from school, cooking my dinner while my mother worked. Over the next number of months I learnt Nana lived with the same grace as my mother, with the same good loving nature. Whose presence was nurturing and calm. We spent hours on the couch watching reruns with my head in her lap while she stroked my hair. Other days she gave me cooking lessons. Taught me about spices and how to stack up flavour. How foods, like people, could be layered. Most of all, Nana taught me how it was possible to love someone other than my mother, without being hurt.

I'm glad of that time, of being able to see my mother be the person she could be. She smoked, taking long drags with her eyes closed.

She drank wine and danced to the radio in the kitchen and when she would see me come in, she would pour me a little thimble of a glass and make me join her. There was always music on those days, and I would happily accept her invitation. We would dance in that kitchen, holding each other's hands and twirling with such giddiness we threatened to fall. Lightheaded as the world spun and my mother the happiest I'd ever seen. With a smile always on her face. Her eye contact with others was now unreserved. It hadn't been her way. It hadn't been part of what made up her personality. It wasn't aloofness or dreaminess that had caused her to avoid another's eyes. It had been fear. Of rebuke, of giving him something to argue about, of annoying him. I tried to imagine having to live your life that way, always trying to second guess what would upset another. All the time that was wasted for her. That would have kept her stomach in knots. The anxiety must have eaten her inside. Yet she must have kept pushing it down. Did she ever feel like she was going mad? Back then I believed I could never do the same, I could never hide those thoughts, or conceal a battle of complex secrets. I was wrong. We can all keep secrets. We can all learn to bury the dark in order to survive.

As we danced, I would notice how the world and my body shifted looser. The confines of our life stripped away. That's where the giddiness came from, where the looseness and the twirling in the kitchen originated. We couldn't quite believe my father was gone. I never once missed that man.

Gloria enjoyed going to work, an outside job never allowed by my father. Although she opened out of necessity, my father had spent or lost her inheritance and anything left he'd took with him and her stash would only get us so far. Money wasn't the only incentive, she found she enjoyed being around other people. A confidence grew in her, earning and spending money of her own. For the first time in her married life, Gloria had the freedom to do what she wanted and spend as she pleased. She took pride in doing her makeup, choosing her outfits, doing her hair. My mother was still beautiful, and the inevitable men came knocking at our door. She closed it on every one of them. When I asked her why, she shrugged and said, 'All of this is for me, not them.'

My life altered too. His disappearance coincided with the start of secondary school and brought a chance for reinvention. The secondary school was nearer than the primary, just a short walk along the strand and up the hill. The freedom of being able to amble on alone made me heady with opportunity. Because I wasn't just my father's daughter anymore. People noticed me as a person in my own right and called me by my name.

My strategy for school was to act differently. Even though most of the students from my primary school went there, Knockfarraig secondary school housed pupils from at least ten other rural primary schools. It meant on my first day, in that first class, there was no one I recognised. Which suited me fine.

I used the tricks of my learned aloofness, even though to me my eagerness and desire to be liked was obvious. On that first day, I smiled at a nervous girl with a soft, round face that walked beside me as we went to find a seat. How terrifying that is when you don't know anyone, with so much pressure. Where you sat determined who you spoke to, who you got to know, who you became friends with, whether they accepted you or began the shun. I switched on my disinterest. Used it. It worked. A tall girl stood at the middle desk with an empty one beside her. From the way she stood, I could tell she was someone. There was no fear for her. She belonged there, or thought she did, anyway. The folding of her arms as we approached told me she would choose. Her scraped back hair sat severely high on her head. She'd pulled her skirt up well above the knee. The mascara and lip gloss gave her an older edge. Definitely not usual behaviour for the first day at a new school.

We both walked towards the desk, the short-skirted girl drawing us near. We stopped in front of her. Looked at each other. Gave each other nervous smiles, knowing one of us had to lose. Who would take it? Who would look for another?

The tall girl leaned towards us. 'Not you,' she said to the other girl. All I felt was relief. I took in her heaviness, her limp hair, and from that I learnt a lesson in how others judge appearances. Without one word spoken between us, the tall girl decided who she would want because of what she saw. That sting would have hurt. The girl gave a defeated, sad smile at me, then moved on in her pursuit of a chair. I didn't even smile back. She chose me. For once I stood against someone else and a person picked me. A girl who was popular wanted me, and that was it, we were friends. Now I wonder what Tessa saw in me, what she decided, as I stood in front of her. Did she see a small, underdeveloped girl who tried too hard to seem aloof? I didn't stop to think if I would like her as a friend. There was no summing up of *her* actions. No consideration of whether I actually should allow someone who could treat someone like that into my life. All I cared about was someone for once was interested in what I had to say. Someone my age wanted to talk to me.

* * *

There followed years I wasn't proud of. Years that I used my new freedom and abused it. Years that if I'd known what lay in store for my mother, I wouldn't have acted that way. Years of trying to be the cool kid and ignoring what I felt in my heart. Years when I hoped a guy would replace the lack of love my father offered. Times I couldn't look in the mirror. Instead, I forced the hurt out through expelling the contents of my stomach. Only while I leant over the toilet, the last retch still choking me, would I feel emptied of the insecurity. For a second I was in charge. The purged, cleansed me would last a few minutes until my jumbled mind took over again.

They were also the most carefree years of my life. Spending hours doing my makeup. Teenage discos. Boys not yet men who wanted the same benefits. Sneaky sips of alcohol and chewing gum to hide your breath when you went home. Trying and failing to hide the wobble of your walk. My mother understood, there was no fighting between us.

'The rite of passage,' she would say and laugh as she helped me to bed. I wish she hadn't. I wish she had demanded I stay in. I wish she had said I was acting out because of my father, that I was looking for love in the wrong places, with the wrong people.

* * *

'Adaline, you know you look so fine.'

A line in the song. I felt a thrill. Before this Cian hadn't shown he'd even noticed me. Braver with alcohol, I said more.

'You think so? Do it then, I dare you,' I said, moving nearer.

'Do what?' He asked, his lips edged closer.

'Say the next line.'

We snuck across the road from everyone at the pier. In an alley, he kissed me. Cold cobbled wall against my head. The smell of salt from the sea. The sound of the waves silenced by the clash and slurp of our lips. It felt pleasant to have a warm body close to mine. A body different to my mother's or Nana. Harder. Less pliable. I liked the tingles it brought. I liked Cian. He was in our group. Good looking, funny. Popular. We had flirted for ages. It pleased me the way things were progressing. He took my number after we finished fumbling, told me he would call. I skipped home.

Losing my virginity at sixteen wasn't my finest moment. It was awkward, as we tried to be quiet in case my mother came home early. It was different to what I expected, or seen on the TV, or read about in books. There was no undressing. No professions of undying love. No unveiling of a wanted possession, no interest in ripping off or unwrapping the present he waited for. We got under the covers, removed our pants and underwear. I spent the time worrying about the angle I lay at or bent over while doing positions we had heard were important. What could he see? Did he like what he was looking at? I worried about how bright the room was, whether my breasts were too small, whether my bum was too big, whether even with a condom I could get pregnant. It never occurred to me he should try to please me, that he should wait until I felt pleasure. It was a relief when it stopped, when he stopped, and I wondered what the big deal was.

But. After he left, and I examined the blood-soaked towel, I thought about the significance. How it *was* a big deal, how I had just given him a part of me I couldn't get back. Something bothered me about it, something I couldn't put a finger on. As I fell asleep that night, it came to me. He hadn't kissed me once after he finished, after we got dressed or when he said goodbye to me even. It was job done and over.

When he broke up with me in the same alley we shared our first kiss, he didn't even finish the end of the sentence. There was no need, I knew it was coming. He wanted out of the conversation and I wanted him gone from the street. There was no shock. As I walked home, I felt disappointed. With myself. For letting a man get inside both my head and my body. I learnt there were other things men could do that hurt as well.

Back in the house, my mother's voice rang out from the kitchen, singing a fast song, in tune and in time. I couldn't drag her good mood down. Instead, I stayed and listened against the wall in the hall, waited until I heard the bathroom door close, then I crept upstairs to my room and climbed into bed.

A moment later a body lay next to me, an arm slipped around my waist.

'What's wrong?'

'Nothing mum.'

'Ah see, there could only be one thing that would make you go to bed without saying goodnight. Who's broken your heart, baby?'

I turned onto my back, looked at her, 'Mum, I'm not your baby anymore.'

'I know. That's what worries me. I can't protect you from the people that are going to hurt you.'

'I couldn't protect you either,' I said.

'It wasn't your job to, Adaline.'

'It's not yours either.'

'OK,' she said, propping herself up by her elbow. 'Well, here's the promise so. I may not stop people from hurting you, but I promise to always be there to hug you after. That I can do.'

'Deal,' I said, as I squeezed her hand. 'I don't even think I liked him that much, it's just embarrassing. I thought it would be different, that I was ready, but I wasn't. I should have been in love, but it felt like I had no choice.'

'He wasn't for you, Adaline. You want a guy that will only want you. Who will drop everything. Don't settle for less. Don't let any man ever make you feel otherwise because that's not love. I thought my love for someone would be enough but they have to love you as much back.'

'Thanks mum,' I said.

'By the way, no matter how old you become, even when you're grey and need a walking stick, you will always be my baby girl.'

She held me then and let me cry. I cried for the ending of my childhood. For stupid mistakes. For things you can't take back or make pure again. She listened as I spoke about Cian and didn't knock him or excuse his actions. In her arms, I had no reason to question that a time may come when she could not do that. I believed her words that I deserved more. I believed she would always keep her promise to be there. I made a promise too; I wouldn't accept second best, I wouldn't make choices I knew were stupid, and most of all, I would let no man touch me unless they showed me who they were. From then on, I would wait until someone proved their love.

Descent

The tannoy woke Andrew with a start, as the high-pitched voice from the flight attendant informed us of the descent. To Paphos, Cyprus.

Andrew turned to me, surprised. His headphones had long since fallen from his ears, his hair on one side stuck up and his brown eyes were crusty from sleep but for the first time since our unravelling, wide and eager.

'Did I hear right? Cyprus?'

I nodded.

He weaved a hand through his hair. 'I loved that place.'

I shrugged at him. It was where we honeymooned. 'It was the only place I could think of that might make you happy.'

He scowled. 'You had to ruin it.'

I opened my mouth to give back, but the plane lurched. A series of shudders alerted me and distracted me. The retort discarded and my silent pleas replaced them. Mini lurches made them faster and more urgent. Who was I asking? I didn't believe in God or an afterlife. The pleas continued anyway. The plane veered to the left, and it convinced me we were about to fall. As we hit a cloud and turbulence, my stomach heaved. The turbulence continued, the plane bumped in the sky. My saliva thickened, the bile rose. The plane rocked from side to side and I became seriously scared. My fears had come true. The plane whistled and rattled. It kept dropping, my stomach was on spin cycle.

Andrew's eyes widened, and I thought for a second he was going to say something or grab my hand. I wanted to say something too, but the words were too big to say if we were about to die. The plane dipped, and I closed my eyes waiting for impact; the plane hit the tarmac with an uneventful, thankful bump. It took a moment for my breathing to settle. A determination came over me, I meant what I said. The holiday would matter.

Some other passengers stood up to leave before the plane had finished its movement, eager to start their trip. They gathered their bags, chatting animatedly, ready for the holiday to begin. I wished I could be like that again. I remembered the last time we took the same flight.

The blanket over us. The giggles because no one knew what was going on underneath. There was always a constant need to touch a body part. A hold of the hand. A hand on a leg. A rub on the back. Back then, when Andrew went to the bathroom, I jittered, missing him. No book needed or looked for on that flight.

We waited until the plane emptied, like we always did. In happier times, we used to laugh at the people as they uncomfortably queued in the aisles - as if that would make the journey quicker. While we would wait, choosing to spend those precious minutes kissing or mocking them. Not even trying to contain our smug giggles when we would stand next to them at passport control at exactly the same time.

Being in the middle of the wing, we were the furthest away from both usable exits points so had the longest wait. Still though, I had to fight off the need to stand and queue like all the other suckers. I wanted off that plane. Even though I would never admit it, there was a minuscule part of me that had a niggle of excitement too.

As I stepped off the plane, the warm, dark night caressed me. Welcomed me. As I sniffed the air of a new country, the stagnant smell of airplane left. The air held a slight heat. My shoulders dipped.

I needed this break.

A relationship, no matter how dysfunctional, falls into roles. We were no different, and we followed them religiously. The mum role, the wife role, the lover. There were too many times I slotted into the role of bitch. Into the stereotypical nagging, whiney wife I swore I would never become. With a smug grin and folded arms, I relished the *being right* role when I could say I told you so. I hated that I rejoiced at his failures, but I still did anyway.

One of those roles was whenever we travelled, I carried all the information. Passports, driving licence, holiday insurance. I can't remember when Andrew passed that responsibility to me, I can't recall volunteering my services. More likely, I took up the reins when the horse ran free. Sums up most of the relationship, actually.

On the way to passport control, I bit my tongue as Andrew fiddled with his phone. Was that the priority at the moment? Who would ring him at two in the morning? It bothered me that I cared. His phone was another irritation. He used it as a screen between us whenever I needed to have a serious conversation. Playing mindless games while I wanted to address real issues, like why we slept in separate rooms, or hadn't been intimate in months but I never ever asked the question I needed to because I knew the retort would be the end all, the never going back from, reply.

I handed both our passports open on the right page to the passport control officer. He surveyed me. I knew what he saw: the dishevelled hair, the tired eyes, the wrinkles. I looked older than my forty-one years. I blamed Andrew for that. All the resentment and anger went to my face instead of out my mouth. I resented more that it didn't affect his features; his baby face oblivious to the burdens I took on mine.

At the luggage carousel, we stood on opposite sides. Remember what I said about roles? Andrew stood at the opening so he could be the first to pick the luggage. As if that could make our holiday happen faster, forgetting we depended on the competence of airport staff and the lottery lucky dip of baggage retrieval. We acted with the same eagerness as the people we mocked on the plane. Hypocrites, I know.

My role was to locate a trolley and then stand at the point of damage limitation. In case by any chance he missed the luggage and god forbid it went around the conveyor again. That would really have annoyed him. As each non-Andrews suitcase lobbed out, I could see the vein in his forehead ready to burst from right across the room. That vein being the indicator on how things turned out in an argument, I'd seen it so much in the years we'd been together.

There were posters dotted around advertising the Cyprus highlights, one with a woman relaxing by a pool, that would be me in a couple of hours. Everything would seem better then. Everything righted itself when I was near the sea.

Andrew's bag was the very last to come out. It would have served him right if they lost it for insisting on keeping all his luggage in the one suitcase. I suggested dividing half into each suitcase just in case, but he refused. Not just him he didn't want inside my things then.

A couple holding hands stopped in front of me and embraced. It sucked me back twelve years when I stood in that very spot. When I kissed the love of my life and thought it would be forever. How much we had changed in that time. That girl I was, open to Andrew's embrace, was a stranger to me now. Andrew was a stranger too.

Now on the other side of the journey, with our luggage in tow, we walked one behind the other. We didn't need to follow signs, our memories led us right. The doors to arrivals swished open and a chorus of men with name boards stood in front of us. I spotted ours and nodded to Andrew in the direction that the Cypriot man with glasses stood while holding a sign stating our names:

ADALINE AND ANDREW LOVE.

Ironic or what?

Oh, Mother

My mother got four good years. Four years of dancing in kitchens; of freedom and of fun. Until fear came looking for her again. Before that time, when the threat of my father's return hung over us like a shadow, we didn't imagine another ugliness would come.

It happened in the shower. While washing, she noticed a lump in her armpit. It was me she told. It was my hand she held as the consultant gave her the news she had Non-Hodgkin lymphoma, as he explained to our blank, stunned expressions what a lymph even was. Or what purpose it had in our bodies. When she spoke, my mother's voice came out like a pleading child.

'Will I lose my hair?'

The consultant gave a half smile, an obviously practised reaction that displayed the right amount of empathy without veering towards being condescending. I appreciated his effort, it made me warm to him, trust him even.

'Not necessarily. This type can be low grade, it can be slow to progress. I would suggest clinical surveillance. If it is faster than we'd like, then it is still treatable. Chemotherapy and radiation would be an option in that case, which would mean a chance of hair loss. But for now, I wouldn't worry about that. We will do tests to evaluate the situation more.'

I was seventeen when I held her hand. In transition year. It struck me how easily a sentence can rip your heart out. How a few words placed beside each other in a row can change everything, can swipe the happy cocoon you hung around your family, ripping it in two. I couldn't breathe, yet I breathed for her because she needed me to be strong. In the consultant's sterile office, that was all I could give her.

At least being in transition year was fortunate, because that year didn't matter to the result of my Leaving Certificate. I could afford to miss days with the teacher's permission. Nana helped too, accompanying my mother when I had a project or assignment.

'I won't let this take me,' she said that first day outside the hospital. Her mouth a straight line.

'How are you taking this so well?' I asked.

She linked her arm in mine and guided me to walk. 'Because Adaline, I'm finally going to discover how to be brave.'

Back home, she kept to her word. Would you believe she blossomed? The words 'sick' or 'cancer' were forbidden; dirty words now banished from our vocabulary.

'I will get better,' she would repeat as her mantra. Her fighting spirit encouraged me, 'You will mum, you will.'

She threw the cigarettes in the bin. The wine reserved for social occasions. She read about the power of laughter and became obsessed with comedies; we would sit on the couch and put a blanket over us and watch funny films on repeat. In those times I was almost thankful for the cancer because it brought us closer; our arms around each other without thought, my days of hanging around with friends forgotten and unwanted. Her laughter reminded me that to take in those moments. There had been too many days before the diagnosis without her laugh. In the future, it could disappear. One day we could get worse news. We could end up hearing the words we never wanted to hear.

Being sick highlights an appreciation of life. Nothing else matters when someone you love is sick. All importance whittled down to life and death. I would have traded our house, every possession, everything worth anything to guarantee she would live. Telling no one, I visited the church. We were never a very religious family, only going on the obligated days, but I figured if there was anything I could do to swing the pendulum of chance in her favour, I was willing. Knockfarraig church was on my way to school and if all seemed quiet I would slip inside and rush to the left alcove; the place where the candles were. I would say three Hail Mary's. It was always Mary I prayed to. If anyone understood me needing my mother, it would be her.

'Save her, please. If you do, I'll go to mass every day. I'll give my life to charity.' I'd whisper, then genuflecting, would rush out of the church.

Gloria went to many support groups for her cancer. Some taught her about stress management. There were beauty classes and music therapy and art lessons. They suggested counselling. With encouragement, our early days stopped being taboo to talk about, and she spoke about the anger with my father she had kept inside. Red meat was out, replaced with juices and vitamins and foods with anti-cancer promises. It was all positivity. Only talk about improvement or getting better allowed.

Sometimes, though, I would catch her looking in the mirror's reflection when she thought I was studying at the table. She would stare off into the distance, her side profile still. Unmoving and unreadable. In those times, the fear slipped through. The lack of expression showed she wasn't always positive. The smile drooped, the chin went down, the eyes clouded. I could never speak or acknowledge those times, because I couldn't allow them to become real. I wasn't sure if that was protecting her or me.

The not knowing lingered. Each check-up hung over us. Was this the one that would tell us something new? Would it be today that they punched us with the bad news? But each one was more or less the same, a little bigger but still not too bad. Monitor, monitor, monitor. That went on for two years and then we got the diagnosis she had worked so vigilantly towards. My mother was practically cancer free. The doctor explained with that type of low-grade Non-Hodgkin's it is virtually impossible to get it completely away. This was the same thing. On the bus home, my mother took my hands in hers and she spoke to me through wet eyes.

'I got better for you, Adaline. This is such a big year. Promise me you'll study for your Leaving Cert. Promise me you'll never have to rely on a man to bring money in. Don't make the mistakes I made.'

I didn't tell her what I should have then. That I was glad of the mistakes she made. I was glad of everything she did because it meant I saw every side of her. I wish I said those words, but the emotion of her being better, of achieving our dream seemed too fragile. Yet forceful enough it threatened to spill out.

I was more aware of my surroundings, more concerned about the people on the bus who glanced at us, in screwed eyed wonder of why two women were holding hands and displaying emotion. I was more concerned about us making a scene than what was important: telling my mother what I thought. Telling her how much I loved her and how blessed I felt to have her with me for longer. I should have taken the time to feel every bit of that moment, I should have got down on my hands and knees and kissed the floor of the dirty bus saying thank you. I should have cried big fat tears of gratitude for the time the Gods awarded us. But we all find out the hard way about hindsight.

The Road

Andrew sat in the front with the driver, even though the man opened the other side door in the back. It wasn't a surprise, he never wanted to be near me and we were used to the space between us. The rift had become our natural state, we didn't know how to act, how to be around each other. I was glad of the distance, being close was exhausting. We had stretched the division of our home life to its extremity that I'd forgotten how to exist as a couple. Everything was separate. Separate rooms to chill out in, separate foods eaten at separate times. Separate beds. The only joint activities revolved around the kids and even then, we tag teamed if we could get away with it. The kids. It killed me to think this might hurt them, how the impact of the decision we made on that trip would affect the rest of their lives.

I took a final look back at the long, low rectangular airport and watched the highlighted palm trees doing their swaying dance. Palm trees were calm trees to me, nothing said welcome more than them.

It was too dark to make out anything on the way. That it was three in the morning meant we were one of the few cars on the road. From memory, the journey took about twenty minutes. With the back seat to myself, I closed my eyes, as the amiable driver's soft voice floated around me, lulling me to the brink of sleep like a lullaby, half listening to recommendations of restaurants and local sights.

The turns in the road brought me back. Every bump I remembered, even though I didn't think I would. It's amazing how much you can recall, how much information can etch into your brain and come to the surface years later, even when you can't see. I knew that place; it touched my heart and ingrained in me, embedded into my memories that still beckoned after all that time. I wondered if Andrew remembered that same journey all those years ago. From the jabber coming from him to the driver, I supposed not. I loved Cyprus. Paphos enticed me. The history, the beauty, the people, the food. It was like a homecoming to a place I've never lived. I couldn't wait to get out and discover it again. Is that what I hoped for? That in rediscovering those places we could rediscover our love also?

'I don't even know where we are going. My wife organised it.' Andrew spoke as if I wasn't sat behind him. 'We came here for our honeymoon, but we didn't see that much of the place, if you know what I mean. The place was dead cheap then, I suppose everything is a rip off now.'

His condescending voice filtered into my stomach and twisted it, making me want to heave. How I'd love to take him down a little, deflate the inflated ego that took over my husband. I reminded myself that wasn't the purpose of being there. Tried to think positive. I used to love his voice, a secret tone inside reserved just for me. I hadn't heard that tone for a long time.

In the car, on the drive to the hotel, his voice grated like blades against my skin. Not cutting but scraping, like razor burn. The water came into sight, as much as it could in the dark. The street lights on the promenade lit up the black sea. It was enough. To know the water was there was enough. I relaxed for the first time in days. Years, even.

The driver pulled into the drive of the hotel. The swanky front glaringly different to the hotel we stayed in the last time. This would be a trip of memories, but I wasn't *that* nostalgic. That last time, a basic hotel was all we could afford. It hadn't mattered, we loved that holiday. I couldn't go back to that hotel, I couldn't highlight how far we had descended. It would only have shone a spotlight on how much we needed the luxuries to distract from the void between us.

I thanked the driver and as I stepped out, he rushed to the boot to help us with our luggage, Andrew stayed in his seat, happy to let me take the bags, too busy getting a tip ready for the man. His role. That's the part he loved, the glory of flashing the cash. The driver looked towards Andrew for a sign, unsure whether to hand me the heavy luggage. When Andrew made no movement, instead of handing them to me, the driver placed the suitcases on the ground and gestured to give him one minute. He sprinted into the hotel, then returned a minute later with a trolley. He loaded the luggage, while I gave Andrew dagger looks for just standing there.

'We'll take it from here. Have you got a card if we need to book a ride anywhere?'

'I have his details,' I said.

The man shook Andrew's hand pleasantly when he saw the tip. He smiled at me and waved goodbye. We walked to the hotel.

'You could have helped him, Andrew.'

'That's what I paid him for, isn't it?'

'You can't buy manners though.'

Andrew looked up at the starred sky. Sucked in a breath. 'Not even in the hotel and you start. I can see how this holiday is going to go.'

I kicked myself. Why did I say anything? 'I just want to get to bed. It's been a long day.'

'Yeah, for both of us.'

We entered the shiny, sparkly lobby. All glamour and marble and bright lighting. The receptionist's name tag said Marina, and she sparkled as much as the lobby, making me feel more tired and inadequate. She was swift and efficient and with no trouble we found ourselves guided to our home for the next week.

The space was two rooms, both modern and inviting. I went straight to the bedroom where the giant bed waited. I didn't switch the light on.

'I'm not even going to get undressed, I'm going straight to sleep.' I said, as I flopped onto it. Andrew picked up a pillow and walked into the other room. I heard him open a wardrobe door outside the bedroom. From the sound, I guessed he found a blanket and was making up a bed on the couch. I was too tired to care. Sleep took me instantly.

Head Down

I did as promised. I studied. Leaving certificate year passed with no issues. For me, the hard part was over. We had beaten cancer. The check-ups reduced to every six months. After that worry, studying was a breeze. My mother became quiet in the run up to and during the exams. Despite my protestations, she tiptoed around the house, afraid to disrupt me. If I turned on the radio and tried to get her to dance, she would shake her head. 'Head down now, Adaline. There's a time to dance and a time to study. You had enough to worry about last year. Now it's time to concentrate.' She never relented. If I sat beside her at the kitchen table, even if it was to study, she would kiss me, pat me on the back and say, 'I'll give you some space. Allow you no distractions, that way you can't blame me.' With a wink, she would leave the room.

As easy as studying was, the exams took over my life. They consumed every waking hour of thought, every dream, every conversation. My body stayed in a constant, jittery state. The importance of that time hung on my clothes, in my brain, in the air. The immense pressure created the opposite effect. I'd done the work. All I needed to do was stay calm. My focus became sharp and decreased my attention to only exam relatable subjects. Anything else needed dismissal. Not everyone was the same. As I entered the examination hall for the first exam, the girl walking beside me stopped at the open door. The students behind tried to nudge her forward. She clung to the grooves of the door frame and let out a wail. I distracted myself with locating my number and once I figured out the direction of my allocated desk, I made my way to my chair. By that stage the girl's wails had turned to screams.

'I can't do it.'

'You can,' a teacher soothed while trying to pry her fingers from the frame.

'I can't,' she screamed. 'I can't. Don't make me.'

That's what exams done to some people. It reduced a grown girl to the actions of a child. Her only resort was tears. She was only voicing our worst fears. I couldn't listen, she was making me worse. A panicky atmosphere seeped into the hall. I was afraid to breathe in its vapour in case her fear infected me. I covered my mouth with my sleeve. It helped.

There were no surprises in the first exam, what I studied came up, I answered as well as I could.

The day was bright and hot, as it always was on the first week of the exams; the only guaranteed week in Ireland you could bank on pleasant weather. On that first break, I sat outside on the grass and discussed the highlights of the exam with some others in my class. I closed my eyes after a few sentences. I needed the sun to touch my eyelids and welcomed the air after the choking hold of the hall. Even though it had gone well, I wished I didn't have to go back in.

Time slows in exams. Life reduces to each question. The only sounds in the hall were the flipping of paper, the tapping of pencils, the scrawling of answers on a page. The silence in between either weighted with panic or disappointment or excitement depending on how it was going. By the time the last day arrived and I closed the door after completing the final exam, a thousand kilos of pressure lifted.

As I walked out, Carol called to me.

'We're all meeting in the Kings if you want to come?'

'Maybe later,' I said.

There was only one person I wanted to see. Only one person I wanted to celebrate with. I felt lighter. Life was now for living. With no more limitations for Adaline. I ran home along the beach way, kicking at the shallow water. For once not caring who watched or judged or how wet I got.

I laughed as I walked into the kitchen, knowing my mother would find my soaking clothes funny. The laughter stopped when I saw her. She sat in the chair holding a tissue. The skin on her face a cluster of red blotches. There was no celebratory smile. Just sadness, a folding in sadness. She was waiting. Ready to talk. Ready to tell me words I wasn't ready to hear. That I would never be ready for.

'All done?' she asked.

'What's wrong?' I asked. The exams already forgotten.

'It's come back,' she whispered, tearing up the tissue. 'I couldn't tell you while you still had the exams, but I can't leave it longer. I found another lump.'

'Oh, mum,' I said. 'Where?'

'In my groin.'

'Well, I'm free now. We'll book an appointment tomorrow. We'll sort it.'

My mother's eyes flicked up at me. Full of sorrow eyes. 'I've already been.'

'You went alone?' I sat next to her.

'I had to. How could I put that pressure on you?'

'How could you take that pressure on your own?'

My mother told me everything. How she had taken the blood tests and the x-rays and the diagnosis by herself. In that kitchen we previously danced, she explained how the doctor told her the cancer had already spread from its point of tumour through her blood. How the lymph node had been a good little worker and served its purpose and passed it down along her body. With shaky words, my mother mentioned the ones I wasn't prepared for. Chemotherapy. Radiation. Bone marrow and stem cells. Immunotherapy.

We told Nana that night. The woman shrunk into herself. Curled in. Her hand covered her mouth as if to hide the shock. 'Oh, Gloria. I'm so sorry,' she said. Nana aged twenty years in front of us. The lines of her face deepened; they dug into her skin. Her skin turned pale, the blood ran away from her face. Her eyes turned almost opaque, as if her sight turned inwards. My mother bent to hug her. It was clear Nana didn't have the use of her legs to stand.

'Don't worry Nana, we're going to fight this. Mum is strong.'

My mother looked back at me and smiled.

'She's the strongest person I know,' I said.

My mother stepped back, squatted down. 'I will mum,' she said. 'I will do everything to get it out of me. I promise.'

Nana clasped her hands in her lap and nodded. But the agreement didn't reach her eyes. 'I'm so sorry,' she repeated.

My mother went to the cupboard and took three glasses and a bottle of whisky that had stayed in the same spot for the previous three years.

She poured long and slow. 'To health,' she said and passed us each a glass and waited with her own lifted. I raised my glass. Nana's glass stayed in her lap.

'Mum, drink to my health.'

Nana raised the glass with a shaky hand but continued to stare at her lap. We clinked our glasses. Nana sipped while we drank and the bottle stayed until it emptied.

I found Nana a week later in the sitting room chair with a cup of half drunk cold tea in her hand. Her skin was even colder. There was no point in trying to revive her. Her open, unseeing eyes told me she was gone. They said it was sudden and she didn't suffer. Their placations didn't help because I knew the truth. Nana suffered. Her death wasn't sudden or old age or a coincidence. What we told her caused her to die. I had witnessed her heart as it broke, as hope faded from her skin. The shock killed her. There was no doubt about that.

The loss left a violent, gaping hole. Seeing her lifeless on the chair made me furious because she left again when my mother needed her most. Even though I hadn't known her most of my life, the years I spent in her company created a dependence she'd ripped away by giving up. I'd let her in, allowed her to love me. Allowed myself to love someone other than my mother, too. Loving her meant losing her hurt more.

We went through the motions, sorting the funeral. Keeping busy does that for grief. The choosing of a coffin, decisions broken down into miniature details. Would she prefer this colour? Mahogany or oak wood? A cross on the side or plain? As the impassive funeral director showed us around the showroom, not caring either way what decision we made; I wanted to scream at him she had mattered to us and what didn't matter was what she would have wanted, but it wasn't his fault was dead.

My mother settled on a casket. Double the price of the others.

'She deserves the best,' she said, running her hand along the polished wood.

She cried once. As we sorted through what clothes to dress her mother in. As she laid Nana's favourite suit for mass on the bed. She lay next to it and smelt the fabric and sobbed.

'I can't believe she's gone, Adaline.'

I knelt on the floor by the bed and with a hand on her legs, we let the tears come.

'I don't know if I'm strong enough to get through this without her,' she said.

'You've got through worse without her mum. You're stronger than you know. You're the strongest person I know.'

In the funeral home, she shouldered me to the open casket. Nana didn't look like Nana. Her skin was pale, with a blue undertone. Her knuckles were white, devoid of blood flowing through those veins. Her skin was as cold as steel on an icy day. It was a strange tradition, peering over the dead. I understood the want for a last goodbye but I couldn't understand what reassurance could come from staring at a lifeless body. I did not want that as my last memory of her. What I wanted was for her to open her eyes and tell me it was a joke, that she would help me support my mother for what she was about to go through.

She didn't scare me. Her clothes were her favourite, the pale blue suit bought for a wedding she attended a few months before, where she spun around in our kitchen and asked us how she looked. Her hair perfectly blow dried, the long grey-blonde draped around her shoulders. It was still soft. My mother had insisted on applying her makeup, so the colours were the same. But it wasn't her, wasn't my Nana.

'All dressed up, Nana,' I said. Then whispered so my mother wouldn't hear. 'If you've any power up there, help her live. OK?'

Gloria led the way for what we needed to do.

'They'll shake your hand and say sorry for your loss. If you do not know them or can't think of an answer, just say thank you for coming.'

Countless faces passed by, some known, some strangers. Crushing handshakes that left me wishing I hadn't worn a ring. Limp one's that left me thinking that they didn't care. People standing around the coffin and making signs of the cross and when they moved, I glimpsed her, a blue suited spectacle for every nosey person in the town to comment on. Yet when they turned and offered their condolences, empathy looked back. These people felt our pain. The anger I could deal with, their sympathy I could not. The tears would not stop. My mother slipped me a handkerchief and squeezed my hand.

After the funeral, I watched her weave her way through the guests, greeting and checking if they needed anything. The perfect hostess.

You wouldn't tell from looking at her about the diagnosis she'd received two weeks before. You wouldn't believe she was sick. That woman was a world away from the lady knelt on the floor with her face in steaming stew.

After we buried Nana, something changed in my mother. The cigarettes came back. The drinking became more consistent. She ate what she wanted. Sugar became her friend again. The fight left her and there was nothing I could say because I felt that way too.

On an evening in July, one month since she told me it was back, I sat on the window seat and read. My mother tapped me on the shoulder.

'Will you come downstairs with me?'

I followed her down with a feeling of dread. There was something bad coming. She poured us both a glass of brandy. I waited for her to speak.

'I always knew it would come back. I think in a way I never believed in remission. What I wanted was a little more time. I've thought about this Adaline and I don't want you getting mad or trying to convince me but I'm not going through with chemo.'

'So you're just going to give up?'

'No. Hear me out. The results of the scans came back. It's spread. They could take away chunks of me. They could give me operation after operation and remove the biggest threats first. They could give me chemo, but I asked them to be honest and they admitted it's very slim that I would survive. When I pushed them, they said none of them would cure me. It's too advanced. If there was any hope I'd survive, then I'd do it, but all it would do is buy me more time. Would it be quality time? I don't think it would be.'

'You're choosing to die.'

'I'm choosing the way I die, Adaline. How can I explain this? My opinion didn't matter for a very long time. I was never in control when I lived with your father, I had to do whatever he demanded. These last few years I learned I loved having a choice. Now, I get to choose. I can do what they suggest, where life will become hospital appointments and stays and operations and sickness from the medications before I die then, anyway. I'm tired of thinking about being sick. I want to live for however long I've left. I want to enjoy the rest of my life.'

'Mum, please. I can't lose you.'

She cupped her hands around my face. 'My love, nothing is certain in this world. I could have walked out the door today perfectly healthy and crossed in front of a truck and had no time to say goodbye. This way we can take in every moment. It's a blessing, you'll see.'

At first we made an effort. We planned nights out, eating in restaurants, going to the cinema and theatre. Dancing anywhere we could. We spent days on the beach, where we shook off our layers and ran as fast as we could, then dived in. As we dried, I sat behind and wrapped my arms around her and held on tight as her shoulders rocked with sobs. The role reversal apparent, it was my time to help her through.

She saved us that, saved us years of operations. She also took away days and months of determination as we vowed to fight. Denied us hope but also removed the hopelessness as she picked out clumps of hair from her clothes, from her bedspread, from the floor. She couldn't cancel the inevitable pain, though. Unlike the hospital visits, and even though she said she prepared for what was coming, Gloria couldn't avoid the overwhelming sadness of her final diagnosis. The words that still brought me chills when I heard them now: *Terminal. Palliative care. Management of pain.*

That day we went straight home and lay in her bed, where I pulled the sheets over us and we stayed there, unmoving, lost in our own thoughts. In the darkness, when I thought she had fallen asleep, she spoke,

'Please don't worry about me, Adaline. I've loved my life.'

'Are you scared?'

'A little. What if I've lived my life all wrong? Not followed certain rules. Not been religious enough. I've made plenty of mistakes.'

'You've been a brilliant mum.'

She lay on her side, to face me even though we were in darkness, her breath close to mine. 'I have one regret. I should have left your father the second I found out I was pregnant. Everything before that I would never change because he gave me you, and you are the very best thing that happened to me. But I should never have forced you to witness the way he was, I should have ran before you knew him. I hoped we could change him, that the love of his family would make a miracle. That was too much to put on you. All those years I stayed, made you stay. I worry you'll bear the scars of his presence. That he embedded into your bones, that he caused tiny fractures that will one day splinter and shatter if too much pressure is on you. Like it did to me. Don't hold in the hurt until it metastasizes. That's what caused them, I'm sure. Lumps of resentment and hurt formed that I pushed down for so long they had to get out somehow. I felt those lumps inside me before they existed. They had to grow because I didn't learn how to let go of them. By the time I did, they'd grown too much. They'd burrowed their way into nodes, made their moves, attached to places we'd never expect to find them. Please, Adaline, don't be like me. I see the way you distrust people. How you are afraid to meet new friends. Go out and love Adaline. I don't want him to ruin your life. Or get ruined by not fixing me.'

'He won't ruin anything, I won't let him. I am your child, not his. You give me enough love for two parents. More. Regret nothing, Mum, please.'

'Promise me when you meet a guy you won't just listen to his words. Watch his actions. I never did, I fell for the lines, heard only what I wanted to hear. A person can learn the right things to say. It's in their actions you really discover what's in their soul.'

'I promise.'

The next words came out in a whisper.

'I'm going to a hospice. It's already arranged. I want only happy memories of me here.'

'Mum.'

'The hospice will know what needs doing. You can be my daughter, not my carer. That's how I want it to be.'

I nodded. Afraid if I tried to speak, the tears would come.

'But before that, before I give in to it, I want one more day. One day where we take it all in. I want to get up before the sunrise and watch it from the garden. A day with my daughter where we go out for a meal and eat whatever we want. All our favourite foods, until we burst. Then I want to sit on the beach with you. You Adaline, the love of my life. And when the sun sets, we will pop a bottle of champagne and toast to life and death.'

'Done mum. Whatever you want.'

I didn't dare move. We fell asleep with our limbs entwined and stayed that way all night. Before the morning began, I stirred when she tiptoed to the bathroom and placed my hand on her pillow and felt damp cloth. There were no tears from me, I knew what she needed me to be by then.

The day wasn't perfect. The reality didn't match the dream. She only managed a few bites of food. She tried to be cheery, but how could she be, really? I watched my mother as she stared out at the water. As she said her last goodbye to the sea. The champagne didn't bring the celebration she wished for. We sipped in silence, the sadness too unbearable for words.

In the hospice, as I watched her slow decay, the weakening of health and will, I understood what she meant about the knowledge of her death being a blessing. For me. It allowed me the time to come to terms with her passing. It couldn't be a blessing for her. Towards the end, after watching her suffering dragged out, I wished for her death every second. I couldn't stand her agony any longer. Or her fear. It was present behind the flickering eyes. If there was somewhere Gloria could run away to she would have, and I'm ashamed to say that gave me hope because that meant there was still fight left in her. Where there is fight, there is hope and I hoped for a miracle.

Every day when the nurses came to check, or when someone from Knockfarraig or her tailor's shop visited, once reassured that they wouldn't leave until my return, I ran down to the chapel and bargained. I made pleas and wishes. Prayed and begged. A calmness came while there. It helped me cope when she groaned. Those times gave me the strength to continue when she would look straight at me but not see, too lost in her pain, in her thoughts or depression. The unfairness of it would gather and form a knot in my chest.

It was when the defeat came that I worried. When the fear left. When she deflated and gave in. New symptoms and fresh moans stacked up to form until I realised she wouldn't ever leave that hospice or even that bed. To see her swollen, her cancerous nodes expanding and distorting her beautiful body. Never again would she be the Gloria I once danced with. It hurt to watch. Her apologetic glances, as if it was her fault, hurt even more.

One day, in the middle of August, I placed an unread piece of paper in her hands. What was wrote held no interest for me.

Her eyes didn't give any sign at first and I didn't hurry her. My mother, who quit school before her exams to spend a life with my father, needed the moment. Then the reaction I hoped for came. A cracked lipped smile spread across her.

'Oh Adaline. Well done,' she said, even though the words came hard now.

I didn't tell her I already deferred. Or that the only reason I applied for fashion was to follow in her footsteps, with dreams of working together. There was no point if she wouldn't be alive to see it.

They say the dying leave when you aren't with them; if you pop to the shop or get some food or go home to get a change of clothes. Knowing this, despite the reprieve I prayed for, I wouldn't take any chances. I never left my mother's side. Even going to the bathroom, I left the door ajar and talked to her incessantly because the shame of someone walking in and seeing me while I urinated was less awful than my mother dying. I needed her to stay the longest time she could, to drag out every second. It was selfish, and I knew it. I wanted longer, regardless. To see this woman once vibrant and kind, as she lay disrobed of her elegant clothes, mortified at having to resort to being cleaned and changed. Stripped of her freedom, of her body as she knew it. The face in the mirror, not her own. It took every wonderful part of her and ate into it, consumed her bit by bit until all it left was a shell with a slight resemblance.

I didn't hold on just for selfish reasons. I hoped for the perfect moment when I could tell her all she meant to me. When she would recognise those words and with it, we would both accept it was time. The movie death. The tearjerker goodbye. I didn't reckon on how much pain she would be in without drugs; how much cancer hurts. So the nurses directed me to increase her morphine, and I agreed. My mother became sluggish and incoherent while still trying to force words out that would take hours on my part to decipher. I struggled with that. My mother, so present in consciousness, in life. Would she have opted for the drugs if they asked her instead of asking me? Would she have spent her last few days coherent but in agony? This is something I carry. I made my choice, I couldn't live with the sight that I caused her any more pain. Only when I'm dying, will I know. When they drug me to ease *my* pain and I want to say words that won't leave my mouth and realise it's too late.

You always think you have more time than you do to say the things that matter.

So, instead of a quick death, I watched her die slow. I wouldn't allow her to leave on her own, even though her journey afterwards wouldn't include me. I wouldn't sacrifice a second less than the reaper allowed. So I sat and held her hand as she gargled, and her breath rattled in her emptying chest. There is no other sound like the breath of the dying. It is distinct and abnormal and unforgettable and always the last memory.

There were no loud declarations of love. My mother died the way she lived, opening her eyes once to look at me. She gave a slight smile, a smile that told me more than any words could: she loved me, she had always loved me, and she knew I loved her back. That it was time to go. With that, she closed her eyes. I listened as the shallow breaths became shallower. She left me with a quiet dignity because she knew no other way.

After the nurse confirmed her death, I stayed on. I didn't want to leave her alone. I stayed with her until the nurse put a hand on my shoulder. A hand that told me it was over, it was time to leave. I looked at that nurse with raw, swollen eyes.

'She was all I had left.'

'I'm sorry,' the nurse said. I could tell she meant it. There were no words that could comfort. Telling me how much my mother loved me was just a reminder her love wasn't available anymore. She was no more and with her, her love left too.

The only two people who loved me were gone. One already in the ground, the other soon to join her. The woman who held me when I was sick, who rubbed my back when I was sad, who scooped me up when I came home and cried because no one wanted to play with me, who fed me at her breast, who sang me to sleep at night. Who held me in the dark when I was afraid my father would come in. Now no more.

By then, the law deemed me an adult, able to live an existence without another, but it took everything. It was only me and her in life, with the brief time with Nana in between. Her funeral passed in waves of pain. To this day, I still do not know how I was capable. Many came, many helped, no one significant stuck in my memory. It reduced my vision. The edges of my sight became soft and out of focus. It was hard to concentrate on anything but minute details. The feel of the soft fabric of my dress between my fingers. The nasally voice of the priest. The colour of the coffin. The taste of tepid tea.

The one thing that stood out was later, as the night progressed, Tom, the owner of the Kings bar turned to me and said: 'Your father was the biggest prick I ever met.'

After, a hush fell in the bar as the crowd waited for my reaction. I lifted my full glass and looked Tom in the eye.

'I'll drink to that,' I said and drained every last drop.

My mother helped as much as a dead woman could. Even in certain mortality, I was always at the forefront of her plans. She organised as much as possible, with a stack of paperwork tied together on her desk next to her sewing machine, with a note displaying her neat, laboured handwriting: *'Open after I'm gone.'*

Of course, she had known when she left for the hospice she wasn't coming home. The stack contained all the insurance documents and bank details, with enough in her account that I could pay for her funeral and get by until the insurance kicked in. It was never enough to counter the loss, but I found myself at nineteen, alone, but a homeowner.

The safety of money allowed me to descend into depression. I could lie in bed all day and sleep. I could wake up in the middle of the night and watch brain cell dissolving TV and zone out. Because thinking was the enemy. Thinking meant the reminder of loss. That year I never saw daylight, never once opened the curtains, only shopping for food or alcohol at night. Everything became weighted. My steps dragged. Motions harder to manoeuvre. My voice developed a thickness to its lilt, thickened with pain. Why after everything she went through, did my mother have to die? She had suffered alive. I suffered alive.

The agony of her loss didn't get easier, but after months of doing nothing, I needed to feel a want. The human spirit isn't meant to stay alone. To stop the thoughts of my mother lying dead in that bed, I needed to do *something*.

Small steps were taken. My room first. I bundled up anything I didn't need. Same with the kitchen, then the bathroom, all the areas I couldn't ignore. Mundane tasks gave me satisfaction: the clearing of cobwebs, the emptying of clutter, the reward of seeing handles sparkle, cleansed of my accumulated fingerprints.

I avoided my mother's room for a long time until its calling became too strong; until I could ignore it no longer. It was time to confront the ghost. When I opened the door, she was back with me. The smell of her perfume in my nostrils. The colours she chose on the walls, her yellow flowered bedspread, everything in the room a reminder of her. That day it was enough to lie in her bed and smell her pillow. To pull the duvet she had slept under, over me. I spoke to my mother in that bed as if she were still there. Lay the other pillow under the duvet and pretended she was lying next to me. The night took me that way.

As I slept, my mother stood over me. With a smile I missed, she stroked my face.

'Find me, Adaline,' she said. 'I'm here.'

Even as I slept, I knew it was a dream, but the next day her words stayed. A new energy came on me and I opened her wardrobes. It was too much to give the clothes away, too soon still for that. But there was pleasure in going through her photo albums, flicking through times when someone caught us mid hug, or mid laugh, or mid breath. Before.

'What do you want to tell me, mum?' I asked as I stroked a picture of her face. How I missed her. The silence in that room was too much.

Her jewellery box on top of her drawers called to me. I ran my fingers along the contents. Her wedding ring, long discarded; there was no way she would have wanted to be buried wearing it. Her emerald drop earrings, her favourite. My favourite too. I slipped them in my ears. All this time I had not thought of them. It made me excited for what else I may find in her room. Under the bed lay stacked perfumed boxes of my baby clothes, memories stored away for me to find. I held them up to my nose and even though they tore at my heart, the tears never came. The search continued behind windows, under her mattress, in the pockets of her clothes. It was in her top drawer I discovered my mother's gift. A note. With my name on it.

I sat on the bed and opened it with shaking hands.

Adaline,

I know it will be hard after I've gone, but I want you to be happy. Because you made me happier than I ever thought was possible. I'm sorry I didn't encourage you more to make a life outside of us because maybe it wouldn't be so hard on you. But you were my life. Everything involving you brought me joy. Promise me you'll be happy. For me. Please live for me. Love for me. I don't know what awaits me, but I would like to believe I'll get to see what happens in your life. That I will get to live through your happiness. I swear if I can, I will. I love you, Adaline.

My body folded in on itself and I slid off the bed onto the floor. Her words couldn't even seep in. All I felt was the loss. That night the grief seemed to stack up and take me over and I cried for my mother. Cried that I wanted to join her. That life wasn't worth staying for. For the unfairness of God or whoever was in charge, to let a woman, my mother, Gloria, finally have freedom and then take away that happiness. To take away the only chance of joy. The tears came because I missed her. For the fear of doing *anything* alone without her. With rage about her painful outcome instead of my father. The tears fell until there were none left. As I sat on my mother's bedroom floor with the note still in my hand, I emptied everything.

The next morning the sunlight snuck into a gap in the curtain and for the first time since she died I pulled them open. With puffy eyes I squinted, then let in fresh air, the window latch stuck from lack of use. I gathered up my towel and put my bathing suit on under my clothes, and I set out on the short walk to the beach. Dropping my things on the sand, I ambled to the water and collapsed into it and tried to cleanse the pain away. I gave myself to it. The water pounded me, covered me, sending me head over heels, but once done, it pushed me to safety; to its sand. Then I swam.

It was a new beginning that day. It wasn't a goodbye. Just conscious movement. My mother's suffering deserved more. I owed it to her to live. I went home and applied to become a nurse.

When my mother began to die in that hospice, as her body embarked on its journey of disintegration, I witnessed the different strangers coming in and out of the room. Doctors and nurses so accustomed to the role they only saw my mother as something to observe, as if she were solely the cancer that was eating in to her, watching emotionless as they recorded the inevitable progression. There were others who were kind, who called us by our names, who recognised the people behind our titles. Who seemed to share and understand our pain and treat us with dignity and respect. Who listened to our wishes. They were the pioneers for my career decision, my reason I became a nurse, because I wanted to be someone like them. I wanted to be there for people's last hours. I wanted to give a fraction of light to their fear, to the darkness. Everyone needs kindness when they suffer.

Sunshine

I woke to a new day. A sunny, fresh day with opportunity in front. The inevitable excitement bubbled in me as it always did at the start of a holiday before boredom and disappointment set in. The sleep had done what it meant to. I walked out of the room to see Andrew fast asleep on the couch, his too tall frame causing one leg to hang out on the floor. He'd feel that later. He looked like a stranger to me, really. The days of knowing what he thought or cared about had somehow melted away. What I knew was I wanted a nice day.

I checked my phone, nine in Paphos, which meant it was only seven in the morning in Ireland, my brain still on school run time. What were the kids doing now? The thought brought an emptiness to my gut. Probably eating breakfast around the campfire. I hoped it didn't rain the whole time; nothing makes a kid more miserable than being soggy in a damp tent. If they were nervous kids, I wouldn't have dreamt of leaving, but I knew the only issue for them would be coming home. They needed a break as much as us. When I'd talked to Ken, the Scout leader about my plans, he'd reassured me, if in the event something happened, they were the best people in a crisis. There were flights from Cyprus at least twice a day. I could get to my babies in nearly the same time it would take to drive to where they were from Cork. Annie was on call if I needed her. I prised my clingy fingers away from the phone.

I picked up my suitcase dumped by the door and rolled it into the bedroom, unconcerned about the noise. Nothing would wake a sleeping Andrew. I unzipped the case and selected a summer dress and wedges. I smoothed my unruly hair back into a bun. The off the shoulder dress would do. I grabbed some cash and slipped out of the room on a mission. From the lift, an arrow gave directions to the breakfast area where I waited, as the sign requested. The room was a cacophony of scrapes from forks and knifes on plates. Of slurping of tea and coffee. Of laughter from people relaxed and enjoying their life. I waited. Although I couldn't resist peeking around the sign, where a massive buffet displayed cooked meats and eggs and pastries. After a minute, the maître d strode towards me.

'Hello, sorry for the wait,' the young man said with a smile. He smiled at me as if he knew me. His dark curly hair framed brown eyes. A younger, darker skinned version of Andrew. He wore an expensive fitted black suit jacket and trousers with a white shirt.

'Hello. No need for sorry, I can see you're busy. I was wondering, we got in late last night. Is it OK if I order breakfast and you send it to the room later?'

'Of course. What would you like?'

'That is the question. Everything looks tasty.'

'Leave it to me. What time would you want it?'

'Whenever it suits. Leave it an hour or as late as you can. Breakfast for two, please. For me and my husband.'

His eyes flickered to my ringless wedding finger. What did that say to people? I took the rings off when my hands became swollen while pregnant. Then I didn't wear them in case they scratched the babies. The babies were now in double digits.

'Thank you, Nicholas, is it?' I said, pointing to his name tag.

'Yes, Kyria.'

'Kyria?'

'Like Madam.'

'Kyria is nicer than Madam. Please call me Adaline though.'

'Ah, like the song.'

'Yeah, like the song.'

Nicholas left singing: 'Oh Ad-da-line.'

The reception area was full of people. With a long line of excited holiday makers, comers rather than goers. I weaved past bags and bodies. Marina, while still busy, waved at me from behind the desk. How was she still here? I walked past her and into unexplored territory. Down a ramp that led outside to a flowered roof of intertwined purple blossoms. Shades of pink shadows floated on my skin. The sun was already strong. On leaving the walkway of flowers, my wedged feet touched smooth stone. Which led to the biggest pool I'd ever seen, made to appear as if it sloped off into the sea. The result was the sight of various blue for miles. Elegant canopy beds dotted around in a square surrounding the pool, their chiffon drapes billowing in the breeze, inviting me to lie down. Those calming palm trees dotted in between. Even the less important, peripheral loungers were cream rattan bases with dark grey, full length cushions, no beat up old stackable sun loungers here. It was opulent and inviting. I breathed out a little of my weariness. Worth every penny.

There was a song playing in the background, adding to the holiday feel. A mother dipped her baby's feet into the water. An elderly couple sat straight in front of me. The woman fussed around the man. He sat, docile, with his eyes closed as she covered him in sunscreen. Feet and legs first, back next, then his chest. She even applied it to his face with gentle, careful strokes as if he was her child, incapacitated of doing those simple things himself. Once finished, she kissed him on the top of his head. He responded with a rub on her arm. It caught me in the throat.

That was love.

Their version of it, anyway. What was love for me? For Andrew? I didn't know the answer anymore. I had split and lost myself. This trip I would find it again. Find me again.

Closing Doors

The grief didn't just stop. It stayed and became comfortable. Became a companion. Being a student nurse kept me busy, and I welcomed the distraction. It was the moments when I rested I disliked. That was when the pain devoured me. I would stare at the walls of the house she had loved so much she never ran from, that she worked so hard to keep, that she brought me home to when her life seemed hopeful and full of promise. The house they entered after their wedding day before the abuse started. Every room reminded me of her, still full of her love, that I had to shut the doors. Afraid if I opened them, the draughts would carry the essence of her away. Knowing if I opened them, I would let in the pain again and it would take me over. If I succumbed, if I allowed myself to feel the complete pain, a worse depression would floor me. My grief for her made me light-headed. It stuck in my throat, not sore but just there, as if I swallowed something that lodged and wouldn't leave. I carried it with me, affecting my eating, my speech. A darkness shrouded and shrivelled me with such intensity, I barely remembered how to function. I spent my days taking in information. Then once home, I'd climb into the only bed in the only bedroom I'd allow myself into, where I would pray that sleep would take me.

Those first two years of nursing, my grief left no energy for anything but study, and I welcomed that, invited that, becoming top of the class. I loved learning about the anatomy. The mechanics of the body fascinated me. The different systems and how they functioned, the reasoning behind how all the cogs worked. Later, discovering the medicine that would counteract the issues. Those two years were the loneliest of my life, even though all my life I had been lonely. Surrounded by a class of others, there was a void hollowed out from where my mother had been and nothing or no one could fill it. The other student nurses tried to get me to join them on nights out, but fun wasn't an interest of mine. I didn't want to get to know them or feel the guilt of laughter. There was only enough room for one emotion and I chose sadness.

The only other choice I made was to just keep my head down and study. To exist and hope the magic of time made things a little easier. The sense of loss didn't get easier. But the shock of the loss dulled, the reeling and the panic of it tamed. The human condition is built to adapt, and I did. With slow gasping steps, I learnt to survive without her love, without my mother's protection.

As you get older, there's this misconception that your body sags, but I haven't found that to be the case. Rather, you stretch. Your body, like your life, stretches and expands. I lamented my thighs in secondary school, yet I would kill for those legs now. I wish I could go back in time and tell that girl now what I know. That she doesn't have to do it; putting her fingers down her throat won't uncover the happiness she's searching for. That all she's doing is trying to claw back a little control of her life. I'd tell her being thin won't make it easier, I found that out when I forgot to eat after my mother's death and any excess on my body gnawed away, until I believed I wasn't really there anymore. I wish I could tell that thin girl to love herself. I tell the today me to try even now.

To prise me out of the bed, I followed a regime. Alarm set for the same time every morning. A shower before anything else. Forced myself to eat something before I left the house. Committed to walk the beach at dawn before catching the bus to the university. It helped. I looked forward to that walk. When I saw the sunrise, it was hard to feel alone. A good start to my day.

It was on one of those mornings I noticed marks in the sand. Carved words into the wet. There was no one near.

What a great day to be alive!

The words might as well have punched me. I walked to a dry patch and sat on my leather bag, in order to not get sand all over me.

'What a great day to be alive,' I said.

My mother might as well have spoken to me. I hadn't kept my promise. I wasn't living life to the full. Or honoring her. My day's priority was only concerned with going through the motions, a half existence. I wasn't diving in headfirst to opportunity; my toes were barely dabbling in the water. What would she have given to see that dawn? How much would she have wanted to sit beside me on the sand now? I closed my eyes and remembered those days again on the beach. With her behind me, when I was afraid to move. Even then, I'd known what time I had with her was limited.

I hadn't done what she asked of me in her note. While I watched the waves, I told myself the truth. I wasn't happy, I wasn't loving being alive. There on that sand I made another silent promise to my mother. To live. The promise I should have made on her bedroom floor. This time I would follow it through. From that morning I began saying yes to all the things I previously refused.

As much as I enjoyed the learning part, I came into my own in the few weeks each year when we were on placement. For some, the thinking on your feet was too much, with many dropouts.

During placement I sucked the information in, I learnt, and then I met Annie, the nurse appointed to train us on one ward. A redhead who was as far away from the fiery, angry stereotype as you could get. As I introduced myself, she burst into song. My song. The Adaline song. Annie, with a needle still in its plastic packet, about to take blood from a patient, now used the needle as her microphone.

'*Oh Ad-da-line. Why do you look so fine?*'

She moved the needle towards the patient and the patient sang the song. Out of tune, but with passion. '*What can I do to make you mine?*'

Annie danced around the ward with that needle, pointing it at every patient until they joined in.

'*Compared to you she don't mean a dime,*

I'll give her up if you give me some time.'

A stern-looking nurse entered the ward. They all stopped.

'*Let me prove I'll walk you down the line,*' she sang in an impressive falsetto.

Every person on that ward sang the chorus, including me.

'*Cos, there's a fire in you,*

That lights a fire in me,

Oh, can't you let it be?

Give in to your destiny.

Take me out of this ag-o-ny.'

The whole ward finished and then broke out in laughter. It was the perfect welcome. That was Annie. She could change the energy in a room. She could make the dying laugh. She brought giggles and kindness and fun. I knew right then I was safe with her. There was an authority to Annie, even though she was only four years older. She advised but didn't scold; the best type of person to mentor someone. She talked to us students as people. In Annie, I found a friend. Finally, laughter entered my life again.

I began joining her with the other girls for Friday night drinks in the city, staying over in her little apartment around the corner from the hospital. We would sleep top to tail in her single bed, if we went to bed at all. I made friends with the other nurses; I let people in to my world. Unfurled to the possibility of someone, someday, loving me. I opened myself out and permitted Adaline to love someone other than her mother. I believe doing that, allowing myself to love, brought Andrew to me.

87

Breakfast

I returned to the hotel room. Andrew had shifted from the couch to the bed. At least when the breakfast arrived, the staff wouldn't see where my husband slept. I lifted Andrew's suitcase and placed it in the double wardrobe by the corridor. It crossed my mind to hang his clothes for extra brownie points, but I decided against it; I wasn't in *that* good a mood. It was my time to relax too. My holiday too.

Instead, I softly clicked the bedroom door shut and sat on the sofa to look around the room, since I barely glanced at it the night before. It was everything I looked for in a stay. Separate room for sleeping, with a seated area to relax. A kitchen for making snacks. Modern. Clean. I admired the lights. Three massive globes hung above, suspended from the ceiling in the middle of the room. The décor was elegant. All muted colours and luxurious velvets and satins. I made myself a coffee from a fancy machine that took longer to figure out than if I'd boiled a kettle. I opened the curtains and light exploded. It wasn't the usual small balcony I expected, but an outside area. It took a while of fiddling with the door before I slid it open; my fingers wouldn't work with the excitement. As soon as it moved, the sound of the waves took me to the water. Took me home. I closed my eyes and ingested the smell of the sea and let the heat warm my bones. The chance of a proper hot day in late October in Ireland was long gone, so I welcomed the heat blast now. The outside was more like a rooftop, designed as an extended room, with two rattan sun loungers identical to the ones at the pool placed in the middle. A glass dining table and tall cream rattan chairs to one side, and a couch with a sun canopy attached for shade on the other. With a panoramic view of the pool underneath and the sea beyond. Perfect. I sank into the couch and sipped my coffee and tried to let the heated air clear my thoughts and troubles.

A soft rap at the door broke my attempt. I skipped to it, swinging it open to a trolley full of cloches and another grinning Cypriot. I loved the Cypriot people. If they smiled, it was genuine, not some fake expression plastered on because they had to. Not an 'inside they hate you' smile you'd get in some countries from overworked or underrated staff. Servers sick of the rudeness or sense of entitlement from some tourists. Or maybe the Cypriots were better actors.

The man's name tag said Kostas.

'Can you bring it outside?'

Kostas wheeled the trolley out to the balcony, and I helped him move the cloches to the table. There were juices and pots of tea and coffee. They had even provided side plates and cutlery, even though the kitchen had them. I handed him ten euros. He stepped back, waving his hands.

'No, it's included.'

'I know. Take it anyway.'

Kostas grinned. 'Thank you. Ring down when you're finished, and I'll run up and collect the plates, Mrs. Love.'

'It's Adaline. Thank you.'

Kostas walked out humming the song.

On the balcony, as I overlooked the banquet on the table, I felt a stir of excitement. The smell made me salivate. Possibility spread out. It also gave me an idea. In the bedroom, Andrew's mouth gaped open, still away to sleep. That gawp nearly changed my mind, nearly made me turn around and go out to that balcony to eat the food by myself, but

I pushed myself forward. Because what would be the point of coming here if I did that? I had to try. I sat on the edge of the bed nearest to him and stroked his forearm once. His eyes snapped open, not used to the intimacy. I waited for him to adjust to the surroundings.

'I was thinking, as it's the beginning of this holiday, we could try a fresh start ourselves. Call it an apology for being tired last night.'

He nodded, unsure.

'I ordered breakfast. It's on the balcony if you'd like to join me?'

He nodded again.

I let him get dressed and thought longer than I should about where to sit. I was nervous. If I sat on the couch, it could seem like I was distancing myself. I chose a chair at the table. Andrew flashed an uncomfortable smile as he stepped out of the room, his cheeks puffed from sleep, but his expression widened as he caught sight of the view. It surprised me how much I cared about impressing him. He sat opposite me at the table but turned his chair sideways to face the view. As I lifted the first cloche, the multiple colours of watermelon and mandarins and strawberries zinged on the white plate. Various wild flowers draped across the space next to the fruit. Another cloche unveiled a true Irish breakfast; a heart attack on a plate piled with fried bacon and sausages, eggs and mushrooms, the oil glistening in the sunlight. The last cloche revealed pastries of baklava and almond croissants. The sweet scent of the baked goods mingled with the salty scent of sea and fried food. Andrew dived in, heaped his plate with a bit of everything. It bode well that he didn't begin eating after he filled his, but took another plate and filled mine. I followed by pouring us both tea. The effort felt nice.

It's funny how you can know so much still about someone you barely acknowledge. How I knew exactly how he liked his tea. How Andrew knew to give me extra mushrooms but ignore the fried eggs. Those little details can make a marriage if you pay attention.

You can destroy one with the information too.

'I was thinking after this we could go for a walk up to the mosaic museum. I always loved walking along the harbour and we never checked it out the last time,' Andrew said through a mouthful.

'Sounds great,' I said, and I meant it.

We ate the rest in silence, both knowing we needed slow steps. This fragile peace between us could disintegrate if prodded.

I ate too much. Back home, I restricted my food allowance, but I made a vow on the plane that I intended to keep, determined to do things differently this holiday. Too stuffed to walk, we sat for longer than planned. After a while Andrew picked up the paper Kostas included with breakfast and settled on the couch, his head resting on the arm and his legs spread out on the seat while I tackled the suitcases. Remember what I said about roles? I didn't mind, it was my little way to keep the momentum of friendliness going, and anyway, I had too many clothes that would wrinkle if left folded and forgotten too long. I worked quickly, over the years learning many strategies to unpack fast. There wasn't much work in it to be fair, having packed most of my clothes with the hangers ready to go. Andrew was different, he hadn't even bothered to fold, preferring the pick and dump option. Which meant he couldn't pack as much, resulting in fewer clothes to hang. Two creased t-shirts, three shirts; picked because they were from the front of his wardrobe rather than preference. Ten boxers and fourteen pairs of socks. A pair of flip-flops and walking shoes. One pair of jeans, two trousers and two swimming shorts. My husband, the minimalist. I shook my head, knowing he would get frustrated with the lack of clothes in about two days, which would mean a trip to a clothes shop to rectify. And a suitcase shop. I pushed the negative thoughts to one side. I didn't mean to always go there, habit, I guessed.

After I finished, I walked back to the balcony where Andrew was dozing. There was that niggle again. How easy to start another argument - while I unpacked, Andrew slept. It wouldn't matter that he hadn't asked me to do it. There was always a need in me to let him know how much I sacrificed for him, anything to make him feel bad. Well, not this time. Different meant no sniping, no whinging. I retrieved my unread book from my bag, laid a towel on the sun lounger and lay. I opened the book on the first page, but my eyes drifted to the sleeping, unaware Andrew lying on the couch in his boxers. He was still handsome. I still found him attractive. In all the years we were together, we never had a problem sexually. Until we stopped. But before that, we always worked, always paid attention to each other.

A drip of sweat beaded on his lip. I worried he would burn lying there in just his boxers, the sun already hot even though it was still morning. I watched his stomach rise and fall, the line of black hair like an inviting arrow running from his belly button and disappearing. For the first time in a long time, I let my mind go there. Maybe on this holiday we could be intimate. If we were truly going to try, wouldn't we need to try that also? Unwelcome images flooded me then. I shivered them away. No, I was not ready for that. I closed my eyes and allowed the sun to take me away.

Andrew

I met Andrew in the summer. The day was hot, with clear skies. Every day I walked on the beach before the start of my shift, to rid myself of the lethargy that clawed for me every moment of existence. Even though I functioned well now, even though I allowed fun and laughter in, the morning still brought grief as fresh as if it had just happened. The walk helped me hide it, and I hid it like a shield. Yet I carried it still.

I had started my thirty-six week paid internship. For me, it was about time. After nearly four years of thinking and learning, now we were getting to the action. The hustle of the hospital, the adrenaline pumping worry that time was not on the side for some people, the fear that patients' lives were in your hands. I discovered I loved nursing; for my extra modules, I leaned towards palliative care, wanting to be the one the dying saw when they closed their eyes. I wanted to call them and their family by their names, to treat them like the person they lived as, not the patient. Not the ailment they would die from. It was exhausting, often thankless work, but I found I was good at caring for people.

The bus route for the city drove along the coast, so whatever time my shift for placement was, I would get dressed and walk the strand to the bus stop in town. The sea always nudged me towards the right frame of mind. Sometimes its image was the only thing that got me through.

If ever there was a day that could give a glimmer of hope, it was then. The type of blue sky you see in paintings that you dismiss as being too perfect. There was a light breeze that swept over my skin and as I stood on the main beach, the sea glistened. The calm water urged me to go in. There was still time. I removed my soft, flat shoes and picked them up and walked to the water and let the waves kiss my toes. The coldness of the sea made me gasp. The sun bounced off my clothes and impregnated my skin and when my toes became accustomed to the water I made small circles in the sand underneath. Minor tasks soothed me back then, I found if I focused on the monotonous action, it cleared my brain of any other necessity.

On the beach, in my nurse's uniform, with my shoes off, I allowed the waves to lick my feet. Allowed myself to catch a piece of that bright day in Knockfarrig before I needed to jump on the bus to the hospital. I felt eyes on me. Someone's interest burning like the sun into my skin. I turned and saw a dark-haired man, similar in age. He was watching me and when I looked right at him, he continued to stare. He smiled at me, with a smile that told me he would be unavoidable. That smile told me all I needed to know. His head dipped as he walked towards me, but he didn't shift his dark eyes away.

I didn't notice I dropped my shoe into the water until he picked it up. His fingers trailed water along my palm when he handed it back.

'You'll have wet feet,' he said.

I walked to the dry sand ten paces. Then placed the shoe upwards on the sand. 'It'll dry.'

'Going or coming?' he asked. Then laughed at my confusion. 'Your uniform. Are you finished or starting?'

'Starting,' I said, avoiding his eyes, embarrassed I hadn't understood.

'I'm Andrew. What's your name?'

'Adaline.'

'I like it, it's different.'

He was the first man I'd met that didn't mention or sing the song. There was nothing the same about Andrew.

Andrew was tall and dark with kind, brown eyes. A shy smile gave off a need for someone to love him. It startled me that within a second of seeing him, I wanted to be the one to give it. As unbelievable as it sounds, I loved him. Or at least the idea of him. From that first glance. From the trail on my palm. From the first time I told him my name. I heard of love at first sight before, but for me, it was love at first sound. I never heard a voice like his. No one spoke my name the way he said mine, as if I were the only one that could hear him. His voice was clearer to me, every other voice muffled in comparison, either insincere or mediocre. His pitch operated on a different frequency, it drew me like an animal's mating call, except it wasn't only sexual. It drew me to him with no choice, the urge to go to him predetermined, our destinies already decided. I discovered that day you can fall in love in a second. You can see something in someone and know instantly who they are.

We sat on the sand on a towel he laid out and waited for my shoe to dry.

'I'll have to go soon or I'll miss my bus.'

'Where do you work?'

'Cork Hospital.'

'I live near there, in the city. One of the lads at work told me about this place, so I drove down here for a swim. I could drive you. It might buy you more time?'

I nodded my agreement. I took his offer of a lift, happily, gratefully. It was crazy and impulsive and stupid to take a lift from someone I didn't know, but already he wasn't. It was years later that Andrew became a stranger.

'I can't believe I've never been here before, this place is something else. It's like stepping inside a postcard. What with the little shops and the bandstand and now you.'

He didn't look away, kept smiling like what he said was normal. I felt my cheeks redden.

'Do you live in the town?'

'Just up the road really, the beach continues on for miles, my house leads on to it.'

'I'd love to live near the sea. It must be peaceful.'

'Sometimes,' I said. 'Not for everyone. Some people learn to ignore it. I couldn't though; for me, it's always in the background. It balances me. Everything can change, but the sea will still be there. It has moods, though. And magical powers.'

'Oh yeah?' He grinned, interested, not mocking.

'Yeah. Like in a storm. The way it lashes out, in any direction. It's mesmerizing. To the point you feel yourself drifting near. Even though to enter the water would mean death, there is beauty in its wildness.'

Andrew's hand tipped against my fingertip on the towel. My whole finger became static.

'And the magical powers?'

'It helps me find solutions. Anytime I have a problem, or I feel overwhelmed or sad, I come down to the beach and listen. It helps me.'

'I can understand that,' he said, watching the waves.

Those eyes. They frightened me. Trust me, they asked. They also begged me not to mess him around. Can you know someone from their eyes? Scientifically, they are only organs. Just different shaped, various coloured orbs that reflect light and filter colour, yet Andrew's eyes were more than shapes and shade. They drew me in. They were eyes I hadn't known I'd searched for.

Andrew's car was a ten-year-old green Fiat.

'I'm sorry, it's not much, but it's all I could afford on a trainee architect's wage.'

'Don't be sorry. I don't even have a car.'

He opened the door for me. The interior of the car was clean. It smelt of aftershave. A smell distinctive and fresh, a smell that became associated from then on as Andrew's. I sat and Andrew closed the door with a click rather than a bang. He ran to the other side. Grinned when he sat beside me.

'So you said you're an architect?' I asked.

As he started the engine and drove, I took in the details of his hands. His long fingers, the short bitten fingernails, his loose handling of the wheel, or how his left hand gripped the gear shift. It prevented me from looking at him. *He* kept looking at me though, enough for me to worry he'd crash the car. To make eye contact was too intense. Too much after a void of solemnity. I fell back on my practised playing it cool. But not by too much. I wanted Andrew to know I liked him, but I also knew to not show over eagerness, to not show how much I already thought I needed him.

'Yeah, I work in town. I just qualified.'

'That's a very grown up profession.'

'There's nothing more grown up than saving people's lives, Adaline.'

I liked the way he looked at me when he said those words. Sincere and searching. We didn't probe each other with serious questions. Neither of us asked about each other's family history that day. We only spoke of us, about the surface of us. We marvelled at each other, at the trimmings that made the other person.

'You have beautiful eyes.' Him.

'So do you.' Me.

'The colour of your shirt suits you.' Me.

'I love a girl in uniform.' Him.

The journey was the shortest it ever took, only seeming to take minutes before we arrived at the hospital. My mind was whirring about what to do next. Should I ask for his number? Or was I reading too much in to it? For all I knew, he did this all the time; he was just a nice guy who gave lifts to random strangers. Even though my fingers went to the door handle, I didn't yet pull.

'Well, thanks. I appreciate the lift.'

'I'd like to see you again,' he said.

'I'd like for you to see me too.'

He leant over. I knew if he kissed me it would differ from other men; everything was already different. There was no awkward moment. My lips meshed with his. The taste of him made me want to skip work and stay in the car.

He took out two business cards from his side door. Handed me one. 'I know it's pure cringe but I have to have them for work.'

'I'm not taking that. If you want to speak to me, you'll have to call me,' I said, handing the card back. There was no way I was making the first move. He wouldn't take it. He offered me the card and a pen.

'Grand. Write yours down and then we'll both have the others. Just in case one of us loses the card.'

I raised an eyebrow. 'Are you planning to lose the card, Andrew?'

'No, I'm planning to ring you the minute you get home. What time would that be exactly?'

'I'm on a twelve-hour shift, I'm afraid, so I'll probably roll in to bed.'

'Another time so. I won't lose it.'

With reluctance, I left Andrew's car. As I waved goodbye, I walked straight and slow, aware he still watched. I fought the urge to skip. He didn't start the car until I waved again from the lobby.

By the end of my shift, my jaws hurt from grinning. The shift was uneventful, which I was thankful for. No deaths. No patient in major distress. A good one.

Annie was the first person I told. The only one I wanted to know; I wanted to keep Andrew secret from the world, afraid if I mentioned his name out loud he would disappear or in a place as small as Cork, that they would know him and not like him. Or worse, been with him.

Somehow he would become tainted, and being with him couldn't be tainted. I wouldn't allow it.

I finished my shift at the same time as Annie, on the walk out I filled her in on my eventful car journey. My stomach flipped. There was Andrew, in the same spot as before. Waiting. He got out of the car when he saw me, ran around to the passenger side and, looking embarrassed, walked towards me. Annie, always fast on the uptake, dropped back and pretended she needed to make a call.

'I promise, I'm not a psycho stalker or anything, but I just didn't want you having to get the bus on your own. Thinking about it now, it probably seems creepy.'

'It's not. It's sweet.'

'I couldn't drive away for ages. I sat here and was kinda numb. These things don't happen to me. Before I knew it, an hour had gone by and then it didn't seem so unreasonable to come back here when your shift finished. If you have a lift it's cool, I don't want to get in the way, I just wanted to see you again.'

'I could do with a lift.'

'Really?'

'Really.' I grinned. Playing it cool with Andrew was over. I waved goodbye to Annie, knowing she'd understand. It would save her waiting with me at the bus stop.

I spent the journey telling him about my shift. It distracted me from talking about us. When we stopped in my driveway, Andrew looked at the dark unlit house.

'All out?'

'There's just me.'

'You live alone?'

'Not so much through choice.'

'What? Something happened?'

'My dad left a long time ago. My mum died.'

'I'm sorry.'

'Don't be. It's not your fault.'

I couldn't stop my eyes from welling. I looked out the window, embarrassed.

'Adaline.'

'Andrew,' I said, looking back to him.

He kissed me, then stroked my face. 'I like you.'

'I like you too.'

I opened the door and stepped out of the car.

'Before you change your mind, can I lock you into a date?'

My heart nearly jumped from its chest. 'Definitely.'

'Is there somewhere nice down here? I can drive down. That way if you want to leave you're near home.'

I arched a brow. 'Do you think I'll want to leave? Is there something you're not saying? Are you going to grow horns or unleash deadly secrets on me?'

'No deadly secrets. I just want you to feel safe. And you might just decide you don't like me after all.'

Andrew looked so vulnerable when he said that it made me want to nurture him and devour him at the same time. This man had been hurt. This man did not want to hurt me.

'I doubt that.'

A silence hung there. Pleasant. Confirming.

'You could just call to mine?'

'No. The first date has to be special. It has to wow, so you'll remember it. What's the fanciest place in Knockfarraig? Don't worry about money, I'm paying. I just secured a project for my boss that should see a nice fat bonus, so I'm celebrating.'

'I've heard Greene's is nice. It overlooks the beach. I've often wondered what it would be like to eat in there.'

'See, that's what I'm looking for. Greene's it is then. When suits?'

'I'm on nights till Thursday, which means Friday I'm wrecked. How's Saturday?'

'Saturday sounds perfect. I'll book there so. Say seven? Or eight?'

'Seven,' I said. That way I would have longer with him.

'Great. That way we'll have longer together.'

I stopped my mouth from gawping, smiled instead.

'I'll pick you up at quarter to?'

'Quarter to is perfect.'

'Can't wait.'

'Me too. Goodnight Andrew.'

'Goodnight Adaline.'

I closed the car door, got out my key. Andrew didn't start the engine until the key was in the lock. Didn't drive off until my door was open. I waved as I closed the door. Then put my head on the cold wood to check it wasn't a dream.

There was no waiting three days to ring. No games. No chasing or hiding who we were. He rang me the moment he got home. His voice breathless from running to the phone.

'Here's your stalker again. Greene's only had a spot at half past seven. I didn't want you to think I was late.'

'Call at seven. You can leave your car and we can walk there. At that time, the beach is lovely.'

'See, you're helping with the wow already. Saturday then.'

'Till Saturday.'

It was the first time since before my mother died that someone danced around my kitchen.

* * *

As I got ready for the date, I took my time. Every stroke of shadow on my eyelids, every strand of hair was brushed to incite a reaction. The nerve ends celebrating in my stomach made me nauseous. Excitement was rare and overdue. In front of the floor-length mirror, I made a full turn. The black dress was worth the money. The long-sleeved satin clung. The deep v neck was just deep enough to allude to more. The skirt stopped below the knee. Barely any skin was shown, yet it was sensual. The perfect first date dress. I hoped.

The doorbell chimed five minutes early. It didn't matter; I had been ready for an hour. Andrew was as handsome as I remembered. He paced from side to side. It bode well that he was as nervous as me, I couldn't stand cocky guys. He wore a grey shirt and black jeans. The grey brought out the darkness in his eyes.

'Wow,' he said. He shook his head. Those eyes stayed on me, I silently thanked my dress.

'Come on then,' I said, clicking the door shut. I grinned as I walked ahead, pointing in the direction that we needed to go. He ran to keep up, fell in line with me.

'Can I link you, this hill isn't kind with heels.'

He held out an arm. 'Gladly.'

As I linked him, I smelt Andrew's smell, not woody like most men's aftershave smelt like, the kind that always attacked my nostrils, his was as fresh as the sea. I resisted the urge to dive my nose into his neck.

'So talk to me. Tell me as much about Adaline as you can.'

'There's not much to tell.'

When we reached the end of the hill, I veered him right to the dirt path that led to the beach. We stayed linked. He stopped when the water came into view.

'Look at that. Start there. What's it like growing up with the sea on your doorstep?'

'Lonely sometimes. Freeing other times. I've known no other way, so I don't know what it would be like living somewhere else. I never take this view for granted, though. It never gets old. There's a bit of a mermaid in me. What about you, where are you from?'

'Oh, I'm a near the city boy. We moved around. I've lived in Barrack Street, the Lough, Togher, Ballintemple. That became our longest home. I moved out of there at eighteen. Stayed in digs on the Western Road. Now I live in a house share on MacCurtain St. It's pretty rough, total lads place, but it's cheap and near work, so.'

We stopped on the sand. The sky was ready for a picture; the sun sinking into the sea.

'With a view like that, I wouldn't want to live anywhere else either.'

I undid the straps on my heels and looped them around my finger. 'We have time to walk in the water if you'd like? It's usually warmed up after the day's sun.'

'This date just keeps getting better.'

We held hands as we walked on the sand. Andrew rolled his pants up to his knees. Dark hairs covered his legs. My stomach flipped at the sight. His warm palm against mine. The sunset. The breeze flipping my hair away. Then the taste of him as he kissed me. We didn't make it to the water.

'I'm sorry, I couldn't wait.'

'I'm glad you didn't.'

We kissed until the sun disappeared, causing Andrew to check his watch. 'Come on, I'm starving.'

I expected a spectacular view from Greene's. What I didn't bank on was how the restaurant would give you enough to see inside that you needn't look out the window. The ceilings were high. High arched windows led to a veil of minuscule suspended lights, shimmering like a ceiling of diamonds. A man in a full on three-piece suit greeted us.

'Did I under dress?' Andrew whispered to me.

'No. Did I?'

'No, Adaline, you definitely didn't.'

The man led us to the last remaining arch. From this height,

Knockfarraig was all sea and sky. Moonlight now reflected on the surface. Andrew held my seat for me. I slipped into it.

'Thanks. So how are we doing so far?'

Andrew sat and taking the hard backed menu that looked more like a book from the server, nodded his thanks.

'Well, let's see.' He strummed his fingers on his chin. 'I have a confession. My friends call me Mr. Picky.'

'Is that so?'

'Wait, hear me out. It's not as bad as it sounds. I just always imagined this perfect first meeting. Like I'd seen in the movies. In reality, nothing ever lived up. I'd meet girls who were everything I could want on paper, but I don't know, it just wasn't there. Then I saw you Adaline. I saw you from the distance. You caught my attention straight away. You were completely unaware of anyone else on that beach, lost in your own world. I wanted to go to you. As you walked along the beach, as you made circles in the water. It was like the sea pulled me to you with the tide. Then I spoke to you and you ticked every box. My perfect first meeting.'

'Wow,' I said, feeling the heat burn on my cheeks. 'Thank you. No pressure for this date then.'

'Relax. I've an inkling we'll be grand. I don't expect you to be perfect. Life isn't perfect. I just wanted to know when I saw the person. I wanted the spark.'

'And you feel you got that with me?'

'I think so,' he said, busying himself with his napkin.

I wish I could recall the food we ate or the rest of the conversation, but even as I sat with him the evening blurred.

As we left the restaurant, we walked through the town instead of the sand. On the pavement, Andrew placed his hands on both of my arms and side stepped me onto the inside. The first time he did it, I continued speaking, not paying the gesture too much attention. The next time I crossed over him to point out where the lighthouse was, he did it again.

'Why do you keep moving me?'

Andrew stopped walking. He shrugged.

'To keep you safe. In case a car came along.'

I giggled. 'What, you'd stop a car from hitting me?'

'I'd try. If I was the first hit, I'd take most of the impact. I just want to make sure you're safe.'

'I can look after myself, you know?'

'I know,' he said.

Andrew was the only man I been with that held a door open for me, who moved me from the outside of the pavement, just in case. I hadn't known how special that would make me feel. As a woman, I probably should have been outraged, but it thrilled me, because it meant I was precious to him, and he wanted to keep me safe. I didn't tell him how that gesture made me feel, how I knew it was Andrew's way of showing he cared.

At my door, there was no speech about going home or saying goodbye, no protesting that it was late, no back or forth about what we wanted to do next. I opened the door and let him in and as soon as the door was closed we melted into each other. Of course there was worry; that I would take a chance and he would be someone other than what he portrayed. But my want for Andrew outweighed my fear. It felt right.

I wished I kept my virginity for him. I would have loved to give Andrew that gift. He would have known what a present it was. He would have acknowledged the significance. Being with him proved what I experienced with Cian wasn't love. It was a first want. It was fumbles and pretence. A teenage need or obsession or unrequited infatuation, but definitely not love. There was no comparison. Andrew was different to other men who showed their interest, who acted like

I would be a commodity. I'd seen it many times on the nights out with Annie, the lads who once they acquired the girl, would look for another to move on to. Andrew looked at me like he already knew me. He saw *through* me, knowing what I thought instead of by the way I acted. He gave me a quiet affection, an undercurrent, a steadfastness. He wanted me and knew he would never not want me, and that was that. It was unnerving and new.

Andrew listened to what I had to say. Wanted to listen. He was interested, and he wanted to see me, every part of me. He didn't care that my breasts were smaller than I liked, or that my bum was bigger than I wanted. He loved it, loved my body. Andrew showed every inch of me he loved me.

After the first time, Andrew stayed over and woke me early. There was a clammy film on my skin from the warmth of the day and the unused to closeness of our bodies.

'You look even better without makeup.'

I looked away, shy then. Being bare skinned didn't bother me; I wanted him to see me, the true me, flaws and all, but it was the validation that made me feel exposed. The compliment.

'Let's go to the beach. Right now.'

'Do you have swimming shorts?'

'No, I'll go in my boxers. Come on, I dare you.'

'Come on, so.'

We ran into the water and gasped as the cold water splashed us. I turned to run back out, but Andrew lifted me and I wrapped my legs around his waist. He waded out further until the waves touched my toes. He kissed me and asked, 'Trust me?'

The sea water caught in droplets in his dark eyelashes.

'I trust you.'

Andrew lowered us both into the water until we submerged. The cold pricked every nerve ending. Sharp stabs of ice invaded me.

Andrew kissed me again while underneath, and the cold didn't seem as bad.

After the swim, we let the sun dry and warm our bodies and held hands covered in sand.

'You're lucky living in this place.'

'I am.'

Andrew kept his eyes on me for a long time, I closed mine shielding them from the sun.

'Ad, come here,' he said.

He stood and held out a hand and I took it and followed him to the wet sand. Andrew picked up a stone and wrote:

I love you.

I picked up a stone and wrote:

I know. I love you too.

It reminded me of another day. A day I found another message scraped into wet sand. It felt like a sign. I kept those stones, put them in a box frame, so I held that day in time; the first memento of us.

We fell into a life with each other. There was no unsureness or playing games. Having my own home at twenty-four had its merits; no parents to curfew or time how long the boyfriend stayed in your room. Andrew opened up my heart and he also without even knowing made me open up every untouched room in the house.

It became normal to meet at mine. When I worked a long shift, he would let himself in beforehand and spend hours cooking something for when I walked in the door. He never officially moved in, we never had that conversation, just a key handed over when I was going to be home later than him one day. Yet it was an unspoken agreement that he would be there. Any moment less than always was too unbearable to contemplate.

There was nothing but us then. Andrew's touch, his love, his voice, it got me through each day. There was nothing for it but to immerse myself in him, the relationship now a requisite for my salvation. Not that I was needy, and he was the strong one. Rather, our mutual neediness met in the middle, because each of us understood the other's requirements and matched it perfectly. When he looked at me, I was sure I could see my future was in the reflection of that stare.

In bed one evening, I spoke to him in the dark:

'Andrew?'

'Yeah?'

'How come I've never met your parents?' I didn't finish what I wanted to ask. Was he embarrassed of me? I knew both Andrew's parents were alive, but they were just as absent as mine.

Andrew stayed still. 'I don't mention them because they would ruin it.'

'Ruin us?'

'Maybe. Dad was in and out of my life. Even though Mum was there, she may as well have not been. They were both absent. It was like my mother took everything he threw at her and placed it inside. When he would disappear, which happened often, she would drink day and night. Never spoke to me. Never interacted. Never acknowledged I was there. When he returned, she shifted to the perfect wife. Fetching, doing everything not to annoy him. Which included ignoring me so he wouldn't get jealous. I could understand it when he was around, because I could see why she would be afraid, but when he went I couldn't. It was like she blamed me. She certainly didn't act like she cared. Early on I learnt to look after myself.'

'Andrew, I'm sorry.'

He prodded himself up on the pillow. Moonlight slivers from the open window highlighted his face.

'When I was younger, I wished my father wouldn't come back. I believed she would love me then. It would have definitely been safer at least. Even if she never spoke, I could deal with her silence. What I couldn't deal with was the threat of him. Adaline from what you've told me, we had the same type of father. Do you know what my main childhood memory was? Bars. Whole weekends being sat at a table, if I was lucky, with a packet of crisps, a chocolate bar and a glass of red lemonade. Other days it was just with my imagination. No other kids, no phones or toys or playground. Only the threat in my dad's eyes to sit still and behave and don't run riot. And a mother quietly sipping like a saint in the corner.'

'I had that too. I'd take a book with me though.'

'We didn't have many books in our house, I stopped bringing any back from the library as he would rip them apart on purpose, knowing I would have to explain why I wasn't returning them. Boredom always won against his threat. He'd hit me, anyway. I'd explore the little areas around the bar for something to discover. I climbed trees. I'd scale them in seconds and reach the top branch and feel like a king. In one bar, there was one tree that was taller than the others. I swore I would climb it, but the height put me off. I mastered the rest first. They got easy, and the boredom came again. So I started small, only scaling to the first branch. I got to know the bottom of the tree. The next time I got to the second branch but there was an enormous gap between that and the next one with no grooves to latch onto. So I climbed back down. The tree became my Everest, I lay in bed and ran through ideas: *lasso a rope to the next branch and swing, ram a peg in it,* or *stop being a scaredy cat and just do it.* The next time I did. The climb up seemed motionless, every branch easy to scale. I didn't need to look where the next foothold was, I sensed it. When I reached the top, I felt triumphant. I could see for miles. Streets and even roofs were below me. The buildings were beautiful up there. It made me want to be part of that, to design places like that. It was one of the best feelings I've ever experienced, apart from meeting you, of course.'

He squeezed my leg to reaffirm the point. 'Until I looked down and realised how far I'd gone. How far from the ground I was. It was the first time I panicked. My palms got sweaty. Sweaty enough that I was sure I would slip. I kept seeing myself fall. The air felt heavier, thicker. Then I lost all sense. I felt around with my feet, but no matter which way I tapped, there was no branch below. I started gasping for air. My lungs wouldn't fill enough. It was getting dark, and I knew the longer I left it, the worse it would be to see. Then a man I recognised came out for a smoke. A man known to my father. Without thinking, I shouted to him for help. The man was drunk enough that he didn't even cop on where the voice was coming from. Looked around him as if a ghost was talking to him until I called through gasps that I was up in the tree. He looked up and nearly lost his balance. As he shouted for my father, I realized what would happen. The man would go in shouting and the entire bar would run out, including my father. I would have caused the cardinal sin. A fuss. I placed my two fears together; side by side. The fear of my father would always win. With a white flash of panic, I let one arm go and my body dipped down more, and I touched a branch. I did it again, with no sense of what was below me. I swear Adaline it was as if something was guiding me. Another branch, then another. I almost laughed with exhilaration, I was going to do it. The dopes would all come rushing out and would see me sat on the ground quietly playing. They would mock the drunk man and tell him to go home and the crisis would be over. But I was too caught up in the daydream to pay attention. A branch ripped into my leg, causing me to let go, and I fell the rest of the way. Broke my arm. I'm not sure if it was from the fall or from my father when he saw me on the floor. It was the only time I caused a commotion. Didn't stop me climbing trees though because after I fell, my fear disappeared. Because that was the worst the tree could do. It wasn't the tree's fault. I'd caused the fall. If I'd kept it together, I wouldn't have dropped to the ground. I learnt to conquer the fear. Actually, the fear of it drove me on. Does that make sense?'

'It does.'

'When I was about thirteen, I started training. Purely to one day overpower him. As I gained strength, I grew braver. He knew it too. He got more savage. No matter how hard I trained or hard I pushed my body, he would always get the better of me. Fighting back only made him worse. But the pain was worth it because every time I hit back reminded him his time was nearly up. The night he used my guitar to smash up the living room was the last straw. I lay in bed fuming. It had taken me months working part time to save for it, and now it was in pieces. Until I heard him thump up the stairs and all went quiet. I snuck into their bedroom and watched that brute. As a lob of drool ran down his chin with his mouth open, it came to me that might be the only time I would find him undefended. I tiptoed away and came back within a minute. I placed the cold tip of a screwdriver near the vein of his throat. With a bare touch of the skin. I was ready. My hands shook so much Adaline. Not because I was scared or he would catch me, but because I could do it without hesitation. I promised myself, swore, if my father stirred I would act, I would see it as a sign to do the thing I wanted. Anything would have counted. A flickering eye, a moving hand, a cough. I waited. The sign never came. As the minutes went by, uncertainty set in and I lost my nerve. The next day, when my father punched me hard enough that it chipped my tooth, I cursed myself for waiting for a sign. If God was real, how could he allow someone to be that cruel and get away with it? I decided I would make my own signs from then on. Before dawn, swearing vengeance, I snuck back into my parents' bedroom with that screwdriver. My mother and father's side of the bed was empty. Gone again and she was downstairs, still drinking. I could never understand how life always spared him, always saved that ogre.'

'Oh, Andrew. I'm sorry.' His pain was a mirror image of my own.

'Don't be.' Andrew sat up straight, clasped my hands in his and then kissed my fingers. 'I get it now. Since I met you, I see I *was* spared.' He laughed at my confusion. 'If I'd killed him, they would have sent me to a detention centre or jail and I'd probably still be there now. We wouldn't have met. It's like we're linked Ad. There are reasons for it all. Us having a similar upbringing. Me going to Knockfarraig on a whim. It makes me think something was looking out for me all along. Looking out for us.'

I understood what he meant. A million invisible strings tied us together. The links of my life played out to me while I lay there. If my mother wasn't diagnosed with cancer, I wouldn't have become a nurse. If I wasn't a nurse, I wouldn't have been going to the hospital that day at exactly that time. If I wasn't lonely and full of grief, I wouldn't have forced myself to make that walk on the beach. I wouldn't have met Andrew. I still couldn't accept why we had to suffer, but I opened my mind to the possibility that a plan was in place.

The Walk

We left at noon, all suntan-lotioned and dressed. I carried a big bag full of all the essentials we might need as the day unfolded. Andrew brought himself. Another role we were used to. As we walked away from the grounds of the hotel, we stopped at the entrance, where a small crowd of three people examined the floor. There were looking at a section of mosaics.

'Imagine they made these before we were even born. Even on your doorstep here you step back in time,' Andrew said, shaking his head in disbelief.

'It was one of the reasons I booked this hotel, modern inside but steeped in history.'

'You chose well.'

I smiled at his compliment. He didn't meet my smile, continuing to study the mosaics.

'You ready?' I asked.

'Sure.'

Andrew didn't seem sure, his expression had changed to serious. I'd hoped for one good day. Just one before the darkness descended on us again.

'Fresh start, remember?'

He looked at me, his eyes threatened tears. Not what I expected at all. He smiled, even looked grateful for the reminder. 'Fresh start.'

Like the mosaics, Poseidonos Avenue brought me back in time. To our honeymoon. Everything was the same, only irrelevant details were different. The uneven cobbles, the restaurants; some with different fronts and different names, but still gave out the same feeling, with the same invitation.

Andrew and I were walkers. As a young couple, we would spend countless dates in the countryside exploring and searching and then when we found ourselves in a field or woods or somewhere completely isolated we would discover ourselves in each other. Back then we would walk for miles without a word, content to just walk, just be. Now the silence was different. It weighted us down, the unsaid shouting loud in the quiet between us. We walked to the start of the harbour, both knowing the way, the castle in view at the end of the pier, the boats bobbing on the water in front passing the many restaurants getting ready for lunchtime traffic. The place was full of activity, from the tourists strolling in their shorts and t-shirts, from the waiters and waitresses rushing to see if we would come in or busying themselves preparing tables in case you did. As we walked, the palm trees sashayed, the waves kissed the rocks, and I breathed.

'How about we check out the Park, then come back for a bit of lunch, or are you already hungry?'

'Andrew, I don't think I'll be hungry after that feast, not until dinner anyway.'

He chuckled. 'Yeah, we were like savages all right. Archaeological Park it is then.'

We went right for the Park instead of left for the castle. Plenty of time to revisit it all.

'There's something magical about Paphos, isn't there? They remember their past and link it with their future. Isn't it protected from change?' I said.

He nodded. 'Yeah, it's classed as a world heritage site and it should be, it deserves respect.'

Andrew paid the fee, and we walked on what could be mistaken for a dirt road; a nowhere road; a sandy, chalky path with parched grass and shrubs that you would never believe could lead you to travel to another time.

The foundations of a once lived life laid around us, resorted now to only bricks and pieces of rock. In some areas there were large square deep holes with stone stairs. I tried to picture another woman my age, using that space to feed her family. Was she happy there? Andrew's eyes sparkled, an architect in his element.

It was the mosaics that drew me. Inside were walls slatted with light coloured wood, with high rectangular windows near the ceiling that ran the length of the building. Across from the entrance were bigger panels of glass, so plenty of natural light poured in. We walked on a walkway of darker slats of wood. The images spread out before us. Andrew pointed to some mosaics that were interlocking shapes and patterns.

'They called these geometric mosaics,' he said. Walking on, he pointed to another mosaic. 'See the colour transitions? They knew then how to make the body and skin have shades of light and shadows.'

We stood in front of greatness, standing against wooden rails looking down at art made from people long dead. In The House of Dionysus, I marvelled at the intricate, repetitive designs that framed the pictured mosaics inside. The men depicted in the porcelain jigsaw looked back at me with their knowing pursed lips. What had they witnessed? How had they lived and died? I wondered too about the picture in front of me, a dog on the left side, with two robed figures in the middle. A smaller figure hovered at the right corner. A figure with wings and a bow and arrow. Was he Cupid? Who waited to send his arrow into the potential lover's way and join them forever. Was love just a random selection by the Gods? I know there was no choice for me. I never asked Andrew did he feel the same. Back then I didn't feel the need to ask, I already felt I knew the answer. Now I didn't have a clue.

'How many hours must this have taken? Even just to make the colour for the tiles. Then to piece together the picture. The faces. They had some patience,' Andrew said.

'Time was different then. Beauty took time. They understood their time would amount to glory, that their work would last forever. They didn't have the distractions we do.'

'It would be nice to get back to that. To lose what distracted us.' He smiled, moved closer.

'Lose the gadgets?' I said, arching an eyebrow.

He screwed his eyes. 'I'd throw the gadgets away if you stimulated me another way.'

One man embedded in the mosaics below sneered up at me. 'Time to go,' I said.

'So what, Adaline? We give up and don't look around the rest of it? How's running away from everything working for you? I thought we were doing things differently here.'

I took a breath. 'We are. I'm trying. Can't you see I'm trying?' My eyes watered, but I stopped myself. Andrew hated when I cried. 'OK, sorry about the gadget comment.'

'OK.'

'How about walking to the lighthouse?'

'Sure.'

We continued on and walked, but my comment set an unrest between us. Those unintentional few words reminded us of the conflict that we pretended we could hide. Like the mosaics, it still lay there broken into tiny pieces for us to see.

I missed the kids. This was the longest I'd ever gone without speaking to them. I itched to ring but they didn't carry their phones with them during the day, so I would have to settle for a five-minute call in the evening when they would both rush through the day's activities so loud and so fast with both of them talking at the same time they would cancel each other out.

After an unenthusiastic linger around the lighthouse, we returned to the hotel, stopping for an ice-cream at a kiosk on the way. The heat was powerful, and coupled with the disappointment of how our interaction went, made me tired. All I wanted to do was to lie in the sun.

'Do you want to go to the pool?'

Andrew nodded, looked away, took a lick of ice cream. The pool area was busy. All the fancy canopies were full, but we located two sun loungers together. I laid out two towels, we didn't say a word as we lay next to each other, him on his stomach, me on my back.

The water lapped at the edges, spilling over. I listened to the gurgle of the filter. To some melody in the distance. To the song of birds. All sounds that floated to me and I batted away. They were unimportant, yet there, keeping me in the present when I wanted to slip into sleep. I tried to take myself out of the impending sadness, the way I'd learnt years before. My thoughts tried to reason with me. He was trying. We would find an outcome. Even if we couldn't work it out, I could enjoy this moment. When I was back freezing in Ireland, I would wish for sun again. I took a deep breath and tried to relax. There was nowhere I had to be. There was no one I had to mind or keep an eye on. For once, I could be my priority. As I closed my eyes, inviting sleep, I felt a hand hold mine.

Two Locks

The first time Annie and Andrew officially met, I kept it casual. Arranged it so Andrew picked me up while suggesting to Annie at the end of our shift she say hi. Their meeting each other made me nervous, I already knew I could never pick between them. As we linked arms, I led her to his car.

'Annie, this is Andrew. Say hi Andrew.'

'Hi Andrew,' Andrew said.

Annie didn't laugh. There was a sizing up between them. Narrowed eyes, then a nod of the head from Annie.

'Ye hungry?' Andrew asked.

'Starving,' Annie said but didn't smile.

'How about coming to Ad's? There's a roast in the oven that's big enough to feed the whole hospital.'

Annie didn't answer, just looked at me. I raised my eyebrows.

'There's wine too,' Andrew said.

'You should have started with that. Come on then, I'm hungry,' she said as she opened the car door.

That was it. Annie, who burned porridge, was won over. After dinner, Andrew was won over too.

Adaline, Andrew, and Annie. Triple A battery, as Andrew used to joke. The weekends we were all off work, Annie would call to ours to have a boozy picnic on the beach if it was warm enough or a fire lit inside if it was cold. We stayed in Annie's or Andrew's if there was a gig in town. Mostly, we stayed in mine, my house was bigger than theirs, with no one else taking space except us. The three of us together made sense. There was never a feeling of Annie being a spare part, Andrew liked her company and being around each other every day of the week meant we enjoyed having someone else there sometimes.

'Andrew, come on, as a man, tell me, why am I single?' Annie asked one evening that was turning to early morning.

'Because you've always chosen dopes. Let me bet at least three guys you've been with cheated on you.'

'More like all of them.'

'See, you can't pick them. You're a nice, attractive, funny girl, but if you had ten men in a lineup, you'd go for the arsehole,' Andrew said, pointing at Annie with a wavering finger. Said finger then pinged the air. 'You know what, I've the perfect person for you.'

'Call him now, tell him to get here yesterday,' Annie said and then hiccupped.

'I will. I'll call him now.' Andrew checked his pockets for his phone.

I laughed. 'Andrew, it's four in the morning.'

He batted his hand at me. 'No worries, he'll still be up.'

His phone was on the table, I didn't tell him; it was much more amusing to watch him look. He found it. Swayed as he scrolled through his phone.

'Here we go.' He dialled. 'It's ringing. Shush.'

No one was talking.

'Joe, my man. Annie is here. You're gonna love her. Just your type. Redhead. Beautiful.' He winked at Annie. She gave him the thumbs up. 'It's in Knockfarraig. At Ads. I love her man, yeah. Oh, get here yesterday.'

He hung up and threw the phone on the couch.

'What did he say?' Annie asked.

'Nothing. Voicemail.'

I poured us another drink, smiling at Andrew's use of the word love.

The next day, as we tried to sober up, Joe rang back. Annie hid her eyes between splayed fingers when Andrew spoke.

'Joe's up for it if you still are?' Andrew said, his voice croaky.

Annie moved one hand away and studied Andrew. 'Can I trust you?'

'Trust me,' Andrew said.

Annie looked at me for help. Barefaced with mascara smudged down as far as her cheeks and her curls unbrushed and wild, she looked so young and pale, so vulnerable, so hungover. I shrugged. 'I don't know him, Annie, but I know Andrew. Trust him.'

'Go on sure, only if it's a double date though,' she said, dropping her hands into her lap in defeat.

'Hair of the dog to calm the nerves?' I asked, pulling a bottle of beer from the fridge.

'You know me too well.'

I could hear Andrew making plans for the following weekend, I smiled when he mentioned a bar in the city. Andrew always knew how to take the pressure off, no restaurants or magnifying glass intenseness of an actual date; a bar would be fine. Like our first date, Annie could leave quickly if she wasn't interested.

* * *

We got ready in Annie's on the night of the date. Annie kept reapplying her makeup; kept sizing herself up in the mirror. Changing her top, then trousers. After going through her entire wardrobe, she settled on the first outfit she tried on. It reminded me of how nervous I had been with Andrew.

'You look beautiful, Annie, don't worry.'

Meeting a friend of Andrew's for the first time left me just as nervous. Even early in the relationship, I knew it would devastate me if anything went wrong.

Joe had orange hair. Annie broke the ice, thumped Andrew on the shoulder.

'So were you thinking, let's get the two people I know that are foxy together, cos they're bound to have loads in common?'

'Not just that,' Andrew said, acting offended.

Joe grinned at Annie. 'That's our children screwed, anyway.'

'Not if they get my hair,' Annie said, grinning back.

'Have you a problem with red hair? Are you foxy-ist?'

'To be fair, yours is more copper.'

'And yours is more auburn.'

They were snogging within the hour.

It turned into a messy night, of drinking and dancing and drunkenness, but also with sparks of possibility. We all ended up sleeping on the floor of Annie's. The last words Andrew mumbled before he passed out was he was the best matchmaker. After that we became Triple A.J.

Those days were such fun. Wild and full of laughter and escapism and atrocious hangovers the next day. I could let loose with these people and they wouldn't judge me. They would encourage it even. I found if it was a hard day at work, if we lost a patient or had to tell someone bad news, being around them helped. Andrew helped. Annie understood. Joe made me laugh. I could feel my life expanding and I liked it.

Andrew and I sailed through those early years. Wrapped in our own love chrysalis, everything else faded into insignificance. Even the likeable friends once Annie met Joe. Especially the unlikeable ones.

When going out became less, we blossomed in our company. Side by side on the couch, reading. Side by side in bed, not reading. The silence didn't need to be filled with Andrew. I didn't need to bat away his attention; it felt good to have his focus on me. For too long, I stood in the shadow of my mother's death. Having someone shine headlights on me was inviting. He was the best distraction. I swore Andrew was a gift from my mother because he was nothing like my father, he was soft-spoken, kind. The opposite of the rough, gruff man I hated. It's funny after years and years of living with someone, you can see the likeness that you were blind to. I would never have believed back then that Andrew had even a possibility of nastiness inside him.

For a year, Andrew kept his digs he shared with three other lads in the off chance that we may break up or have an argument or just want space, but those times got less and less until there wasn't a point in paying the money anymore. When it made more sense to acknowledge there was an us, and the us was permanent, it was time. So he would stay and use his own key and we would journey to the city and come home together in the evening. Home. Our home now, not a house I just slept in anymore. Not a house I survived living with my father in or an area I danced with my mother at or a place I just existed despite my grief but a home I looked forward to getting to, of sharing with.

I mentioned earlier that I didn't possess a fire in me. Well, meeting Andrew lit something inside, just like the song. All the quietness and isolation and loneliness after my mother's death, disintegrated. I took all that pain and turned it into love and shocked him and me with the ferocity of my passion for him. I let go fully and gave Andrew every part of me, and he returned my love with just as much.

How can I explain how much I loved Andrew? It was in my waiting for him to speak, dying to know what he would say next. It was in the way his lips moving fascinated me. Loving Andrew meant laughter and cuddles and phone calls when he said he'd ring. It was days off, spent in bed and staying there until evening. It was the smell of him. It was stained sheets. It was my stomach growling with hunger but not wanting to leave our sanctuary. The easiest thing I've ever done was fall in love with Andrew Love.

We just fit. We both held an exact key to the other's lock. When we were intimate and reaching climax, I used to think we held the secret of the universe. Intercourse held the answers to life. It *was* life. All meaning. In orgasm, we became one, melting into the energy of the world. At the pinnacle of pleasure, everything seemed to come down to us; what could ever be more important than what we were both feeling then? In that exquisite few seconds, I knew the answer to all life's problems and the answer was love. That somehow our sex life could right the wrongs of all the hate in the world, because it freed us from all of life's shit. All problems unnecessary and unimportant; what mattered was me and him and the connection we felt, doing something solely for pleasure.

The years moved quickly, time being sucked from us with the completion of exams; the move from being a student to a qualified nurse. Andrew finishing his degree and after I presented him with the keys for my mother's shop, opening his own architecture firm with another architect he worked with called Donald. Time filled with holidays and days on the beach, with friends' birthdays and social occasions and being in love. We spoke about our future as if it was somewhere in the distance, not needed then, not ready for yet.

I settled in palliative care. Being there for a person's final moments was an honour. When they were unconscious, I would talk to them as if I knew them; I felt I did: a freckle on an elbow, a lock of hair that always fell to a certain side, a gap between a tooth. I cared for them, too much maybe, but I always called them by their name. The unconscious hear us; I've seen enough evidence of that. Palliative care is always life and death; the blessing of life and the intense leering of death reminded of. Intensity always forces closeness. However, as the years moved on, I found some deaths unshakeable, especially the young; their wish to live and the unfairness was too hard to shake off, and I wanted to by that stage; I was tired of death haunting me. With Annie's recommendation and encouragement, I moved to Accident and Emergency. They needed a nurse with palliative experience when someone near end of life came for severe pain management.

For our five-year anniversary, we booked Greene's again, reserving the same table. As I got ready, Andrew rang me from the car.

'Adaline you'll have to go ahead, I'm caught in traffic and I'm after spilling coffee over my trousers.'

'I can ring the restaurant. Ask them to move our booking for later.'

'No,' he said. 'Don't. They were booked out when I reserved it, that's why we had to get the earliest. I won't be long, just order a drink, anything you want. Champagne. I'll be as quick as I can.'

'OK, see you soon.'

Andrew hung up.

I avoided the beach and walked to the restaurant by road, not wanting to get sand on my new trousers. Or walk on the beach without him. Walking in heels down the hill was a reminder of how much I relied on him. I slipped off my heels and walking barefoot, I batted away my doubt. Andrew used a tone I hadn't heard before, never with me, anyway. At the entrance of the restaurant, a flash of red hair caught my attention across the road, disappearing into the corner shop. It couldn't be Annie, she knew I was out tonight and was working, but her hair was a distinctive, rare auburn. The shop beckoned, I passed the restaurant. Andrew stepped out just as I arrived at the shop's door.

'I thought you were going to change?'

Andrew frowned. 'I am. I just ran in to get a card.'

'Did I just see Annie?'

'No.'

A vein in his forehead bulged, I'd never noticed it before. The way he answered made me cautious, the pit of my stomach sent signals he was lying.

'Are you sure?'

'Go in and check if you don't believe me.' He gestured to enter.

'No, I believe you. I'll go up. See you after you get changed.'

Before I took the stairs, I waited for my heart to slow. There was no coffee stain on his trousers.

The restaurant differed from five years before. A place can look identical, but because of how you feel it has changed. This time the high ceilings and arches were vast and overwhelming. Alone, I felt all eyes swivel in my direction. The busy waiter ignored me at first, then seeing I was on my own, huffed.

'My partners delayed,' I said, then kicked myself for sounding apologetic. It wasn't my fault. He promptly led me to our table. Timed perfectly on our first date, the earlier time meant the sunlight obscured the view. It was too hot on my face.

'Can I get a drink please,' I said to the waiter's retreating back. He stopped and cocked his head in wait. 'A glass of house white would be great.'

'Sure,' he said.

I tried to pretend I was relaxed. As the servers busied themselves around me, I concentrated on the view. My lone seating brought glances from the other guests, they probably thought I was being stood up.

Andrew arrived at the table looking flustered. He sat across from me, without the usually compulsory kiss hello.

'Sorry for the delay,' he said. He looked guilty. He waved at the waiter, waited till he was near. 'Can I get a double vodka please with lemonade?' He pointed at my barely touched glass. 'Do you want a top up?'

'No, I'll wait.'

'Can we just order a bottle of the house white as well?'

'Sure,' the waiter said.

He never drank vodka with a meal. Something was up. As he reached for the menu, the smell of him wafted. I closed my eyes and breathed it in for a moment. This was Andrew. My Andrew. The Andrew who would not hurt me; who had never hurt me.

Give him the benefit of the doubt.

I started fresh. 'How was work?'

He examined the menu.

'Awful. I was just heading out when this guy came in. Total time waster, but I couldn't get him out the door. Had to listen to him for nearly an hour before he said he just wanted to evaluate the price of his house.'

I smirked.

'It's not funny.'

'It's kinda funny.'

Andrew drained his glass. Thanked the waiter for the bottle of wine and we waited as he poured. I raised my glass. 'Let's make a toast.'

Andrew raised his and smiled at me. 'To us,' he said, then drained his glass in one go. He refilled his own and stared out the window. It wasn't like him to not top up mine too. I picked up the bottle and poured my own.

Andrew's leg jittered under the table. He was drinking too fast. Kept looking at his watch or his phone or out at the view. He avoided my eyes. I needed their reassurance, their kindness. It worried me he couldn't meet mine. His eyes couldn't lie to me.

'Is something wrong?'

'No.'

'There is something, I can tell.'

'There isn't.'

'Then why won't you look at me Andrew?'

Andrew dropped his fork onto his plate. 'Stop asking. There's nothing wrong.'

'Don't seem that way to me.'

'Christ. I bring you to the fanciest restaurant in Knockfarraig and you spend the night looking for problems.'

I sulked. Picked at my food. The sea bass that was the price of a full day trainee's pay lost its flavour. My mood turned it slimy and inedible. Andrew's phone beeped. 'Finished?' He asked, shoving his half eaten plate away.

'I guess,' I said. I felt like crying; Andrew would never forfeit dessert. Something was up, I could taste the souring. Could feel the tension. Could see Andrew's discomfort and his want to not speak. The perfect night I counted the days to, looked forward to for so long, had turned into a nightmare. As he stood at the counter and paid the bill, he turned and looked at me, his expression apologetic and I knew in the pit of my stomach, it was for what was about to come. He didn't put his arm around me as we left the restaurant.

The breeze on the strand was welcome. A cold blast to the face had a similar effect as splashing me with water.

Andrew walked up the steps to the pavement instead of staying on the beach. We were heading home, which meant no further celebration. I pushed down the disappointment. He didn't move me to the inside of the pavement, walking ahead a little instead. His silence highlighted the surrounding sounds: the waves, the wind, the distant sound of music.

Andrew turned and walked back to me. 'I'm sorry, OK? I didn't want to ruin your night.'

I stopped and waited for the breakup to continue.

'I've just been nervous. I wanted this night to go perfect and instead of us having a chilled-out evening, I've over thought it.'

'It's OK,' I shrugged, not even trying to hide my relief. Of course I accepted his apology, I would forgive Andrew for anything. At least he wasn't dumping me.

The music drifted louder, a pleasant tune with a melody I didn't know. 'Why were you nervous? You know you don't have to impress me.'

'I was nervous because this is the most important night of my life.'

He blocked my path, pivoted me sideways, so I faced the bandstand. Candles lined the pathway, making a lighted trail. Andrew held my hand and walked me towards the stand where candles circumnavigated the circle. As we walked closer, the music became louder.

'Andrew, what is going on?'

'Let's celebrate properly.'

He pointed to a bucket containing a bottle of champagne. There were two champagne flutes on the floor alongside a radio. I poured the champagne into the glasses.

'This is a lovely anniversary present.' I said, swiveling to pass Andrew his glass. He was on one knee. Annie and Joe were standing on the path. Annie was already crying.

'Be my wife, Ad.'

Elation. Relief. The emotions pummelled me.

'You didn't even have to ask.'

He slipped the ring on my finger. Two diamonds side by side. It was the perfect fit.

'I liked the two stones together forever. We can always change it. The jewellers said there was no bother.'

'Andrew, you chose it. There's no other one I would want. I thought you were breaking up with me.'

'I'm sorry Ad, I was nervous it would go wrong.'

Annie and Joe joined us, Annie checking out my ring, Joe hefting a slab of beer onto the green. We lay on the grass with the music playing. A warm feeling sat in my tummy, whether from the champagne or the hope that bubbled inside me. After my glass emptied, I didn't drink another drop. I wanted to remember every second of that night. Surrounded by my three best friends, but the only person I wanted was Andrew and for us to be alone. As the night descended and the temperature dropped, which in March was early, arm in arm, we walked to the house and I waited for them to announce they wanted sleep. As Andrew stood up to go too, I placed a hand on his arm to stop him.

'Don't go to bed. I don't want this night to end yet. I've an idea.'

I packed a plastic bag with a bottle of wine, two plastic glasses and a blanket to sit on and led Andrew out the door. It was the dead of night. There was no one else on that beach; no houses overlooking or cars, just us and the sea. Alone, we sat on the blanket and watched the stars while sipping warm white wine. Andrew hung his jumper around my shoulders when I shivered, but I stopped his hand and removed the jumper. The shiver wasn't from the cold. I wanted to show Andrew my appreciation for the night he had just given me. To thank him for the bandstand, for gathering my friends, for the ring. For changing the path of my life, first when he met me, and again when he asked me to marry him. I wanted to show him the things he could expect if I became his wife.

I stood, taking my time. The light from the moon reflected and lit my features, and I wanted that. I used that. I pulled my top over my head, dropped it onto the sand, exposing my lace mesh bra. His favourite. Nice and slow, I kicked off my shoes. Undone the buttons of my trousers, taking my time to tug one side over my hip and then the other. Andrew placed his hand on mine to stop me, but I pushed his hand away. I wanted to do it. I wanted it to be all from me; to give myself to him. There was power in the submission, in giving my body completely to someone else. As I pulled off my trousers, I never broke eye contact. In just my underwear, I straightened and allowed him to look over me and relished Andrew's want. I unhooked my bra, pausing before I let go. As the seconds continued, Andrew's eyes widened until they were as open as they could be, as if he needed every bit of space of sight to take me in. His expression was serious. No laughing now. My bra dropped on to the sandy floor. Arching my back, I let the moonlit sky highlight my nipples and breasts.

In that blue hue, I was a woman of power. Cleopatra, or an Amazonian warrior, or a Greek goddess, or just Adaline. I played with the elastic band of my underwear, coiling my thumb underneath. The plan when I started this was to take it off and walk to the water, but I realised Andrew had as much power over me as I had over him. Seeing his want made me want him more. As my thumb stalled, Andrew took over. Holding both sides of my underwear, he tugged it off.

Sex that night was different. My body reacted with more intensity than any other beautiful orgasm. This time every sensation and nerve became alive. With expulsions of pleasure, that made me see long bursts of different colours. As Andrew, my husband to be, climaxed, I already knew I was pregnant.

Sunburn

A tightening in my skin woke me. A warning to go into the shade and apply more sunscreen. I moved to a seating position, pulled open my bag, took out a kaftan, put it on. Andrew was no longer by my side. It surprised me how disappointed his absence made me feel. An annoyance rose too. Why didn't he tell me he was going somewhere as a courtesy? I picked out my book from my bag and succumbed to the words of the author the New York Times listed as its new bestselling must read.

A child screamed, followed by a splash of water. My instincts instantly searched for my own children. The boy was fine. No need for alarm. He was about five, and a man I presumed was his father was playing a game of lifting him a little out of the water and dropping him, so he splashed.

I was about to get back to my book when I noticed Andrew in the distance. He was sitting at the bar and there was a blond woman beside him. How long had he been there? I tried not to look, but I couldn't help it. I took in the lady's tanned long legs. Her body language as she leant into him. The way his head tipped back as he laughed.

I looked away.

Was Andrew speaking to her because he thought I was watching? Or was he hoping I wasn't? I didn't know which one I'd prefer. I bet Blondie had the perfect body. Didn't have my flaws, didn't have the scars. The book remained open on the same page. I stared, but I'd gone somewhere else. Just like that, Andrew hurt me all over again.

Needing a distraction, I removed the kaftan and threw it on the lounger along with my sunglasses. As I walked to the opposite side of the pool, I smoothed my hair and secured it into a bun to distract and conceal my vision of them. I sat on the pool edge with my back to Andrew on the off chance he checked on me. The last thing I wanted was eye contact. I slid into the water. It was cold; a pleasant sensation from the heat. I went all the way down, touched the bottom of the deep end, then pushed back to the top. I bobbed on the surface, letting my body accustom to the chill and kept my eyes averted; I did not want to witness the sight in front. I swivelled to face the length of the pool. This time, when I pushed off, my arms sliced through the water. I swam laps until my chest pounded; until I'd had enough. On the climb out of the pool, I couldn't help taking a glance. The bar stools were empty. It took me a moment to pinpoint my sun lounger. Andrew sat on his one. He watched me while holding an empty glass in his hand. And another full glass in his other. Was I just being paranoid about the blonde? Had he actually done something wrong? It wasn't a crime to speak to a woman in a swimsuit.

Give him the benefit of the doubt.

Still, it hurt. I couldn't keep his gaze.

He handed me the plastic glass of beer. The rim had beads of condensation that ran back down into the drink. The beer was warm. I took a drink anyway.

'Thanks.'

'It's probably warm. I didn't want to call you out of the water. You seemed to be on a mission.'

'I was,' I said, embarrassed. I sat on my lounger and wrapped the towel around myself.

'Where did you go?' I cringed as the words came out. Always with the questions. How needy. Andrew didn't seem offended.

'I was checking out the hotel. It has five restaurants. Five. I was talking to one of the staff, Nicholas. Sound guy. He recommended a few spots. Thought maybe we could check one of them out tonight.'

I bit my lip with a smile.

'What?'

'Nothing. It's just nice to see you excited.'

As I sipped my beer, I thought about us. About how people say first love is the sweetest, so much so that everyone remembers how they felt. But what if you don't ever break up and instead stay with that person, knowing love never got better than that? From the very first moment, I knew that whatever life would throw at us, no matter what Andrew ever done to me, I would be his and he mine.

The problem with staying with your first love is time.

That initial, intense love can't maintain itself. Life gets in the way: grocery shopping, bills, bosses, intrusive relatives and unlikeable friends, tragedies and treachery all test love. Can twist and taint it.

Could we untwist it? Could we unravel the knots that bound us? Was it possible to start again?

It still surprised me how we got to that point. To the disintegration of our marriage. When we were younger, I thought our love was invincible. I won't lie, I was even smug about it. Nobody loved like us, nobody communicated better than us. I had to have him; I had to feel him inside me. I was insatiable for him and he loved it. In every conversation with anyone else, I thought of him, wished it was him I was speaking to, looking at, kissing. I pined for him even when I could see him. If we didn't breathe the same air, it disappointed me.

The older nurses, on break in the canteen, would berate their relationships and while they talked, I judged them for being harsh on their partners. Their relationship just needed attention. Instead, the opposite of love expelled from their mouths. I was convinced those words determined how their partners acted. But I hadn't lived their lives yet. I hadn't seen what time can do to a relationship. How it can corrode the greatest of loves, how it rusts and rots and strips away all the good, so it leaves you with only a carcass of feeling. The shell that's left is the only memory of what once was. On the days I heard those women speak, I would go home and hug Andrew tight and swear I would never become them. I swore I would never forget to love Andrew. I didn't realise those women spoke those words to survive, to continue to survive the shrivelled marriage that conjoined them.

You marry the person you love expecting to be with them for the rest of your life. But you have no clue that person will change so much it leaves you looking at a stranger; a stranger that knows everything about you. Who you once opened yourself to, hoping for the acceptance you longed for, but after the years rolled on, they judged and despised you. They got to know you and decided they didn't like you after all.

There should be a disclaimer at the marriage ceremony, a thirty-year money-back guarantee. I'm not saying I would have been queuing up for the refund, but you can tell a lot about a person after they marry. After the chasing goes and forever flaps like a red flag in front of you.

The Entwining Of The Love's

We married near the end of spring. During my favourite season because everything blossoms. When the winter is over, and you are thankful for the bursts of sunshine and the colours that emerge from the ground after the bleakness before. There's always excitement for spring in Ireland, with hope this year an actual summer will follow, that the wet weather and dark days disappear for a while. Before rain and reality hits again in June and there's flooding.

The weather blessed us with a beautiful day, Annie swearing it was because she left fourteen Child of Prague statues outside her house overnight. It didn't matter, I would have married Andrew in a typhoon. I would have walked into that storm without a glance around me. I still don't know if that was naivety or plain love, all I can do is give you the truth and that was how I felt.

There wasn't a big wedding, what with Andrew's family and my father out of the picture and the only two people I wanted, other than Annie and Joe, lay under the ground. We opted for a cluster of people. A few of Andrew's friends from school. Donald, Andrew's business partner and his wife Regina. Joe's mother. Annie's brother. A couple of nurses that had become night out buddies.

It was small, but we took our vows seriously. I did, at least. We did the God thing, because back then marriage was church, the only way to get married in Ireland. We married in Knockfarraig, in the centre of the town. It wasn't an elaborate affair, no fussy church flowers or puffy dress for me. Instead, I wore my mother's wedding gown, a timeless silk long-sleeved number that cinched in under the breast and then flared out. Used as my something old, I wanted to wear the dress so a piece of my mother would be with me. It was also similar to my first date attire. Having learned some tailoring from her, I added a layer of beaded hem on the v of the neck and above the waist, hiding the tiny bump that grew inside.

Annie made my bouquet from hand-picked bluebells, and shop bought lilies. In that church, I walked the aisle alone. The only way I wanted to. I walked to Andrew, seeing no other. That aisle was too long, every step too slow to leave single life behind me. More than anything, I wanted to become Mrs. Love. Andrew's reaction when he turned was unforgettable, his expression changing into multiple emotions. Relief. Fear. Awe. I understood because my own feelings mirrored his. His hands flopped to his sides, devoid of movement. Mine clung tighter to the bouquet. He was even more handsome in his suit.

As we stood before the altar, before the priest, in the practically empty church, I took short gulps of air to combat my nervousness. Andrew's hand trembled as he lit the candle, as frightened as me. While we said our vows, the world dissolved. With clammy hands, I stood in front of a man and promised to love him. In the same spot my mother stood, asking another man to love her. She would never have chosen the life he gave her. How can you know who you're really marrying? Or what life has in store. None of us know the way the dice will roll; only the years can tell you that. Only through incidents and altercations and observations and conversations will you discover who you truly ended up with. Marriage is like standing on top of a cliff with water below. You don't know whether you will crash against the rocks or dive perfectly into the water when you leap. All you can do is jump. At the altar, I didn't have that information, but I looked at Andrew and he appeared so afraid, I forgot my fear. Remember what I said about roles? Those vows started them; it obligated me to help. As we said I do, our baby kicked inside me. The very first kick I'd felt. I saw it as a sign.

Afterwards we walked the two streets to the beach, giddy with the momentous words we had just spoken. Our succession of friends sang my song and passers-by clapped and smiled. Buoyed with excitement, Andrew scooped me into his arms and carried me to the sand. We took photographs on the beach, at the exact spot of our first meeting, and I didn't mind when the hem of my dress got wet. Some of our guests waded in, the men's trousers rolled up to their thighs. The women kicking off their heels and whooping at the cold hitting their legs. The sound of laugher when the trousers unrolled and people splashed others. Afterwards, we held hands and went to our special place. Greene's. It had to be there, where Andrew brought me for our first official date, where we also ate uncomfortably before he asked me to marry him.

We married on a Tuesday, so the restaurant was happy to give us the space between the end of the lunchtime rush and dinner service, ours for a little while at least. We ate scallops for starters and sea bass or steak for dinner, and as I looked at Andrew who was looking back at me, I couldn't think of another time I had been as happy. The day was calm, with no fuss; exactly as we wished. As I watched our guests laugh and eat, as I held Andrew's hand under the table, my joy mingled with slight sadness, the happiness bittersweet, because I knew that this day was the best it could ever be. I had reached the pinnacle of happiness and nothing that ever came after would be as good again.

Dinner

Stephanos was a restaurant on the harbour overlooking the water, one that Nicholas recommended. Andrew shook his head at the menu, as if he couldn't see one thing he'd eat. As if the menu had only one page of options instead of six. Another annoyance. Andrew had turned into one of those typical tourists I cringed at, who wouldn't dare try local cuisine but insisted on chips and ketchup with everything. In those early days, he wasn't like that. He would try new things in a restaurant, or concoct food experiments at home, but that was when he was still open to newness and life and me.

A man sat down beside us with a coffee.

'Irish?' he asked, with a smile.

We nodded. I wondered if it was the pale skin now in places threatening to turn red for me. Or the typical tourist loud shirt on Andrew.

'We Cypriots and Irish are the same. We both come from tradition and morals. Both are countries with two sides. Both have a country that has been at war with itself,' the man said.

'The troubles seem to be over in Ireland,' Andrew said.

'Yes, they are meant to be for us too,' he said and lit a cigarette. 'Are you here for long?'

'A week, it's our first day.'

'You still have plenty to see.'

'We've been here before for our honeymoon and loved it. We always wanted to come back, we swore we would come every year, but then the kids came along and something always got in the way. It's still my favourite place in the world besides Knockfarraig,' I said.

'Mine too,' Andrew said. 'Lot's of great memories here.' He flicked his eyes away when I looked at him.

'Stick around after your meal. It's the owners birthday, there will be celebrations, you don't want to miss it. Have you ordered yet?' the man asked, standing from the table, his break over.

'No.'

'I can suggest a few things if you like?'

I nodded.

As I looked out to the water after ordering and absorbed the surroundings. I had spoken to our children. Even with their mobile data switched on, there wasn't enough reception in the woods for a video call. Their pixelated faces caught mid pose, which only caused frustration for the precious time. Instead, I let their excited voices comfort; I sat back and listened, even though they made no coherent conversation. They were safe. They were happy and having fun. They were not missing us at all. Everything is much simpler for kids, it's adults that make life complicated.

With that information, I gave myself permission to relax. I was in a beautiful restaurant, in a beautiful country, but still. This trip had brought so much back. Andrew's hand moved nearer to my plate. More eye contact. More conversation. Smiles instead of grimaces. Yet we skirted along our issues. We couldn't go there yet. The threat of the needed conversation hung above me, ready to swoop down. Not tonight. Please Andrew, not tonight.

The starter came. I bit into a salty combination of halloumi cheese and lountza ham. I smacked my lips in pleasure. My earlier assumption proved wrong; Andrew didn't order what I expected, he asked for the same as me. There was a bending of us both instead of the rigid way we previously went about our life. The bending leant us closer. A resemblance of the man I fell in love with revealed itself. Andrew was enjoying the food too; he licked his lips after the last bite of the smoked pink lountza.

The stifado came next. It reminded me of an Irish stew, but instead of the use of potato, there were whole small onions. With the taste of red wine in the sauce. The beef fell apart when I bit into it. Andrew ate happily, his relief apparent that his dinner wasn't too far away from what he was familiar with. It carried the rest of the meal along. There wasn't much conversation. Our eyes flickered from the food to each other. After we'd finished, Andrew seemed ready to go, trying in vain to get one of the staff's attention. They were busy. The man we spoke to earlier cleared the room; loudly scraping tables and chairs to each side. The clearance allowed me to see a dance floor at the back. Four men shifted stools together, then sat in a line. They fiddled with instruments and music started. A guitar. The sound more like a pluck than a strum. Flitty, lively, a violin moved fast. A man came out dressed in traditional wear, the same as I'd seen in the tourist brochures. Black boots, black pants. White shirt, red waistcoat. He was on a mission; focused and ready. Another man in the same style walked behind him. They raised their arms wide, out to their sides, in line with their shoulders. Andrew looked uncomfortable. This was exactly what I needed. The men stood opposite each other. They twirled in unison. The men raised one leg each, kicked out, hopped, twirled again. Their twirls were graceful, the timing between them impeccable. The waiter who spoke to us earlier, sat on an empty table next to us.

'See? like the Irish. Another way we are similar. This sounds a little like your traditional music?'

'It does. The dancing is a bit like Irish dancing.'

The men became faster. Moved in close to each other, moved back out and twirled. Both bent their knees and dropped to the ground, bounced straight back up again. Weaved between each other, twirled, got faster.

'They make it look effortless,' I said.

'They don't even break a sweat,' Andrew said. He smiled, relaxed a little. The music shifted in tempo. Two more men came out. The first two stood aside. These two started in the same way as the last. Then more leg raising, kicking one leg behind, touching the foot with the hand. Twirling faster, arms out wide. Each time they did a high kick, or a complicated move, one of them shouted, 'Opa!' encouraging us to do the same. The music stopped. It ended too soon.

A different man walked in to centre stage, took a glass and a napkin from another, showed it to the crowd. The glass was larger than a shot glass, smaller than a tumbler. One dancer took another glass, the same size and shape. He made an exaggerated show of the glass, walking along the crowd. He placed the glass on top of the other on the man's head. His movements steady.

'Opa!'

He placed the napkin on the rim of the glass, then balanced it on top of his head. They upped the tempo now. Another of the dancers took three glasses and worked the crowd. The man bent a knee, allowed the placing. He stood up and sauntered the length of room.

'Opa!'

The dancers now handed out glasses to the crowd and invited them to add more until the man balanced at least ten stacked glasses. He walked as normal, as if it was perfectly easy. There was a flow to his walk. An elegant grace.

'Opa!'

The waiter next to us popped two glasses onto our table. Andrew smiled like a child, and I had to do it, I had to smile back. The man with the glasses on his head came to our table and knelt down. Andrew went first, with no bother. I was afraid. It would be awful if I was the one who would topple it, to ruin the whole thing. I took a breath. Placed it on top. It stayed. The man swayed, and for a minute I thought my fear would come true. He winked at me, then moved on to the middle of the floor. With a final twirl, he gestured his walk was over.

'Opa!'

Each of the other dancers took turns in taking the glasses away until there were only two glasses left. The man placed his hand on top, bent, and with a flourish removed them with the napkin and showed them to the crowd like an offering.

It was my turn. The dancers appealed for someone from the crowd. People shied away and eyes looked at the floor. The dancer with the glass walked straight to me, held out his hand, winked again. His smile said *trust me*. I took his hand and he led me to the dance floor. I stood unsure, embarrassed to have a roomful of eyes on me, afraid too in case I messed up his instructions. Andrew watched, not with his usual indifference but alert, interested, even. The man instructed me to hold out my arms until they were in line with my shoulders. I complied. He stood by my side and done the same. The hand nearest mine held out a napkin. He nodded his head in a gesture to take it. As I did, he pulled on the napkin and brought me nearer, guided me to where he wanted me to follow. He twirled me and weaved me around that dance floor. As I twirled, I became lighter. Around I spun. On the spin I caught sight of Andrew, our eyes locked in place for a second. Each spin I looked for Andrew's eyes again. As I span, I heard laughter and realised it was from me. Still giddy, the dancer led me back to Andrew, the clapping from the other diners ringing in my ears. Andrew's shoulder bumped mine, in solidarity rather than accidental.

They handed us plates and encouraged us to gather on the floor. The owner, the man with a *birthday boy* banner around him, took one plate and smashed it onto the ground. The shards scattered in various directions. The violent gesture made me flinch. The man from earlier pointed to those shards.

'Another tradition of ours. It is said to raise spirits. Try it. It will make you feel good.'

He took a plate from the pile on a table and jumped before smashing his. He looked at his mess with glee.

I shrugged at Andrew, 'Here goes.'

The man was right; there was joy in that movement, in the smashing. It brought an instant release. I took that plate and I smashed it with all my force, as if the breaking was a metaphor for the tension between us. Andrew broke his with even more enthusiasm than me. The energy in the room was fast-paced, frenetic even. The noise was overpowering, but I didn't care; we were laughing together, and that was rare. By the end, by the time the last person threw the last plate, the floor was a ceramic jigsaw.

We sat at our table, our chests heaving, Andrew's eyes bright. The crowd dispersed to their own seats. The music slowed until it became just a background melody. The lighting lowered, with people chatting amongst themselves, separate again. We drank our wine in gulps after the exertion.

'Ready to go?' Andrew asked.

I didn't want the night to end. I didn't want to walk out of that restaurant and revert to ourselves, but I nodded yes, anyway. Andrew placed a hand on the small of my back as I stood. Our arms touched against each other at the counter as we paid. We walked alongside each other as we made the journey to our temporary home. Not with him in front or with me behind. I accepted what was going to happen next. I invited it, in truth.

As we entered our room, we said nothing, no small talk or turning on of lights. I walked straight into the bedroom and with my back to him, I slipped out of my dress with slow, encouraging moves. One strap first and after a pause the other. I gave him a moment to see, then turned around to show Andrew all of me, to offer myself to him. He wasn't there.

The sitting room was in darkness, so I struggled at first to work out where he was. Andrew lay on the couch with his back to me, already feigning sleep. I closed the bedroom door.

On the bed made for two, I let my mind run. Had I misread? My cheeks burned with shame. How foolish to get caught up in the night's excitement, to think after a day, we could slip back into love. After one good night, I'd let myself imagine, and betrayed my resolve. Cyprus did that. Every street we walked, I saw us as we previously were. I felt the love we once had.

I was twenty-four when we met, Andrew twenty-six. Can you forget who you are when you've been with someone for that long? I loved him fiercely, terrifyingly. The force of that love so strong I couldn't express it. I would have done anything he asked, anything. I lived to feel his breath on mine.

In the darkness, a thought hit me, to love someone that much gives too much responsibility. After you lose the momentum, you carry the burden of trying to make the other person happy, like it's your job or something. Like it isn't down to them.

My mind went to our children. To Sophie, in particular. Things were very different back then when we first met in the late nineties. Life was more stereotypical. In Ireland, if a girl slept with many men, they labelled her a slut. That was her title, having to wear that judgement like a noose, with sniggers or whispers if you even talked to a man again, whereas the men that slept around got high-fives. I worried for Sophie that things were still the same. Teenage years for every generation were harsh, but now bullying was sneaky. Bullying got you in the places that were safe. They could reach you anywhere with a phone. All a kid needed was mileage on someone. Or I worried maybe the opposite was true now, maybe the pressure was on to sleep with as many people as possible. Sophie had a good head on her shoulders. I hoped we'd given her the tools to deal with what life threw at her.

I hoped Sophie wouldn't have to compromise herself for a partner. Yet if she wanted love, she would have to. It was easy to say love accepted all, but it was foolish to think you were going to agree on everything. One had to give in. Hopefully not the same one all the time.

I thought about all those things as I lay alone. Instead of the thoughts I should think about, the issues between us, the real hurts that caused us to be where we were. I still couldn't go there. The pain was still too much.

The Honeymooners

At our wedding dinner, I surprised our guests. As Annie offered me a glass of champagne, I shook my head and stood and stretched my dress around my stomach so they noticed the bump. I would hide it no more. Andrew's voice broke as he told them the news.

'We're having a baby.'

I sat to a chorus of congratulations, relieved I didn't have to keep up the pretense of why I wasn't drinking. Then it was our guest's turn. It never occurred to me they could keep secrets too. Annie handed me an envelope. Inside were two plane tickets. For Paphos, Cyprus.

'We know you planned to drive around the coast and just book cheap bed and breakfasts along the way but you only get a honeymoon once, so we all chipped in for one big wedding present and booked some flights.'

'But I don't own a passport.'

'Well, that's the other thing. You know when Fr. Mackey said you needed to get photo's for the ceremony?'

'Yeah.'

'Well, we persuaded him it wasn't really a lie if it was for the greater good. It was scary how little it took to convince him. The photo was for your passport. You know Sean's a guard?' I nodded at Sean, Annie's brother. 'He sorted the signing of the form and photo.'

Sean saluted me. 'I think I could vouch for you.'

'Andrew, did you know?'

'Joe, the dope, let it slip about a month ago. All good though cos it gave me enough time to get my passport and book a hotel. Nothing fancy, what with our loans for the business, but Cyprus is the country of love, so who cares what the hotel is like. The second trimester is the safe time, right?'

He looked at me with such concern. Combined with my hormones and elation from getting married and being surrounded by the people I loved, the surprise pushed my emotions over. I burst into tears.

'If you don't want to go you don't have to,' Annie said, looking concerned.

'It's not that I'm worried, I just can't believe you done this for me. For us. Today, I've never felt so much love. Thank you all.'

The honeymoon was sedate and lazy and perfect. Cyprus in May is a beautiful time. The ground not yet parched, drunk from the rain of winter. The flowers bloom in the still mild sun and cooling breeze. The locals invite in the masses of tourism after the slower season. We soaked up the time together because we knew the honeymoon would be the only chance left for a just the two of us trip. Soon it wouldn't be just my stomach that would grow.

I've heard people say marriage is only a piece of paper, that it changes nothing, but I disagree. It changed things for me and Andrew. It secured us, strengthened our love. We needed the other to make that declaration. It deepened our commitment. Our love was out in the open, we had shown how much we cared for the other and saying those words made us take it more seriously.

Using the pregnancy as an excuse, we stayed near our hotel most of the time. With late nights to bed and later mornings to rise. In the afternoons we would stroll along the harbour and get an ice cream. Or lay on sun loungers by the pool and let the sun take all our stress away.

We visited the castle and afterwards sat on a row at the Odeon, the amphitheater with the lighthouse in the background. Andrew took a picture of me on one of those limestone steps, holding my minuscule bump. It was a beautiful time. The morning sickness that started at six weeks had given a reprieve, I wasn't to know it would come back with ferocity two months later and last throughout the rest of my pregnancy. Sitting on those steps, I was unaware of the impending gloom of sickness. I was only glad it had ended. My fear at our wedding of never being able to match that level of happiness was unjustified. As I smiled into that camera, I was the happiest I'd ever been. My skin tanned and with the glow they talk about in pregnancy, before the swelling arrived that changed a woman's lips and hands and legs. The wedding planning rush behind us. The sun on my skin. Sophie in my stomach. Andrew looking at me through a lens with love in his eyes and a smile on his lips. There were no problems on the horizon. No heartbreak yet. The loneliness abated. The pain of my mother still there, but now I remembered the good times instead of the misery. Back home, Andrew insisted we get that picture blown up bigger than the rest, saying, 'You never looked more beautiful, Adaline.'

He was right. When I looked at that photograph, it was like looking at a person who knew all my secrets. That possessed all the secrets to life. That woman looked right at me and reminded me what it should be like. Reminded me it was still possible to feel happiness again. In that frame she stays blissfully unaware of what was to come. I wouldn't tell her if given the chance; I would want her to stay ignorant. I wished I were still.

Most afternoons we sat in bars at happy hour when it got too hot to sit outside, where I drank virgin cocktails and Andrew sipped beer. Pleasant afternoons where we would people watch or I would read and Andrew viewed sports. We accumulated a few Greek words and practiced them often in the bars or grocery shopping, or in taxi's or speaking to locals. We said little, but we repeated the same words often: 'Yasou' (*Hello*) or 'Kali-Mera,' (*good morning*) or 'Kali-Nichta' (*good night*) or 'Ef-haristo,' (*thank you*)

We found the effort softened the barrier of language and showed our willingness to learn, to adapt to the culture we were stepping on. We used them to show respect. It was also fun. Andrew's favourite word was a different one. 'Ya mas,' meaning cheers. He used it regularly; I didn't mind.

On the first day, as a surprise, I booked a trip as a wedding gift for Andrew. A flight for our second week, to Egypt for two days. What better gift could you give an architect?

The flight to Cyprus had been my first time abroad and was full of expectation and wonder. The flight to Cairo was different. The plane was a little thing. This jet was the first inkling of my falling out of favour with aircraft. Even though the journey was only an hour and a half from takeoff to touchdown, it damaged me. The windows were grubby, the space inside limited and stifling. The pilot was visible *and* touchable. I regretted my decision to refuse the longer boat trip, my reasoning at the time being the sea could bring on my nausea again. I hadn't factored in the turbulence and ricketiness of the plane. Andrew got me through. He clasped one hand while my other hand stroked my belly. He made jokes, pointed out boats or landmarks or quirks from the other passengers.

Even though it was early morning in May, Egypt was already hot. Even though I dressed accordingly in loose light linens and comfortable walking shoes, a slick of sweat gathered under my breasts and over my lip as soon as I stepped out from the plane. I pulled my hair back into a bun, the back of my neck damp where the hair met skin.

Within minutes of entering the grounds of the Giza Plateau, I had grit in my eyes, in my mouth and hair from the Khamsin, the wind covering my face like a hot blanket. The haze from the heat faded the triangular pyramids to floating shadows. The Sphinx sat on a blanket of beige below. As I neared the limestone walls that surrounded the area, the blocks joined as if the Egyptian's only laid them yesterday.

'I thought we would walk amongst ruins.'

A passageway led us to an opening, and then the Sphinx was there. We held back from the guide, choosing not to listen, only staying with the tour for the protection against the many touts that called us from outside asking if we wanted a picture taken, or if we wanted to ride a camel. They meant no harm, every person has to earn a living, but we had heard they were more aggressive with the tourists sightseeing on their own.

The look on Andrew's face was worth the flight. We stayed with the Sphinx for a long time. I watched the light hitting its face.

'This has always been a dream of mine. To see what is possible to design and build. There's a million ideas running through me right now. It's inspiring.' Andrew put his arms around me. 'And it's all down to my beautiful wife.'

'Wife still sounds funny.' I nuzzled his neck. 'I love being your wife. I like doing things that make you smile.'

'Thank you Adaline.'

We lost ourselves to the quiet. Even though there must have been at least a hundred people dotted around the Sphinx, I think everyone was experiencing the need for silence. Words weren't enough here; each step humbled me. We were standing amongst legend; we were walking on the ground of Pharoahs. We followed the sandy path to the pyramids. Andrew pointed to a tomb, the sides sloped, the roof flat.

'Mastabas. Cemeteries. Where they buried the elites of the old kingdom.'

The pyramids called us towards them. A man swept excess dust into a tray as we passed. I wondered if he ever cursed the task and called it futile. I hoped he knew his hard work wasn't; he was uncovering beauty; maintaining wonder. As we neared the pyramids, I kept my eyes down. The ground was uneven, and I was afraid of a fall, of landing on my stomach.

'I thought it was going to be smooth like the bottom of the Sphinx. I always believed they were three smooth walls.'

'No, it's brick on brick. Not brick. Slab. Block even. Imagine the weight of each one. Or how they must have determined the exact angle to get the triangular shape.'

'How would they have moved those blocks? They're huge.'

'I read about this before. Wet sand. Researchers think they wet the sand to prevent any friction when they dragged them along.'

'You'll think I'm thick, but I always thought they made them from sand.'

'Some were, but those collapsed.'

Andrew pointed to the outside bottom of the stones. 'There's been restoration here. You can see the difference in parts. See here? The stone is weathered, the beatings from a thousand sandstorms have worn the surface down.'

The next thing to do was go inside. I eyed the narrow entrance, the steep steps into the pyramid, I had read about the inside, about the tight spaces, the heat, the claustrophobia. I rubbed my stomach; the panic rising.

'I can't go in there, Andrew.'

'Are you OK? Are you feeling unwell?'

'No, I'd just freak out with the lack of space.'

'Come on, we can skip it, I've seen plenty. More than I ever thought I'd see.'

I placed my hand on his heart. 'Go Andrew. You need to see it and I need a rest, walking in this heat is tiring.'

'You've got your water?'

I pulled two bottles out of my bag, handed him one.

'I don't need to see it,' he said.

'You do. You have my permission. Go. Now.'

Andrew grinned and joined the line for the stairs. I smiled at his excitement. As I sipped and waited, I realised it was the first time since we met that I'd chosen to be apart from him.

At three the next morning, we rose and dressed. On the bus journey, we watched night become day with eyes swollen from the dust and grains. We entered desert surrounded by only sand and stone. In the distance stood multi coloured curved domes. We were near. Rainbow coloured shapes like light bulbs hovered at alternate positions in the sky; some hot air balloons had already departed. The bus stopped, and they directed us to one that still lay on its side. Orange flames flashed and disappeared inside it. How did the flame stay sideways? Surely the natural inclination for fire is to go up, to reach for the sky like we would do later ourselves. Our balloon was a patchwork of coloured squares, the most colourful of all the ones I could see. The nicest one. A good omen.

There were at least twenty other balloons, all at different stages of flight. Some stood, still not suspended as people climbed into the baskets. I thought there would be less. A man with a red cap looked over the side of his. The imposing orbs loomed over us. The closer we approached, the more menacing it grew; the flame just added to the element of danger. The balloon next to us took off, leaving the ground not at an angle but ascending straight up, like a slow elevator. Until the people in the basket became dots in the sky. The red cap shrunk until it was a tiny circle. I tried not to imagine how much distance you would need to get that small.

To get into a balloon, you climb over its basket. My height was an obstacle; Andrew cupped his hands together, and I used it as a step.

On reaching the edge, I sat. I held Andrew's hand as I lobbed my legs onto the other side and slid down into it. Inside it wasn't one open area but divided into sections, giving us a space of our own. Little loops of rope hung from the inside walls. As if holding them would keep you safe. Twelve people. I didn't include the uniformed driver in my count. He was different; he determined our passage in the sky.

We were on the ground, and then without fuss, we were not. There was weightlessness, a lightness as we left land. The basket swayed. The flame burnt. The smell of gas singed the inside of my nostrils. There was a tag on the side of one belt. I played with it, looped it in my fingers, my way to distract me, to anchor me to something real while we went through an unnatural action, while we floated. I made the mistake of reading what it said. I should have known what it was. A disclaimer. *The owners of this balloon cannot be held responsible for loss of life or limb.* Until reading that, it hadn't even entered my thoughts. Only when I was up in the air with no other options and no way of getting off did that come into realisation. We were servants to the wind. We would go wherever it decided. No amount of pulled rope could change that if it saw fit. Slaves to the air. With only a thin floor of wicker dividing us from the sky and dropping to my death. I clung to the edge with one white knuckled hand. The other held my bump in protection, as if my skin placed near my baby's heart could stop or reassure us from plunging. Up in that sky I could taste the fragility of life. I hoped I would survive to see my baby being born. Until I left the ground, I never felt danger from being in the air. What fear the little plane to Cairo had planted, the balloon now cemented and turned to stone; I was not a fan of being airborne. What if I never saw my baby? A multitude of ways we could die bombarded me. The balloon could go limp and fall. A hole in the latex. A gas explosion. A loss of gas. A rogue spark catching some material. A frayed rope from years of deterioration as rats gnawed through it every night. More balloons joined us in the sky. Surely we could crash into them? Surely things went wrong. Below us minuscule cars drove on a road, journeying as normal. Safe in their vehicles. Safe like I should have been.

'Andrew I don't like it.'

'Watch the horizon, Ad. Don't look straight down at the ground. Look at the skyline. See how beautiful that is.'

The land became sights. Curved cliffs on my right. Green grass to my left. And then sky met sea met land. It stretched out. The world faced us.

His voice stayed soft, his breath against my ear. 'It's like heaven. How could you be scared of something as beautiful as this? How could anything scary happen to us watching this view?'

Andrew was right. The sun hit the horizon. A yellow dip touched the ground where land merged into sun. An orange globe bigger than any balloon spread out in front of us. Deep blue framed it. I dreamt of seeing a sky like that. I looked up at the canopy of colours on my roof of latex and despite my fear I was thankful. I was with Andrew. We were here looking at something we would never see again in our lifetime. Something we would never forget. Something I would make sure I would never repeat either. Then we were lowering slowly. The desert ground became buildings. Artifacts. Hollowed walls that once held people safe. Now victims of disintegration; now particles of dust and desert. We hovered past walls with door frames and roofs still held in place at parts. As we neared land, I wondered how we wouldn't topple when we stopped. The driver directed us to sit, to hold the ropes on the sides. In case we toppled over, I supposed. In case you fell out and the balloon landed on you and crushed you into flat bone. I could sense the land below us; could tell there was little distance between. I braced myself and worried about the bump; worried about my bump. There *was* one and several shudders too, but we landed on sand, softer than hard ground, more like pillows. Many men waited to help us out. I resisted kissing the ground. It was too cliché. Instead, I kissed Andrew and silently thanked the sky for allowing me safe passage.

155

The Dip

When I woke, the room was still dark from the blackout drapes, but light filtered from underneath. Being careful not to wake Andrew, I found what I needed in the kitchenette to make tea. Once made, I slipped out to the balcony.

The thoughts I shouldn't think about were there. I let them seep, let the darkness descend even though the sky was brightening, and the day was already stunning. The depression coiled. At the same speed the sun came up, the weight of bad feeling shrouded me.

I shouldn't have come. It had been a mistake.

I felt the pull. The sadness hooked into my skin and climbed up and over. It threatened and lingered. It would not go away. I had a choice; I could shake it off by doing something that I'd learnt; something that would shift that feeling or I could give in to it. I welcomed it. I encouraged it and offered myself up. Even though I knew the repercussion; how hard the inevitable, eventual need to scrape off the ground would be. I wanted to lie down. To succumb. To be devoured by self-pity. To climb into bed and pull the duvet over my head. I wanted to sacrifice my body to the darkness.

The glass door moved, Andrew stepped out. He smiled at me. I didn't smile back.

'Are you OK?' he asked. His vein expanded. He looked concerned.

I shook my head. I couldn't speak. If I did, I would say I felt the sun was mocking me. Its brightness highlighted how stupid I'd been for thinking he could love me. I couldn't say those words, those words that would prove my belief. Instead I cried, not silent tears but sobs because the sun shone a spotlight on the pain I'd tried to hide. Of the things that ruined me and Andrew. In an instant he was over, and he was holding me.

'We'll be OK. I promise we'll be OK. Just talk to me. Tell me what I can do. Everything that happened was unbearable, but we can find a way.'

I opened my mouth to speak about the reasons that broke us. Those brown eyes searched mine, and I wanted nothing more than for him to kiss me. The distraction would be better than the truth. He looked like he wanted it too. His eyes flickered to my lips and back to my eyes, setting an intention. Asking for permission.

There was a knock at the door. Andrew let go.

'I'm sorry, I ordered room service as a surprise.'

He disappeared into the room. Through the open door, I saw the lovely Nicholas enter. Andrew helped him push out the trolley to the balcony. I wiped at my face, embarrassed. Nicholas smiled, misreading my discomfort.

'Late night Kyria. You Irish, you know how to drink!' There was no malice in his words, meant as a compliment. I gave as big a smile as I could muster.

'Nothing this breakfast won't fix.'

Nicholas laid the cloches on the table. 'I will be quiet, in case your head is sore. Stephanos was good, eh?'

'It was amazing. Thanks for recommending it.'

'Well, if you like that, your going to love The Meze Tavern.'

I didn't hear the rest. I let their voices blend to background. The sadness was there, dulling everything: words, views, taste, smell. Nicholas waved and caught my attention. Andrew sat next to me and we ate in silence, knowing the moment, knowing the chance for intimacy was gone.

* * *

We walked along the harbour and made our journey to the castle. At the top we watched the boats as they came in and left.

'Can I take a photo of my queen?' Andrew said. There was no sarcasm in his tone. No harshness in his eyes.

I nodded. Stood at the edge. Smiled. Heard the click. 'How about a picture together?'

He gestured to a young girl next to us. She shrugged, shy at first, then took the phone. Andrew walked towards me; the same Andrew that walked towards me that day in the water at Knockfarraig. The Andrew I fell in love with. He stood next to me and draped his arm around me, his palm on my shoulder, his warm hand burning into my skin like the sun. The touch was still familiar; I missed that hand.

The girl handed me the phone; I looked at the picture. An awkward couple stared back. Both unsure of the next step to take; they looked like strangers, yet I knew them; I understood how they felt. It was time to be a little clearer.

'I need to get out of here. Can we walk?'

Andrew's hands went to his pockets. He took a glance at the boats again. 'Sure, let's walk.'

I waited until we were once again on the harbour. 'You're confusing me Andrew.'

'How?' he said as he patted his stomach and shook his head at an expectant waiter. Even that gesture surprised me because for an awful long time, Andrew had only seen himself, hadn't seemed to care what others felt. It pushed me on to speak.

'Last night, I thought it would end one way. But it didn't. You left. I thought I'd offended you, but when you came out to the balcony this morning you acted fine with me.'

Andrew came closer to me, close enough his nose tipped against mine, his dark eyes on me, so close I was sure he would kiss me.

'Adaline,' he stroked my face. Whispered in my ear, 'I will never touch you again until you give me the sign.'

He removed his hand. From his straight-backed walk, the conversation was over. We'd once again returned to him storming ahead, with me behind, trying to keep up.

At the entrance of the hotel, I stopped. I couldn't go back to the room; to the silent balcony or the separate rooms as we dozed. I needed people and the welcome sound of noise. Right then, I needed to blend.

'I'm not going up,' I said.

'Right, well I am.'

He was fuming. That made me angry. 'Well, I'll be at the pool.'

'Have fun.'

He punched the button for the elevator and leant his hand on the wall as if to steady himself and say something. I was too angry to care. It was my turn to storm, this time to the pool.

There was one canopy bed left. I dived on it. It was as soft as I expected. I settled, got myself comfortable, took out my book, stripped my outer clothes off, looked around. Couples occupied every other canopy. Couples who preened and stroked and were happy to lie or sit next to each other. I felt silly. What was an enormous bed for if you had no one to roll around in it? The extra space in our marital one only ever reminded me of loss. Of the absence of him. Its emptiness only highlighted who should lay there next to me.

The pool area was full of almost naked girls. That could never be me, bikinis were a thing of the past. I looked down at my swimsuit. It covered so much. Yet Andrew never minded. It hadn't turned him off.

The time had come. To go to that room and we thrash it out. To say the things we needed to say and leave that room as a couple or apart. At least, an outcome would be decided.

'Space for one more?'

Andrew stood above me. Relieved, I made motions, movement of books, movement of me, movement of decisions made. I couldn't look at him. Instead, I looked at the sky. Blue. Cloudless. The drapes of the canopy fluttered in the brief, welcome wind. Andrew's thigh brushed against mine as he lay down. Moved away as he got comfortable. All I could think about was that space between. That inch of air that divided our legs. His thigh magnetised mine, an energy came from it, drawing me towards him. I felt something below. A wanting. I wanted to smell Andrew again. I wanted to taste him. But what would that achieve?

I stood, too hot, the sweat running and pooling in the curve of my breasts. Through the cloak of my sunglasses, I saw Andrew's appraisal. A thrill ran through me when I saw desire in his eyes.

'I'm going for a dip,' I said.

I turned and strolled to the edge of the pool, feeling his eyes on my behind. Knowing it was Andrew's weak spot with me; his favourite body part. I worked hard to maintain that butt, hours spent in the gym when I could have relaxed or slept, all worth it now though to feel his focus. I stopped at the edge and looked back at him once, then dived in. If Andrew wanted a sign, that was it. That was my way of showing him. The water refreshed me; loosened me. I swam the length of the pool and swam back. Cooler now, I leant my hands on the edge and let my body float. Andrew still watched me. Not as Andrew the dad or Andrew the architect. As my husband, as the man who loved me for all those years. He edged closer until his legs dangled over the end of the bed. He hunched forward, placed his hands on his thighs. I tingled in the water. Andrew hadn't looked at me that way in a long time. He stood up, walked towards me, squatted down when he reached the edge. I was aware of how close his thigh was to my face, of how he covered himself to keep his balance by placing his hands in front.

'I'm going to the room to lie down,'

'I'll join you,' I said, feeling bold.

He nodded and returned to the canopy bed and gathered my bag and waited for me with a towel open wide; he hugged me as he wrapped it around. I slipped my sandals on and still in the towel we almost ran to the hotel room.

It wasn't awkward. It was urgent and carnal and sweet and needed. So fucking needed. I lay afterwards wanting a cigarette even though I hadn't smoked in decades, but nothing else summarised the satisfaction I felt as Andrew dozed with an arm on my hip. That arm. I drifted off into a deep sleep.

Parenthood

Once home from the honeymoon, our life revolved around getting the house ready. Baby proofing and colour schemes and weekends spent loitering in baby aisles. Nights spent with arms from Andrew around the growing belly in protection, falling asleep to names called out in the dark.

'What about Vanessa?'

'No, they'll call the child Ness.'

What's wrong with that?'

'Loch ness monster. No thanks. What about Dylan?'

'No way. Reminds me too much of the singer.'

'By this stage we'll be calling it baby Love.'

'Could think of worse names.'

When night sickness came back, Andrew would grab my hand and help me keep my balance as we ambled down the hill to the beach. We sat breathing in the sea air as I gulped away the nausea with a plastic bucket by my side. When it passed, he held me, and we lay on the sand and stared at the stars. Everything seemed possible with that pregnancy. The excitement got me through the misery of constant vomiting. I couldn't wait to have Andrew's baby.

The labour was routine until the fifth hour. The expected pain was present and accounted for. Until I felt something was different. Something was wrong.

'Please check me. There's something off.' The midwife continued with her paperwork in the corner of the room and flicked my words away with her hands.

'I've seen a million births. It's perfectly normal.'

Andrew spoke then. 'She's asking you to check her.'

She spoke to Andrew, ignoring me. 'Nothing has changed in the last hour. Don't worry, I know the signs. The first baby won't come for hours yet.'

'Andrew, please, get someone for me,' I said, pleading with him.

Andrew looked as if he was about to burst into tears. He had never seen me in this distress and the midwife was telling him it was normal. She walked to the bed and put a hand on his shoulder in comfort, more concerned for him than me. 'Why don't you go out and get some fresh air for a minute?'

Andrew nodded and left the room quickly. The betrayal felt like a punch. The midwife turned to me with a victorious look on her face. 'Now there's no need for the dramatics. If you need my help, I'm here.'

A contraction hit me, floored me. The jolt was to my pelvis, bashing my bone. My words came out broken, hoarse. 'I'm asking you for help and you're ignoring me.'

'I just don't welcome performances, your baby will come when the time is right.'

She fixed her top, sniffed, went back to her paperwork, selected the music station she wanted on the radio. In all my time as a nurse, I had never come across a bad one. I had heard some still existed, rumours of the matriarch that wouldn't listen, that didn't care, that only wanted to be right, that wanted the power. I couldn't believe at my most vulnerable they appointed me with one. In the bed, with no one that cared around me, I cried. Tears of pain mixed with disappointment, mixed with feeling abandoned by Andrew.

The door swung open with Andrew in tow with a man and another younger, kinder looking midwife.

I was drowsy from the pain. My head bobbed with wooziness. My voice came out mumbled and parched from vomiting. It took too much energy to dispel sound. I tried anyway.

'The baby is trying to come. It's knocking against me.' The man nodded at my mumbles, didn't introduce himself, whispered to the older, meaner midwife, listened to her, shook his head. Spoke to Andrew, instead of me. 'Don't worry, this is normal. My wife went crazy at this point too. They can all temporarily lose their mind at this stage.'

I'll never forget Andrew's face. The twisted expression, the division of his turmoil. The vein popped. A man paid more in a day than I could earn in a month was speaking about me as if I wasn't there, as if I wasn't important; questioning my sanity in front of my husband.

'Get out,' Andrew said.

The man guffawed, unused to those words, so much so he thought it was a joke. 'Excuse me?'

'Get out. Don't you speak to, or at, or about my wife like that again. She is telling you something is wrong and what do you do? You question her sanity.'

He turned to the older midwife, 'I'm telling you now, get him out of here and you can go too.'

Everything including my contractions stopped. Andrew squared up to the man. He skulked off in an Armani scent. Followed by the outraged older midwife.

Andrew straightened, the vein stayed. He turned to the midwife.

'Can you stay?'

She nodded.

'If I hear one more condescending word towards my wife, I swear to God I'll wreck this place. The only person's sanity you'll need to check is mine. This woman is a nurse. She is telling you something is wrong. Listen to her. Check her now.'

The younger midwife smiled at both of us. 'I've been waiting for someone to put that man in his place for a long time. Just don't tell him I said that.'

The power shifted. Pain came only minutes later. The midwife checked.

'Adaline, you were right. The baby is trying to come. Stand up,' she said. There was a respect in her tone, an urgency too. Andrew helped me.

'Push your right leg towards me,' she said. I couldn't raise my leg. There was no energy reserve left. The pain jolted in my pelvis, head thumping against bone. I was about to pass out.

The midwife stood under, then in front of me. She held me upright, 'Dad, I need you to lift her right leg towards me. Do it now.'

I recognised the calm tone, the one used by nurses when they were suppressing their panic. 'What's happening? Is the baby in trouble?'

'Adaline, I need you to help now. Lift your right leg up to your hip, OK.'

The strength wouldn't come. 'I'm trying. I can't.'

Andrews arms hoisted my leg into position. The jolting eased. A different pain soared through me, this kind welcomed. The panic left. I was safe. I trusted these two people. I had a man next to me who wasn't afraid to stand up to anyone, who held my hand when life gave us its worst. His eyes were a beacon.

Through the pain, through the exhaustion, my focus was on Andrew's face. When I felt my baby leave my body, I didn't look down. Instead I watched Andrew, waited as his face changed. My payoff. The fear turned to astonishment, to absolute glee. That was it, the look I'd hoped for. Pride rushed through me because I gave him that, my gift to him.

The wait for him to speak took too long.

'Andrew. What did we have?' Our deal was, he would tell me. His mouth trembled, like he couldn't find the words.

'A girl. The most beautiful baby girl I've ever seen,' he said.

'Her shoulder was caught, that's why it felt wrong. Moving your leg gave her the space to squeeze through,' the midwife said with her back to me as she checked the baby and cleaned her down.

I heard the sweetest sound then, a baby's first cry, the sign that life has begun.

As the midwife carried my swaddled child towards me, I looked at the woman properly.

'Thank you. I'll never forget what you just done. I didn't even ask your name.'

'That's understandable. You did such an outstanding job. I'm Sophie.'

'What a beautiful name,' Andrew and I said at the same time.

And then Sophie handed her namesake to me and everything, Andrew included, melted away.

* * *

The next few years were crazy. Filled with the usual things new parents complain about: Sleepless nights, the monotonous rigmarole of feeding and nappy changing and crying and trying to figure out what to do with the tiny thing that had taken over your home and sex life and hearts.

When Sophie was born, we came into our own. Despite everything, Andrew walked around with this grin that could be mistaken as smug-like to anyone else. It was smug, that smugness made me love him more. That time was bittersweet. I felt like I was swimming against the current and didn't know if it was the right direction. There was so much guilt; For not spending enough time with Andrew or being too tired to enjoy Sophie; I needed to split in two. Caught between a

166

baby that needed me in order to survive and a man who needed me to reassure him his world was still in order. It was too exhausting to do it all. People got pushed aside in order to prioritise. Wrong word; there was no priority. It came to a breaking down into logical compartments. When the baby was screaming, what could I do? First, I needed to calm myself as the screams twisted my insides. Next came the nappy check. If it was dry, when was her last feed? Was it wind? Was she just wanting love? If dinner needed to be cooked, that would be the only option that could get changed. I would text him: *Bad day. Fancy take out?*

My nurse's training aided me, the need to put other's needs before my own wasn't so much of a shock, but the lack of any time for myself was. As I tried to cope with that new shiny, soft, living, demanding thing, all while trying to heal. It's a strange experience to cope with the exhaustion from birth while you're left with a baby. A baby loved more than anything, but you've just embarked on the equivalent of a marathon and could sleep for ten days straight. Dealing with a body that still bled and felt assaulted and violated. Bruised and sore and hormonal. The only way to cope was with tears in the shower when no one could see you. Tears for being that tremendously happy and simultaneously distraught. The pain in the breasts when the milk came in. The weirdness when it came out. I felt my husband's frustration. I felt the fraction, the sliver of change, and I resented it, because I was being pulled from every direction. For me, there was no choice.

And then six months came and even though sleep consisted of naps in the day and rocking a crying baby at night, light slipped through. The terrifying newness wasn't there. We established some routine. Some trust gathered in our ability. We had made it this far. We found a way through.

The pain and blood left. The nightmares of birth abated enough to wonder about sex again. Other worries spurred me on that Andrew would become a deprived husband, forced to look elsewhere. I'd heard of it. I'd seen it with other people around us. But I was afraid. What if childbirth changed me inside? I'd heard the crude, smutty jokes from disgusting, drunk men. I expected it would be different, and it was. The first time was like losing my virginity again. Awkward, sore, and with wishes I could get it over with.

But the next time, though.

I didn't expect betterment. Everything became deeper. The trust. The bond. The love. We shouldn't have worried, we still had it.

Just as we found a flow, Henry surprised us. Pregnancy with a one-year-old was manic and exhausting. Once there were two, there was never enough time for me and Andrew. In the pot of time, at the end of the evening, we would reach in and it would be empty. The balance of energy always tipped on one side. We tried to find the time for each other, but the children needed my attention. It reduced Andrew to the background of our life. Whether it was the provider aspect in him, Andrew concentrated on work. Ploughed ahead with projects.

Having children changed me. Worries that wouldn't have been an issue even for a worrier like me came to mind. The randomness of fairness bothered me. How good people could have life taken away so easily. I worried about sharp objects, corners, neck support, over heating or being warm enough. Worried about how much sleep they had, or how little sleep I got, how untidy my house was, how much housework I'd attempted for so little result. I eyed cute animals as potential threats. We avoided shopping centres unless the trip was an absolute necessity; with toddlers each visit led to exhausting arguments of *put that down*, or *no you can't have that.* Or chasing races down aisles with giggling children attempting to break free. And then the guilt of leaving them when my maternity was over. The guilt also from the pleasure I got while working. What I worried most about was being too happy. Waking up with two kids wedged between us with six feet on me, I couldn't believe life could be that good.

Before no time, the children were more manageable. They could understand words, you could reason with them a little. The constant worry abated. We spent summers on the beach. Our beach. Henry eating sand. Andrew and Sophie looking for unusual shells. Me holding the ones they picked for home and thinking of how in days gone by I did those same things with my mother. The whoops of shock when the water hit little feet. The delight. The fun. One day, as the kids buried their feet in the sand next to us, Andrew kissed my shoulder.

'What's that for?'

He grinned at me. 'Does it have to be for anything?'

'No. It feels nice. More, please.'

A multitude of kisses fell on my shoulder. We watched our children.

'We are nothing like them,' Andrew said.

'Who's them?'

'Our fathers. I worried when I was a kid it was hereditary. That when I had children, something inbred in me would turn. It didn't. We haven't carried on their misery.'

I held his hand, kissed his fingers. 'You are a brilliant father.'

'I am, aren't I?' he said, grinning.

The children's laughter floated to us. The perfect moment; the air felt thick with our love.

'Give me another,' I said. My voice came out low.

'Serious?' Andrew said.

'If I could get away with it here, I'd say right now,' I said.

'I want another too.'

And that was how Adam was made.

Thunder

My hunger woke me. It was dark, but the rumbling in my stomach told me it was only dinner time. Careful not to wake Andrew, I loosened myself from his arms and snuck into the bathroom, taking my phone. Easing the door shut, I showered and afterwards took my time applying my most expensive lotions and face creams. I wiped the steam away from the mirror and examined my face. The sun gave me a glow, my eyes looked brighter than I'd seen in years. The last two days had given me the equivalent of a facelift.

My phone beeped. Multitudes of pictures came through all at once of Sophie and Henry. All smiling. In various poses. In their tents. At the campfire. Kayaking. A message followed:

Can't ring going on a night trail.

I sent a quick message back: *Have fun. We love you.*

Later we sat in a restaurant on the harbour and watched the thunder and lightning in the distance. We chose the inside by the window. As we examined the menu, we heard the first drops of rain on the awning outside. The drops turned into a shower. A Cypriot man ran out on the walkway and held his hands out wide in the air. The rain washed over him. In the middle of the street, the man danced. Our server noticed our puzzled laughter as he came over to take our order.

'He's checking to see if the rain is real. We haven't had wet weather since February.'

'Typical that it rains when we leave Ireland. We were trying to get away from rain there.' Andrew laughed.

'It will be hot again tomorrow. It just gives the ground a chance.'

It poured now, fat droplets dripping off the canopy. The occasional flashes of lightning on the horizon relaxed me, too far off to be of concern. I shivered a little.

'Are you too cold?'

'No, it's great, this day has been great.'

Andrew smiled an enormous smile. The vein nowhere to be found. 'We're good together here.'

We walked home holding hands.

On the balcony in our home for a week, we shared a bottle of wine. Each sip loosened us, shifted us closer on the seat until we were on each other for the second time that day and that year.

The next morning we didn't move from the bed, stayed that way until we became hungry, then rang down for room service. As we lay there for hours, relaxed, the thought came to me that Cyprus *was* the island of love, because it managed the impossible; it healed our brokenness, bandaged the scars of our fractured relationship. The old me had returned. The me before kids, the me before Adam and the us before the hurt. I sensed the undoing of the wrong that was done to us both. That *we* did to us.

'Nicholas recommended a restaurant. It's a drive, but it serves with no menu. He said it has the best meze in Cyprus. What do you think?' Andrew said, his lips on my back.

'I think let's do it.'

Andrew snoozed then, his soft breaths displaying the satisfaction of sleep. Sleep wouldn't come for me. I wanted to saviour that feeling. How had I existed without that affection?

Like my first dates, I took my time to get ready, showering and applying my makeup and choosing what I'd wear in order to parade myself to him after his siesta. Because I wanted to again, I wanted to impress my husband.

The restaurant was a trek away, with the last portion of the journey a drive along a dirt track. It didn't give me much hope for what to expect; I wondered if Nicholas sent us to the wrong place. The front of the building didn't allude to much either: rustic brick walls with potted plants placed along a parched walkway. The many cars outside and the amount of people entering assured me it was popular.

'Nicholas said it's not touristy at all. It's where the locals go. He said it's the best.'

The hand painted sign scrawled, *The Meze Tavern.*

Inside the restaurant were white walls with mahogany beams and matching tables and chairs. Dark wood picture frames dotted every available space of wall with images of one man holding vegetables or awards or with arms around other people.

We sat outside, under a huge veranda that had flowers woven into its beams; the perfume of lemongrass around us. An uninterested woman approached our table, she wanted to know only two things: what colour wine we wanted and whether we preferred fish or meat. Simple.

Andrew pointed to a rail beside us. 'There's cucumber. I read they pick all the produce from here. That's how they dictate the menu.'

The woman placed a carafe of white wine on the table.

'They make their own wine as well. No sulphates mean no hangover,' he said with a wink.

Homemade breads and hummus and garlic mushrooms with arti-chokes drizzled in oil and salad with tomato came one by one to our table. Potatoes dripping in fresh herbs and oils. Everything made my mouth water. Plate after plate came out, the woman stating only what each one was in Greek, then English with no other attempt at conversation. There was no contempt or indifference; her words came out as a statement.

'Keftedes. Spicy meatballs.'

Then, 'Souvlakia. Pork skewers.'

Next, 'Afelia. Pork in red wine.'

The portions were small enough to not fill us and they left plenty of time in between. It was pleasant; with no sense of rush there. The woman would serve the same no matter who you were, no matter what your preferences. She would continue to serve in the order the chef saw fit, even after you left.

The next plate she placed on the table were dark green parcels with red sauce oozing out.

'I've heard of this one, it's koupepia. Made from grape leaves, I believe?' I said to her. She nodded, then surprised me with a grin.

Stuffed with rice and minced pork and smothered in a tomato sauce, the taste exploded in my mouth. Andrew closed his eyes while chewing. I waited until I finished. 'You've surprised me coming here. I didn't think this would be your cup of tea if I'm honest.'

Andrew narrowed his eyes. 'I don't get you?'

'Well, you're not usually open to this kind of food. You're not usually open to anything around me.'

His expression changed. 'Before the kids I used to cook new things all the time.'

'And after the kids, you never cooked again.'

I'd gone and done it again. Picked at the scab. This time I knew why. Our happiness was false, I was desperate for us to talk. It was time to rip the scab right off. 'Do you think if we met now for the first time we would still fall for each other?'

His eyes flickered, hesitated. 'I guess not then,' I said, disappointed.

'No, I still find you attractive.'

'But do you love me, Andrew?'

His silence said it all. The absence of words wounded me. The energy between us prickled. Spiked.

'So what? Was this just a last fling? Why are we even trying if you don't love me anymore?'

'You tell me. Frankly, I'm confused. You're like this different woman out here. For over a year now you haven't let me touch you, not even kiss you Adaline and here it's like we are on a second honeymoon, back to the way we were ten years ago but with no explanation, no talking to each other as usual. Are we meant to carry on the pretence for the whole holiday? I thought by coming here we were going to have it out with each other. Shout and roar and scream and cry and then, after we let it all out, come back to each other, but I'm none the wiser about why you went cold. I know Adam changed us but there was something else and if I don't know then I can't work towards fixing it, which means it could happen again. I won't cope with it happening again.'

'So this is all my fault?' I said louder than I meant. Other dinner guests looked over at the possibility of drama.

'I'm in the dark. One day we were happy and the next you blanked me. Out of the bed, out of your affections. A ghost in the house.'

'This is typical of you, your shit doesn't stink, does it Andrew? You have done nothing. No clue, right?'

He hesitated for a second. Opened his mouth to speak. I put my finger in the air to make a point.

'We're finished. I don't want to be with you. It was foolish to agree to coming here. Stupid to believe intimacy would get us back to each other, but it can't; it's too late and you're still an *arsehole*.'

Shaking, I stood, grabbed my bag and walked to the entrance. 'Can you book me a cab please, my husband will settle the bill,' I asked the woman. Another of those roles, Andrew always carried the most cash.

The woman opened the door for me and gestured outside to the taxi's lined up without a reaction. 'There are cars already here.'

'Thank you.'

I left without looking back. I didn't care if Andrew was right behind; he wasn't sharing a cab. With that much anger I would have preferred to walk off the emotion, but the hotel was too far away and I didn't have a clue how to get there. I wanted to get to the room before him, to get to bed and make sure not to say another word that night. Because if I did, if I said what I wanted to say, if I spoke of the truth that lay inside me, there would be no going back. I needed to sleep and be sure. No good came from speaking in anger, it only resorted in trying to hurt; when reaching for the jugular became more important than peacekeeping. For the kid's sake, I would have to finish this amicably.

As the car pulled away, I saw Andrew running out. He put his hand up to hail us down. I looked away.

Dark Corners

The pregnancy with Adam was tough. Not because of sickness or soreness or a variety of symptoms, but because of the enormous amount of energy required to run around after two small children and working shifts at the hospital.

At that stage I had settled into Accident and Emergency. I loved the hustle. The randomness. The way each day was never the same. The shift never dragged, never had the chance to. We were always busy, always full, always short staffed. I loved the chaos and found I was good at it. I found I could take a challenge and break down the problem into logical bundles, seeing exactly what we needed to do next. But by the time I was eight months pregnant, I was over standing all day.

As I made my way from the car park to the hospital for my last shift, I ran through a combination of emotions. Dread for getting through the next twelve hours and excitement for finishing. Annie made sure we worked the same shift that day; it was rare for the two of us to be on together, with too many younger nurses to oversee between us. I smiled at the thought of her, knowing she was planning something. Being my last day, I took in my surroundings more, the smooth path, the freshly landscaped green areas on either side. The difference in paint on the building where the old hospital joined the new extension. It resulted in a mess inside. One-part slap dashed on to the other, old rundown parts joined on to new flashier sections for the public. There was never enough funding, never enough to cover the expense, which resulted in the closure of some wards because even though the rooms were there, the extra beds weren't and the cost of staff and cleaning them too much, so we only ever used them at full capacity. I didn't know it then, but this day would be one of those times.

What I was most concerned about was whether my uniform would stand the duration. My belly, higher this time than the other two, was threatening to pop its buttons. Another reason to want the shift over.

In the lobby, I waved at Jo on the information desk.

'Last day. Lucky you,' she called to me.

I punched the air in answer. Made my way to the staffroom to drop my bag and coat in. There was a note on my locker.

Be back here at six. No exceptions!!!

I chuckled at Annie's note, she'd never let me down.

She was the first nurse I saw that shift and also, later, the last. In accident and emergency, there were horizontal bodies and vertical people everywhere. Packed seats in the corridor. With extra people standing, holding heads, or arms, or green with sickness. There were shrieks and screams. I could smell blood too, like a sniffer dog, I could sense it from miles away.

'What's the story?' I whispered to Annie.

'Ten car pileup. Two already dead. Gas explosion in St Mary's too.'

'The psychiatric hospital?'

'That's the one. Supposedly one patient snuck into the kitchen and found a saw and a lighter. Hacked at the gas line, I guess I don't need to say what happened to him. There's a few lively patients here because of it, to put it mildly. All the critical patients are in surgery or in ICU, so we're left with the more colourful one's. A lot of disruption.'

Disruption wasn't the word I'd use and lively patients were an understatement. Annie looked exhausted, and she had only started her shift. A terrified kid in the first bed was being bandaged up. It wasn't from the pain of his injury though; he recoiled from witnessing the man across smacking his head full force against the concrete wall.

A porter tried and failed to get through the mass of people with a trolley. No one moved. A distressed woman punched one of the trainee nurses. The place needed order. The cogs of my logic turned. A solution formed.

'We're gonna need more space. What are the chances of opening up Ward Augustus?'

Annie looked at me with an expression that said, *'how the hell am I going to get the time to do that?'* I laughed.

'Don't worry, I'll sort it. I'll go down and turn on the lights. Give me the keys and I'll make it look like it was open the whole time. Get a porter to wheel down the more disruptive ones, we can keep them away from the others, get some calm back here.'

'Adaline, did I ever tell you how much I love you?'

I squeezed her arm. 'Only every second day.'

She walked to the desk, and I caught the keys she threw. 'Just as well the feeling's mutual,' I called out as I rounded the corner. I weaved my way through the crowds until I came to the end and skimming past a chair whose only purpose was to block the entrance. I pushed the double doors to a long corridor.

As the doors swung closed, silence greeted me. It was like entering a different building all together. Rarely used, that empty corridor only led to the abandoned, locked, ghost ward of St Augustus. The times I'd ventured down, I always hurried. That corridor and ward always gave me the creeps. It was too empty. Too old. Its silence always too quiet compared to the bustle from the other wards.

The squelch of my shoes on the floor echoed in my ears. It didn't help that the end was in complete darkness, the light switch turned off to deter any wanderers from going further, I understood the reasoning but it always left me feeling exposed. I held the key out for protection, as if a little metal could help me. From memory, I turned right, knowing it took about another five feet to reach the light switch next to the St. Augustus ward. With my shoulder against the wall, I edged along until my fingers tipped the pitch black corner where concrete became a door. I backed up a little, feeling something uneven and gritty under my feet. My fingers felt along the wall for the light switch and when I finally found it, I switched it on. The top door pane was empty except for a few slivers around the edges. Pieces of glass surrounded my feet. I heard a crunching noise. Shoes on top of glass. A man with jittery eyes and a contradictory grin stood in the other corner; his arm covered in blood. His other hand held a long shard of sharp glass.

Edward

I walked through Kato Pafos on a mission, going to a place I remembered from our honeymoon. A church. But a church like no other. Its Cypriot name was Agia Kyriaki, but tourists called it by the name of an inconspicuous column on its grounds, St. Paul's Pillar.

I stood outside the church, where people from another time stood before, with their own set of problems. Those issues, like them, long dead. How had this church lasted the test of time? I came to learn its secrets. Hoping its magic would seep through its pale tan walls into me. A sea of beige rubble lay under my heightened view. I followed the walkway that surrounded the church grounds. The walkway was a recent addition. Back when we last came on honeymoon, tourists were free to roam. I leant against the metal rail and looked down at the remnants of columns and bricks laid and made by ancestors. Every stone had a story. Every step I stood on had history embedded into it. I tried to work out the patterns and structure of that floor, hoping if I could make sense of what the broken puzzle stood for, I could also piece together my marriage.

For two days we had avoided each other, me and Andrew, the silence too strong and overpowering that I didn't know how to start a conversation even if I wanted to. When he walked into a room, I walked out. I went to the pool and read while he slept. He ate lunch while I lay on the balcony.

Once I completed the walkway, my feet causing the wooded slats to clop and clack, I settled before the entrance to the church on a low stoned wall under the shade of some trees, a few feet away from the walkway. The real reason I came was to watch the weddings, which usually ran on the hour from twelve to three. For two days I wanted to tell the various brides to run, turn back, that they didn't realise with those vows you changed everything, because becoming a wife meant giving yourself up. Giving the solitary you away. From that day on, you had to always think of someone else other than you.

But I couldn't ruin it for them, on that floor of ruins.

I recognised the naïve joy the couples shared. It reminded me of our day, and how happy I'd been.

It took every bit of willpower not to book the first plane out after our fight because all I wanted to do was hug my kids. But I knew if I did that, everything I tried to achieve on this trip would definitely be over and I couldn't use my kids to ease my pain. I missed Sophie and Henry. The need to hold them was vast. Nothing could fill the emptiness. Cutting short my break and turning up at the campsite would be for my benefit, not theirs.

An old man with a backpack in his hands stood next to me and stared at the church. He glanced over and smiled.

'Do you believe this is really the spot where they flogged Saint Paul?' he asked. Pointing to further down, where the column sat under a tree.

'Well, it says so, doesn't it? I'd like to believe it's true,' I said, smiling back.

'May I?' he asked, gesturing to the shaded wall next to me.

'Course,' I said, scooting over.

He mopped his forehead with a napkin. 'I chose the wrong time to explore, midday heat is not the best time to walk around. I was hoping for no weddings, it's a lot cooler in the church.'

'Ah, you've been here before.'

'A few times you could say.' The wrinkles by his eyes folded into themselves when he smiled.

'A romantic at heart, so.'

'That I am. You?'

He had kind eyes, this man. His voice was soft, with an English accent and encouragement in his tone, which made me trust him instinctively. 'I used to be. Now I've come here to wonder where it all went wrong. Myself and my husband, we came out here to fix us, but it is unfixable. It's irreconcilable.'

How could I say these words to a total stranger? But I knew the answer. It was because he was a stranger I could talk.

The man didn't speak for a moment, moved his foot over the grains of history on the ground.

'Nothing is irreconcilable. Anything can be worked out. Me and my wife married sixty years ago next month. We got married in this very church.'

'Congratulations.'

'Thank you. We got divorced about forty years ago.'

'Oh. I'm sorry.'

'Don't be. It was the best thing we ever done.'

'I think I understand. At least on this holiday we've tried. But it's useless. We've grown apart and there's too much hurt inside to move on. Even if we wanted to, even if we forgave, we can't forget. We've tried. We've failed.'

'Which one was unfaithful?' he asked.

I looked at him, unsure. 'I haven't spoken to anyone about this.'

'We are strangers in a foreign land. No better time to spill your guts and have no repercussions, almost like going in there for confession,' the old man said with strangely bright eyes.

I took in a large breath. On expulsion, I said the words that terrified me. 'It was him.'

'Is he apologetic?'

'We've never talked about it. He's never admitted anything. Doesn't know, I know, and I've never confronted him because I'm a coward. I couldn't. Even now I can't still. I've been afraid if I lay it out, that would be it, our relationship would be all over and a part of me didn't want that, didn't want to end that.'

'So you decided to stay and punish him instead,' he said, his old wise eyes on mine.

'I didn't. I didn't mean to, anyway. At first I was sick to my stomach.'

The man waited for me to continue. I took another large breath.

'I did punish him. I moved out of our bedroom. At first because I couldn't let him see how hurt I was. Then after, I couldn't let him touch me with the same hands he touched her with. After everything we'd been through, he betrayed me. We weren't that couple. He was meant to be the rock. Andrew was meant to be the unchangeable when everything else warped or threw itself at us. There I was, dying inside, yet he carried on, laughing with the kids, trying to joke with me. I wanted him to hurt like I did. So I blanked him. Then when the hurt got a little easier, I got angry. Not sleeping with him was the best way to get him back. I forgot I was denying myself as well. This trip reminded me how much I missed that side of our relationship. Sorry, I shouldn't be talking to you like this.'

'Not at all. Don't let my age fool you, there's not much I haven't heard or seen, in eighty years. I could tell you stories that would make you blush.' He chuckled, but then turned serious. 'It was me in my case, I was the one. There was no confession either, I just didn't even try to hide it. Carried on in our small town, going to the only hotel. Eating in my friend's restaurant. I wanted her to leave me, you see? I wanted to get caught. Forced her into the decision because I knew that was the only thing she wouldn't put up with.' He sighed. 'Planned it all. Still, it did not prepare me for the look in her eyes or the hurt I caused. I came home one day to bags in the hall. She handed me divorce papers. Without a word, I picked up those bags and closed the door and walked away, knowing I'd got what I wanted. A divorce. But it was different than I imagined. I thought the misery would go the minute I walked away. But it was still there. Being with the other woman wasn't even the reason, not even an option afterwards. Once I left June, I lost all interest in her, all interest in sex. Do you know what's funny?'

'What?'

'The traits you fall for in a person can be the very things you learn to hate. Yet when I was on my own, those were the first things I missed.'

I screwed up my nose. The old man saw my confusion. He chuckled.

'I'll explain. When we were dating, I loved how she knew what I was thinking about so well she'd finish my sentences. Near the end of our marriage, how it used to grate on me. The bloody woman couldn't let me finish! It drove me crazy.' He took a napkin from his pocket and wiped at rheumy eyes. 'Every night I came home to an empty apartment. Before I left, I'd walk into a house full of noise and chaos and now I had the silence I'd craved for, I missed them. Too sorry for myself to cook, I went out to bars most evenings just to be in company. People tried to drag conversation out of me, and I wished then for someone to finish the words. It was one thing that made us, us. All the things about her I despised were the very reasons I fell in love with her. She hadn't changed, it was my perception of her that had. While in that bar, with people around me sharing laughs and acting raucous, I admitted to myself how lonely I was. It took leaving to realise I made a mistake. On my own, I finally saw what I should have seen all along. She didn't hinder me, she enriched my life. I decided I would do everything I could to get her back. It was hard at first, I won't lie, building trust takes time but I had a taste of life without her and I knew I would never take her for granted again. From then on, every day I would show up at the house and help with the children. I would bring food shopping, help cook the dinner, listen to their problems. Every day. My June was the kindest woman I've known. We married again three months later with the children as our witnesses.'

'Oh wow. That's lovely, I'm so happy for you.'

'Do you know what I realised? My infidelity, my scorn, it all came down to ungratefulness. I had no gratitude for my wife and when your life turns that way, everything around you shrivels. Nothing can prosper. Our love withered. When I figured it out that I missed her quirks, I remembered the other quirks about that woman I loved so much. The way she always left a change of clothes out on my chair, ready for the next day. The way she smelt of Chanel because she heard it was Marilyn Monroe's favourite. How great a mother she was. How great a wife. My best friend. It all comes down to that in the end. You know the saying glass full or empty? Well, it's true. You can't be unhappy and grateful at the same time. The minute I started counting my blessings, our love healed.'

'I don't think any reasoning can make me feel grateful for my husband cheating on me.'

'Fair enough, but why did he cheat? Have you ever asked him? Men are fickle, childish characters. At the end of it all, we want to be loved.'

'So it's my fault?' My voice came out needy.

'Not at all. In my wife's case, it certainly wasn't. No, what I mean is, we can hurt the people we love the most, when we are afraid of the hurt they can do to us. Maybe this will force his fear to the surface. Can I offer you a little advice?'

'You have so far. Work away.'

'Say everything you have to before it's too late. He deserves to know that you found out. Even if it's just to finish the book before closing it.'

'You think I should forgive him?'

'No, I don't know your circumstances. I just think for your sake you should say the things you need to. In order to move on. If you still love him, find a way to forgive. Any relationship can work if the two people truly want it to. Just decide what you want. Life is too short. I should know, I got forty more years because I was brave. That's why I'm here. To say goodbye to my wife.'

He took out an urn from the backpack.

'My sons and daughters are meeting me here in a while. I wanted a little time with her before I let her go. June made me promise when she was sick I would make this trip. To scatter her ashes out here in the ruins, in the place we became man and wife. She wanted me to show the kids our favourite spots, so saying goodbye wouldn't be so devastating. That was my wife for you, always thinking of everyone, even while dying.'

Memories of my mother's own dying plans flooded in and the plans I had to make for Adam. I couldn't stop a tear from falling, yet I didn't feel shame for exposing my pain; I felt lighter. I embraced the man who was a stranger five minutes before.

'I'm sorry about your wife.'

He patted me on the back. He broke the embrace to wipe at his eye. His finger shook as he caught his tear. 'Don't be. Those forty years were wonderful. We were still young, your age now I'd say, give or take a year. We still had plenty of time when I figured out I'd won the lottery. Forty years of knowing I am blessed is better than most.' He patted my hand, looked at the church. His lip quivered. 'I live my days now she's gone counting down. Every day drags, I try to take the joy still, June would have wanted that. I love being around my family, and Cyprus has been a lovely holiday, but it isn't the same. I miss her. Now that there's only me to finish my sentences, I don't feel like talking too much.' He squeezed my hand. 'Do yourself a favour, if he isn't the right one, finish it and give yourself the chance to find someone. Don't give up on love.'

'I can't go in there,' I said as I nodded to the church. Some people in dressy clothes were loitering outside. 'I haven't stepped foot into a church since Adam. My son. I didn't want to. I couldn't.'

He gave a slow nod. 'Ah. I'm sorry. It's hard to continue a marriage after that.'

'That wasn't what finished us though. It damaged us. Broke me and changed us, but it was the affair that ruined us.'

He patted my hand. I needed to change the subject because if I didn't I was going to burst into tears. I concentrated on the church.

'I have been in there. Before. On our honeymoon. I remember it's lovely inside.'

'It is. I was never religious, but when June showed me a picture of that church, I knew I could get married there. There is beauty in this place. Historic, peaceful. When I got married in that church, I swear I felt the Gods smiled down on us.'

'Maybe I'll brave going inside. I could do with some peace.'

A car entered and pulled up by the pedestrian entrance near the church. A man got out. Dressed in a too hot suit for the sunny day. His hands wouldn't stop moving, fixing his hair, his tie, checking his pockets, wiping the sweat from his brow, his eyes shooting from side to side like an animal sensing they've become prey from some unseen threat. The groomsman pushed him towards the crowd gathered around the church. We both exchanged glances and chuckled at the man's fear.

'It's a beautiful day for a wedding. Thank you, for everything, I promise I'll talk to him.'

Some voices sounded near, coming towards us, three women and two men.

'Are they your children?'

The man nodded.

'Wow, you were busy.'

'Me and June kept ourselves amused,' he said with a wink.

'I'm going to slip away, leave you have some peace.'

'Let me introduce you.'

'No, I've taken up enough of yours and June's time.'

He held out a hand to me. 'My name is Edward. Thank you for talking to me. June would have liked you, you remind me of her.'

I shook his hand. 'Really? She must have been some woman so,' I laughed. 'Adaline.'

He was the second man I met to not mention or sing the song.

I waved once at his children. Their red-rimmed eyes and sombre glances assured me it wasn't the time to make acquaintances. I ambled to the road but then turned back and watched as they lined one by one on the walkway overlooking the ruins right beside the church. As they scattered their mother and Edward's wife's dust, releasing her back to the grounds, she walked in happier times. A time that paved the way for the very children now who mourned her to be born. I had to close my eyes from their sobs and from the embraces because it made me feel I was intruding on something only June should be witness to. Instead, I followed the last bits of her as they floated. As they mingled with the air and became the breath of the oncoming, unaware new bride beginning her wedding march. I'd like to think it was June's way of giving the bride her blessing; that as the bride breathed June in, she was given an extra chance to have a fraction of the love June did. I hoped so, I really did.

Adam

Adam's death devastated us. One day we were planning a life ahead and the next we weren't. Left only with hollow plans and a gnawing emptiness in my womb. I'd like to say we rallied around each other when our baby died, but it would be a lie. Andrew tried. It didn't matter how many times he reassured me, I couldn't shake the feeling that he blamed me, more than I blamed myself even, for placing Adam in that situation, for causing the death of our son. Because I would have if it had been the other way round.

Blackness took over everything. In the hospital bed, I succumbed to my depression; I wallowed in the hurt and suffering, and I couldn't bear to open my eyes. Everything came on top of me, the grief of losing Adam, all the feelings I didn't let go of when my mother passed, the anger I felt towards my father and the horror of what that man did to me came to the surface and mingled together in a constant unending nightmare. Sometimes it was my father who pierced my skin and slowly plunged the glass into me with a satisfied grin. Other times it was my mother cackling afterwards as she climbed back into her coffin and crossed her arms to go to sleep. Those times were better because even in the nightmare I knew I was sleeping. It was when I would see the real man's face and the blank stare he possessed when he attacked me, that chilled me most of all, because I knew that was real and this time nobody would come and I would die on that ugly corridor floor. When I woke I tried to rationalise it: he was mentally ill, and he thought he had no way out, I'd cornered him, and he didn't think there were any choices.

But then I remember the *slowness* of his attack, how much he enjoyed the glass entering me. His expression showed nothing but detached glee. How he happily slashed at my hands to get them out of the way. How he punctured my stomach and when the amniotic fluid seeped out, he laughed. The paralysis that used to take over me when my father was drunk returned, I watched as the warm fluid dribbled on my soft plimsoll shoes. The man pushed the glass in deeper, turned the shard and then lifted it. I couldn't get his hands away, the pain and shock and the strength of him left me frozen in horror. He lifted me until my feet raised from the floor, until they suspended off the ground. My nurse's logic kicked in. I wrapped my hands around the mans, to keep his in place because if Adam was to have any chance, the man could not pull the glass out. The blood loss would mean he would surely die. I also knew if I let go and he freed the glass, he would continue to stab and stab. He screamed over and over, 'That's Satan's child. I'm ridding you of the devil.'

Those screams alerted the staff. I held on until I saw them, until they struggled him to the ground. The last person I saw before the dark took me was Annie and her auburn hair. Her voice trying and failing to not sound scared.

'You're OK. Everything's going to be OK,' she said.

But I didn't believe her. By then I didn't care what she said, saving me didn't matter, I wished for death too because I knew my baby, my innocent Adam had gone. I felt the life drain out of him and then felt it drain from me. And I welcomed death because it would be better than a life knowing that man had killed my baby. I closed my eyes and let it take me.

I didn't save him. As a mother, that was all I had to do. Just keep my baby safe. I failed Adam. I failed Andrew.

You hear of survivors who emerge from horrific instances and live life to the fullest, who never look back and never take life for granted. That didn't happen to me. I grieved for what happened; I grieved for my baby and my body, and I couldn't do anything to fix it. Conversations were pointless. When I had to speak, it would remind me of how futile talking was, how unnecessary. I craved silence, begging for the voices in my head to calm because all I could hear over and over screaming at me from the inside was: ADAM IS DEAD. YOU LET HIM KILL YOUR BABY.

The surgeon told me I was lucky that he didn't pierce my organs. What he didn't say, what he omitted, was the fact the man did all the damage to Adam. My baby took the wounds instead of me. An inch under or over and it could have been different. If I had a choice, I would have moved that piece of glass, if it meant Adam lived.

When I recovered enough, we had the funeral. I kept all my strength for that because despite the reassurances they could wait, I couldn't stand Adam waiting, frozen in the hospital morgue.

We had to buy a burial plot for Adam, as death wasn't something me or Andrew contemplated for any of us before. The hospital offered to bury him in a shared grave, but I couldn't imagine being buried anywhere but next to him when I died. They held Adam in the hospital's morgue while I recovered, assuring me he was fine and would wait till I was ready, but I would never be ready. I needed my baby to have a ceremony, even though I wasn't religious. The funeral mass took place in the church that held such fond memories for us of our wedding and the other children's christenings. After that day I never stepped foot in a church again, I vowed the next time would be in a coffin when I would join Adam.

Andrew carried the white coffin from the funeral car to the plot. He was so careful, his eyes dead set on the uneven ground, and I could see every step nearer to the open hole broke him more. He grew older the further he walked. I couldn't move, couldn't help. It was too much to watch, with only enough energy to hold the children. When he finished his walk, when he completed his child's last journey and the undertakers took our baby from him and lowered Adam into the black hole, Andrew crumbled to the ground. It broke me to see Andrew break. I went to him then and held him as we cried and that time he held me back.

Nothing was ever the same for us after that. How could it be? Our flesh, our blood was under the ground, our son buried before us. As they tossed the earth over Adam's coffin, the horror slammed into me. The mistake I'd made struck as deep as digging soil. By refusing the shared grave, by burying my baby in a new burial plot, Adam would be all alone.

I kept strong until we put him in the ground. But then I succumbed, and I couldn't do anything else but let the pain flood through me.

There were days I cried for hours, the pain racked through my body, my nerves on fire, my heart hurt, a searing, burning. The rest of me felt empty. Boneless. A void of space that the pain swept into. I knew as a nurse it was grief and I just had to go through it, but rationality on those days went out the window and the pain overtook everything, and I was thankful for it and immersed myself fully. Because the pain distracted me from the guilt. I went to the bedroom and I stayed there. Andrew would open the door and he would see me crying and I would watch him turn his head and look back at the door contemplating walking back out. And I wished he would because I couldn't give him what he wanted, which was for me to be better, to be Adaline again. Or to give him back our baby.

Annie came and tried to talk, tried to make me laugh, but I would turn on my side with my back to her, because I didn't want her. I didn't want the laughter or comfort she wanted to give me. So, she did the next best thing, the thing she knew I needed most; she looked after my children. Free to wallow, I did just that. I tossed in that bed. I thrashed and hit and snivelled and when all of that came out, I just lay there. I begged Adam to take me. Not God, there were no words for him. I begged Adam to allow me to die in that bed because I didn't want a life past that. I didn't want a life without him. Weeks spent unwashed, undressed. Food passed my lips in a catatonic state. Fed by Andrew or Annie, it didn't matter. My body still went through motions and betrayed my will to die. I still gulped and swallowed, still urinated and shat. Still went against my instructions by breathing.

Over a month I stayed in that bed. Then one morning I heard my kids' laughter outside the window. A laughter without me. That they could laugh without me; or laugh at all with everything that happened, annoyed me. While my heart broke, they could still be happy.

Henry's voice travelled up. 'When can we see mummy?'

Annie's voice soothed him. 'Soon. She needs rest now.'

'Does she still love us?'

'She loves you very much. She just feels exhausted and sad. Not with you. Never with you.'

Guilt may as well have slapped me across the face. I had three children. Not just one. Two were alive and deserved my attention. I couldn't do it to them anymore. Andrew, Annie and work could be ignored; they understood my need for bed, but my children didn't. Instantly I craved them, needed them. I threw off the covers and walked into the shower and emerged from the bedroom as their mother again.

They kept me alive. Luckily, they were young enough at five and three to ricochet my depression and not internalise it. Children, I've found, adapt to anything. Older kids rationalise detachment by blaming themselves, but they weren't there yet. I was free to act oddly with them. I sat for hours holding them, playing with them, with my nose up to their hair, smelling their scent, pleading with the world to not take my other babies too.

The hardest part was meeting people who didn't know. They would notice the emptied bump and they would ask excitedly what I had while looking past me to see if the buggy would magically appear. I'd always answer with the truth. 'I had a boy and we named him Adam before we buried him.' Sometimes I got more pleasure out of it than others because a lie would have spared them the pain. My pain could never be spared.

I say that was the hardest part, but that's not true. Everything was the hardest part, breathing was, living was. In the darkest moments, the only thing that stopped me from keeping Adam company in that plot was the other children.

I never returned to work. I couldn't. How could I? Every corner reminded me of my pregnancy, of a time full of promise. Such stupid promise. I could never have faced that corner, the corner he trapped me in, the corner where my baby died.

Maybe there would have been closure if they held a court case, if I could have confronted a monster. But he was just a man who was unwell. Who had a psychotic episode. I didn't even blame him. It was me who tried to talk to him instead of running away. It was me who put myself in that area on my own. The unfear of strangers finally came back to bite me. No, it was always me I blamed.

The Priest

I didn't leave the grounds of St. Paul's Pillar. I waited a few moments for Edward and his children to move to another part of the walkway and then snuck into the back of the church, quickly walking past some seated guests until I reached the safety of a stone archway. On the other side of it, there were seats running the length of the room. The altar positioned at the top of the room, to the left of the archway. Leaning with my back on the stone, it was easy to stay hidden; the guests' attention focused on the bride and groom. It felt wrong though, my intrusion. I listened to the declarations of love. Saw the nervous hand holding from the bride and groom. I felt their fear, their excitement and the love that amalgamated in the room. It was too much. I left.

I trudged up the road but hadn't even reached the top when the anger flooded over me. I turned around for the second time and hung around the walkway and pretended to examine the ruins.

It was time to pick a fight. With the first on my list. As the wedding party filed outside and took photographs alongside the ruins, I marched back into the church. All was quiet. The stone walls gave an instant coolness. The seats weren't pews but individual wooden chairs. The shadowed walls gave off a dullness, with no natural light coming through. Painted pictures balanced in even spaces on the walls. Light filtered from above the altar, leading my eyes naturally towards it. A priest stood there.

'I'm sorry,' I said, about to turn around and leave.

'There's no need to be sorry,' The priest smiled as he said those words. His smile threw me. His voice surprised me as well. He was English. My argument wasn't with him.

'I just wanted a moment. I shouldn't be here. I'm sorry, I don't actually believe.'

He checked his watch. 'A moment you can have. You're in luck there isn't another wedding today, for the first time in months. I'll leave you alone.' He hesitated, clasped his hands. Frowned. 'I'll come back in an hour to lock up unless you'd like to talk?'

I shook my head.

'Fair enough.' He left the altar, then turned back. 'Just so you know, you don't have to.'

'Have to what?'

'You don't have to believe. This can be a quiet place to think. Can I ask one question before I go?'

I nodded. 'You said you don't believe. Did you mean you believe there is nothing after this or is it just God you don't believe in?'

'Both.'

'Ah,' he said, walking from the edge of the altar and leaning on a chair in the first row. 'I see. That can make life feel hopeless if what you're going through isn't going well. If this is all there is, I mean.'

'There can't be anything else. If there was, I'd feel it, I would feel my son, Adam. And I don't feel him. I don't sense him at all. The minute he died, I sensed it, I could feel him leave so if he was around me, I'd know.'

The priest nodded. 'You get what you believe.'

'Sorry?'

'It's why people with a strong religious belief may try to convince you there are miracles. You feel and see what you believe. Have you tried to feel Adam?'

My eyes welled. 'I think about my son every day.'

'But have you tried to feel him?'

'I don't understand.'

The priest gestured to the chair; I nodded. We sat, him in the first row, me in the seat behind. 'When you think of Adam, do you think of the loss?'

'Yes. About how he died. He didn't just die. Adam was murdered. A man stabbed me when I was eight months pregnant.' I expelled a breath, loudly. 'It feels good to say that out loud, I don't get to talk about that, it's too hard for people to hear. It's not just how he died, though. I think about how much I miss him. People don't understand, they think because I never met him, I didn't know Adam, but I did. I knew him from inside. From his kicks, from the fluttering's when he'd move. I could tell he was going to be a live wire.'

The priest chuckled.

'I think about the unfairness. About what he would do now if he lived or what age he'd be, what stage of growth, things like that. If I think of him being around me, then he's really gone and that would be worse.' I stopped. I had never thought of it that way before. A tear spilled out. In this place, I allowed myself one, I wiped it quickly. 'If he's really gone, then the pain will flood in. Anger is better because how could any God do that to a child? He was innocent. He didn't deserve any of that. What did I ever do to deserve that? I lived a life where I feared my father, but I swore to only love, despite him. All I wanted to do in life was help people like my mother and my patients. I am not a bad person, but still the worse thing possible happened and I couldn't protect my baby. God didn't protect my baby. For years, death has haunted me. It followed me no matter how much I tried to leave it. It led me to my career, but it also ruined me. My mother's death. Adam's. The fear of my own. The fear of the death of my marriage. It scares me, yet it's in my thoughts all the time.' I spoke through proper tears then. 'Are they somewhere? Are they nowhere? Can they hear my thoughts? Do they know how much I loved them? Love them.' I let out a groan full of pain. 'Did they suffer? Do they suffer still?'

'We do our suffering on this earth.'

There was kindness in the priest's eyes, far away from the pompous, arrogant priests I believed were the normal.

'Do you know what I believe?' he asked. 'I believe it doesn't matter what God you believe in, in my case I call that power God, but many don't. I believe there is something that watches over us. That gave us the gift of choice. To choose right or wrong. To choose our reactions towards wrongdoing or right. But because of that freedom to choose, it cannot step in when bad things are about to happen. A path has been set and we do not know the full story. But when the time is right, in certain circumstances and only when the person is ready, it will. Only if the person has asked for it. If we do our suffering on this earth, then Adam is in an exquisite place. I believe he is watching over you, as your own guardian angel. You have every right to be angry. You have suffered, and it is completely acceptable and understandable how you are feeling. But feeling this way will not heal you. Take God out of it, do what's right for you. Why don't you ask Adam to send you a signal? Children give signs. They give them all the time. Ask him to show you one thing, to prove he is happy. Has there been any signs?'

There had been none from Adam.

I shook my head. Then I thought of my mother. Of lines wrote in the sand. *What a great day to be alive!* This sparked another memory I'd forgotten.

'After my mother died, a robin kept showing up. It kept on coming to the door and window of my house. Each day it would get a little braver, come a little further. It would look at me, as if it had something to say. That robin would be the only thing that would make me smile. One time it flew into the kitchen, it kept moving from side to side like it was dancing, I swore it was a sign from my mother.'

'Maybe that's it. Maybe that's your sign. Ask Adam to send you a bird.'

'You think so?'

'It doesn't matter what I think. It's what you feel that will help you. Ask for a sign, there's nothing to lose. Now, if you want some time alone, I'll leave you be.' I nodded. 'You are always welcome here. Come back anytime. I promise we don't need to talk about God if you don't want to. This place is more than that. Do you know it is Greek Orthodox? They just allow Catholics and Protestants to marry here too. It goes beyond religion in these walls. Don't let being afraid to die take away from the pleasure from living.'

He patted my hand, and I placed my free hand on top of his.

'Thank you,' I said.

I waited for the church doors to swing as the priest left. The silence followed. I took in the surroundings. The chandelier. The dome above the altar with windows, the light shining down like an arrow. I walked to the altar. Behind, on the wall, were wooden engraved arches with painted pictures with gold features inside. I screwed my eyes at them, then sat on the same chair the priest sat and said nothing for a long time. The church was cool and silent. I gathered my words together.

'No matter what that priest says, I can't forgive you,' I whispered, then closed my eyes at the unwanted religious imagery. 'Adam, if you are around, please show me. Would you have loved birds? I don't know if I can let go of you. I don't know if I want to, but I can't cope with the pain anymore. There's a knot in my chest since you died, and I can't get rid of it. Please. Adam, help me. Show me somehow, please.'

The church stayed silent. I sat until I noticed the passing of time; I didn't want to still be there when the priest came back. It was time to go.

Aftermath

The months after Adam's death, the times I braved the mirror I didn't recognise myself. My eyes were microscopic; shrunken into the sockets. The skin on my eyelids were swollen and inflamed. Under my eyes, red circles blazed against a sea of pale. The woman in the reflection wasn't the same; I didn't know her, didn't want to know her. I looked as broken as I felt.

Even though Adam's death broke me, it didn't break us. We clung to each other; I clung rather, but Andrew needed me to cling. He held me when the panic took me, when the nightmares came for me in the night. Not letting go until my breath returned and he guided me away from the fear that took over. We could never be who we were before, we were unrepairable from that, but we adapted. We found another way.

I existed on the surface, done the school runs, the children's parties, the after activities and you'd never know. Instead, you'd think, how does she hold it together? Nobody on the outside felt the horror that came over me on waking. Nobody saw how I climbed back into bed after dropping the kids to school or how I wouldn't get back out until ten minutes before I was due to collect them. How those hours in between were my favourite time of day because I would put a pillow under my shirt and dream of having Adam still inside me, pregnant again. I functioned. Only Andrew knew. He never mentioned the cereal bowls still in the sink that evening. Or the dinner he brought home because I wouldn't have the energy to cook. The unswept floors and unwashed clothes. I would come down the next morning to a clean house. A hand on my shoulder as he'd pass by. Or a kiss on my head at the precise moment a thought would catch. He innately knew I needed distance during the day. In order to get through I detached, all my energy used to pretend to the kids I was fine.

At night Andrew brought me back. Through him, I took out my anger and our mutual pain. We raged at each other in our bedroom; we clung to each other in the dark.

Until Henry fell in the mud one weekend. He waddled into the kitchen and it covered every part of him. His hair, his mouth, his clothes. Andrew was behind him, waiting for my reaction. Henry shook himself like a dog, spraying mud on me, on Andrew, on the walls. There was mud everywhere; on our clothes and in our hair. It was too much. I laughed. Not a giggle but a proper belly laugh, erupting in me and it wouldn't stop. Henry laughed. Andrew laughed. It was the most wonderful feeling.

'Oh Ad, it's good to laugh again.'

I stopped. My laughter turned to horror. I stood and ran up the stairs and climbed into bed and stayed there for three days. Because how could I? How could I betray Adam's memory like that?

On the third day, Andrew woke me. Dressed me. Walked me to the car and drove for a long time until he parked outside a hotel. He didn't get out. He looked ahead and wouldn't meet my eyes. There was a sign outside the hotel with an arrow saying: *Angel wings ceremony*.

'You need this, Adaline,' Andrew said. He left his seat, came round to my side of the car, opened my door. He held an overnight bag. 'Come back to me. Please Ad.'

He guided me into the hotel and stopped outside a conference room where a woman with soft hair like candy floss waited. She opened her arms wide and I went to her and hugged this woman, this complete stranger, because she looked at me with love instead of pity and an adult hadn't looked at me like that for a very long time. Only my bag was there when I let go.

She led me into a room. There were eight other women sitting in a circle. I took a seat even though I didn't want to sit; I wanted to run. Confrontation always terrified me. Confrontation of the truth was even scarier. The pain on their faces was too obvious. Too normal.

The woman who hugged me joined the circle.

'My name is Ellen. Thank you all for being here. I know most of you don't know what to expect. We are going to spend the next couple of days trying to come to terms with your loss. I will not try to convince you you'll walk out of here a different person. You will never forget your child. You will never stop loving your baby. This isn't about forgetting them, it is about honouring them and remembering them and having a safe place away from other family where there are expectations. Where you have responsibilities. In this room, if you want to cry, cry. If you want to talk, then spill and don't feel any shame for it. Through written work, projects, group and individual sessions we will try to make it easier. The aim is to help you feel some bit, any bit better. You are safe in this room. Safe to talk. Free to talk. You have all got grief in common. You can trust each other. Every single person you look at in this room is dealing with the same pain you are feeling. Every woman here can understand what you are going through.'

A woman in her sixties with grey roots halfway down her head put up her hand to speak. She wore trousers so threadbare at the knees, her pale skin showed through. She spoke in a quiet voice.

'People think because I lost my Patricia forty years ago, I should be over it. But it changed my life. It changed how my life should turn out. I stopped caring about myself. About everyone. It wasn't fair, there were no signs of any problems, everything up to the labour was perfect. They told me after I came around, I had a placental abruption. It killed my Patricia, it almost killed me too. They had to perform a hysterectomy there and then. I had no choice. They gave me no choice.' Her voice cracked with emotion. 'Of course, I couldn't have any more children and I'd wanted to have a child more than anything. Harry wouldn't adopt. He said he couldn't raise another man's baby. I pushed him away after that. Pushed everyone away. What was the point of being married if we didn't have children? What was the point of my existence without Patricia or another child? He left me, of course, had a new woman who was pregnant six months later. Five children he has now. I have to see them around town. When they pass they are all so, so, happy. That should have been me. At my age, I should be a grandmother.' She picked at a knob of wool on her jumper. Her voice came out like a child's.

'I don't want to live like this. If I don't change, I'll die alone. And I want to move on, to see if it's possible to. Time is supposed to be a healer, but it's been forty years and I haven't healed at all.'

The woman sobbed then, and Ellen walked to her and embraced her. I excused myself and found a bathroom and sat in the cubicle. I wanted to be in that room, but I was afraid. Forty years. Those wasted years of that woman's life; I didn't want the same outcome. I flushed the toilet and prepared myself to listen and to talk.

Over the hours, the awkwardness left. Surrounded by other women who had lost their babies too, I felt understood. They couldn't share the horrific way Adam left me. Our circumstances were different, but the loss was equal. Their grief the same.

Then it was my turn.

'I'm angry.'

'At who?'

'At whatever's up there. At myself. Someone decided. Someone has to be in charge. Something let us all get pregnant and then took our babies away before they got to experience breath. A breath! I feel angry, then I feel unbelievably sad, then I feel guilty because I have no right to grieve this much.'

'Why not? What makes you say that?'

'Because I didn't save him. Because Adam never even existed in the world. He wasn't someone we knew. He didn't have a favourite toy or colour. I don't know what would have made him smile. What he would have been afraid of.'

'But he was real to you. He existed for you.'

'He *was* real to me.'

'You're allowed grieve, Adaline. You're allowed to grieve for what should have been. It wasn't your fault. There was nothing you could have done to stop him. Allow those feelings to come.'

'Everybody wants me to deal with it. Like a couple of days here will fix me; I'll do all my crying and then forget all about him.'

'You could never forget him, Adaline. You never will.'

'You didn't?'

'I didn't,' Ellen said. She looked at me with genuine sadness, smiled at the group. 'I lost my boy fifteen years ago. I carry him with me. He's everywhere I go. I blamed myself for my Eric's death. I fell. I wasn't paying attention and missed a step. Before I could move on, I had to forgive myself. You all need to forgive yourself too.'

'You can tell me that, to let go of the loss. You can tell me all those things, but I'll tell you right now, I don't want to. I won't.'

'What do you want, Adaline?'

'What I need is a way to cope. To get through the day. I want to live a life where my other children are happy. Where I won't ruin their life even though inside I'm ruined.'

'So you want to live a lie?'

'No, I want to survive. Can you help me do that?'

She pursed her lips, then smiled. 'Yes Adaline, I can help you do that.'

There was freedom in believing her. A lightness in that freedom.

On that retreat, I realised, I owed my other children a life; I owed them a mother, otherwise I should have died right next to my baby. I didn't. So, I would live on.

Henry, Sophie and Andrew waited outside for me on the day it finished. My heart felt like it was going to burst from the surprise of seeing them. I ran and clung to them.

'I'm sorry I've been so sad.'

'Are you happy now, mummy?' Henry asked.

I smiled at them, every one of them hanging on my next word. 'I am.'

In the car as we pulled off, strapped in to his seat and buoyed by my answer and bright mood, Henry decided it was time to ask another question.

'Mummy, do you speak to Adam when you go to the grave?'

Andrew's head inclined nearer to mine, but he kept his eyes on the road. His hand squeezed my thigh and then went back to the steering wheel.

'I don't go to his grave, Henry.'

'She doesn't need to speak to Adam at the grave. He's in her heart silly,' Sophie said.

I swivelled in the chair so I could see into the back. 'What do you mean?'

'You said when I was scared to stay in my own bed, you're always with us.'

I screwed up my nose, confused.

Sophie rolled her eyes as if she couldn't believe I could have forgotten.'You said before we were born we joined. Your blood made my blood and when I left your body a piece of me stayed behind and moved to your heart. Isn't that where Adam is?' Sophie looked upset by this, by the possibility of being wrong.

I looked ahead so the kids wouldn't see my tears.

'You're right. That's where Adam is. I have a piece of each of you inside me.'

All the counselling, all the tears, all the lying in bed, none of them had the same impact as those words. The comfort that Adam's blood may still be mixed, that there may be even one tiny DNA cell of his living inside, was enough to carry on. It would be a lie to say that was the cure, that there were no more dark days or times when I wasn't floored with the memory of what happened. But that was how I learnt to survive; believing I carried Adam with me. Through me Adam might see life still, may feel my experiences, may still get touched by love.

The No Sign

There was no sign.

I walked towards the hotel, towards Andrew, dreading another confrontation. The images of Adam's death wouldn't leave me. I stopped mid walk.

'I think more of your death than of you,' I said.

I spoke to no one but Adam, not caring who else heard on the busy pathway. 'I think of what you might have been, not what you were.'

I turned right to the pebble beach, sat on a rock, not caring what anyone would think of a woman rambling to herself. I spoke to Adam. 'You were my best pregnancy, you never caused me a day's sickness. I joked if you were anything to go by while I was pregnant, then raising you was going to be a breeze. Do you know how wanted you were Adam? We wanted you so much. Sophie and Henry used to put a big cross through a calendar each night. Trying to explain to your brother and sister why you weren't coming home, why my stomach wasn't big anymore. It was so hard. Burying you broke me, Adam.'

I didn't know how long I had been crying for and I didn't care. I stood, slipped my shoes off, trudged to the water and dipped my feet and remembered that day all those years ago when my life altered. I had felt something then, a pull towards something I didn't understand. By just looking up from the water and into Andrew's eyes. How would my life have turned out if I continued to watch the sand and didn't notice him? I would not have experienced love at first sound, I wouldn't have known the passion of great love. If I hadn't met and loved Andrew, I wouldn't have felt such a massive loss. I sat with a thud in the wet sand.

There would also have been no Sophie or Henry. No honeymoon in Cyprus. No Adam. No make or break holiday.

I felt something then. An urge. I looked at the sky. Looked for a bird. The sky was cloudless. Bird less. I remembered Andrew's no sign, how that turned out for him. How the no sign saved him from a miserable life. How the no sign meant he got to meet me.

'I won't keep looking Adam, show me when you are ready. I love you, I promise I will never forget you, but now I've got to go.'

Cake

I laid out the ingredients on the table. Everything needed for baking a cake. Not just any cake, Andrews favourite, chocolate sacher-torte, a nightmare if you didn't get right. Chocolate work was notoriously finicky: the chocolate could go grainy, the infamous sheen glaze on the cake could be dull, the cream could curdle. That day I would get it right; it needed to be special as we would miss his actual birthday. Instead of spending his day with us, he had to go to a weekend conference in Dublin. His business partner rang me to explain it was unavoidable. Andrew sneakily set up the call, knowing I couldn't argue. Donald's wife was having chemotherapy. It was the first birthday we would miss. Andrew promised we would celebrate when he returned.

I lined the pan with baking paper, then greased the sides. Melted dark chocolate over a Bain Marie. Scraped out the insides of a vanilla pod, added it to a mixer with soft butter and icing sugar. Waited for the bubbles. I reached for the eggs in the box, found emptiness. There had been eggs in there that morning.

'Sophie, Henry, did you use the eggs?' I shouted up the stairs.

Commotion erupted, the two of them barged out of their rooms.

'What?' Henry asked.

'Did you use the eggs?'

'Yeah, I made pancakes, to practice for when Dad got back. I want to make his breakfast in bed this time,' Sophie said.

I couldn't show annoyance, I needed to encourage her independence.

'OK, it doesn't matter. It just means a trip to the shops.'

'I've training,' Henry said.

'I told Jennifer I'd call to hers. We need to plan for the scout's trip. You said you'd collect my uniform, remember?' Sophie said, her hair dangling down from looking over the bannister.

That meant a trip to the city, not planned today. 'Well, I do have to collect something for your dad. Do you want us to all go in later, we could get some shopping and treat ourselves to something to eat?'

They looked at me like that was the worst thing on earth they wanted to do. I couldn't ignore the pang of sorrow. There was a time they couldn't bear to be apart from me, when each one of them clung to my leg every time I sat, so much so sciatica became a permanent fixture. I never pushed them off, I loved how the pain intertwined with the pleasure.

'I guess I could ask Shane's father if you could stay with him if I wasn't back.'

I ignored the relief in my kid's eyes. They loved me, really.

No radio played as I drove into town. After the noise from young children, I learnt to enjoy silence. I liked it to gather my thoughts. After losing Adam, I used silence to think of him, my little game that kept sanity with me.

Maybe if I'd had time with him while he was alive, I would have felt him around me, but I never got to see his open eyes or feel his warm body. After I woke up from the operation that saved my life and took Adam from my stomach, I held him, wrapped in a blanket so I wouldn't see the damage. He was already cold. Dead too long to have any blood still running through. I blamed my unconsciousness on that. If I'd stayed alert, if I hadn't passed out, would I have saved him? If they had put him skin to my skin, would it have kept him in this world? I wondered about that all the time. You hear of it, don't you? You hear of babies that are stillborn who the mother insists on holding and putting to her chest, and the baby miraculously out of nowhere breathes again. The mother's love revives them. I couldn't do that with Adam, he had passed over by the time I touched him.

His hair was dark, with lots of it. His face was perfect, with none of the stretched and spongy alien-like features that the trauma of labour produced. A cute button nose and long black eyelashes.

The words Sophie said to me that day in the car stayed with me. The belief grew in strength over the years and convinced me when they pulled Adam from my body, they forgot a piece. They left a little of him inside. It lay flat, immovable in my womb. My own cells joined it, grew over it. It grew inside me, into a mass, a lump, a tumour even; the scar inside matched the scar outside. My stomach was a cross of scars. First, a horizontal line halfway between my belly button and pubic bone made by a killer. Then, one long vertical scar ran from just below my belly button, from the man who tried to save my baby, and then saved me.

Going into town, I knew it was time, I could do something about Adam without it sending me over the edge. Right before I handed him over, the only and last time I could hold him, the lady who worked in the hospital morgue looked at me in her practiced way, not over pitying but not careless either. As if she understood.

'Would you like to keep a lock of Adam's hair?'

I was so grateful for that. For the gesture. More so for the fact she called Adam by his name. She acknowledged his being, his existence, even if he never got to open his eyes.

I kept his hair at the back of the drawer in a silk lined box. Over time, over the years, I would sit on the bed and stroke it. Years on, his hair still felt exactly the same. Touching it brought back all the emotion of that day. Of waking up to think that I was still pregnant, then remembering the pain of what happened and then the love of holding my baby in my arms. His hair as soft as if he was alive.

He had still smelt of baby. My breasts poured milk as I held him, awaiting his cry, awaiting his suckle, awaiting his tears that would never come. Only my tears came.

I never told Andrew about his hair, it was my secret. My talisman back to Adam. But I was ready to share it. I had found a place that would make secret compartments for jewellery, so you had them near all the time. A watch for him and a locket for me waited for collection.

I walked down from the car park feeling pretty proud of myself; I was making progress. As I crossed the road to the jewellers, a man and woman caught my attention. The man looked like Andrew. The woman looked like Maria. They had stopped outside a hotel. His arm was around her. He brought her head to his chest. She drew back and shook her head. He smoothed her hair back off her face. The way he did with me. The way he smoothed my hair back when I needed soothing. They hugged again. She buried her head in his chest. Then he led her into the hotel.

White rage flashed in me. I wanted to follow them in, drag her by the hair away from him, tear at his face, pound at him and drag them apart from each other, but a voice told me not to; to wait and get all the facts. Trying to calm my heaving chest, I took deep breaths. I approached the glass doors, staying back far enough so they wouldn't see. I needed to make sure I wasn't reading too much into things. They could be just going for a meeting, or I might have misunderstood where the conference was and it was in Cork and not Dublin.

I wasn't wrong. I watched as they signed in. Watched as the receptionist handed over one room card. Andrew handed his credit card to pay for it. They walked side by side to the lift; her leaning on Andrew, him with his arm wrapped around her waist. I watched until the lift opened and they faced each other and embraced before the doors closed.

I stumbled around the same road in town twice, not looking in any window, or seeing the people passing me by. My legs functioned, but I couldn't feel anything. You could have stuck another shard in me and I wouldn't have noticed.

I forgot the eggs. Abandoned Sophie's scout's uniform. Left Adam's hair in the jewellery shop. It took a mountain of effort to drive the twenty minutes to Knockfarraig; it took even more to prepare for the call.

I drank a glass of wine full to the rim and waited for the kids to settle on tablets and computer screens. I played it cool. Made a call.

Andrew sounded flustered. 'Hello?'

'Hey, how's it going?'

'Good. Good. How are things with you?'

'Is the conference over?'

'Just about. I just got to the hotel now.'

'Where are you staying again?'

There was a pause. I could feel Andrew's brain trying to kick into gear.

'Jurys, you know the one by Stephen's Green we stayed in before?'

Dublin. There was the truth, Andrew was a liar.

'Did everything go OK?'

Andrew took a deep breath. For a moment I thought he was going to say something. The fear of it hit me then. He couldn't tell me over the phone he'd had an affair.

'If you don't want to talk about it, you don't have to.'

'Thanks Ad. Been a hard day.'

'I'm sure it has,' I said as I felt my heart turn to stone.

'I'll see you tomorrow night.'

'OK. Andrew?'

'Yeah?' I could tell he wanted to hang up.

'Happy birthday.'

'Thanks Ad,' he said, then the line went dead.

Andrew was a brilliant father. He was the kind who jumped up for the night feeds and let me roll onto the other side to catch up on sleep. Who didn't baulk at the shitty nappies or vomiting children like so many husbands supposedly did. We were the same person, me and Andrew, yet different in so many ways, but the foundation of us was identical.

Some days I would lie in bed and keep my eyes closed and pretend I was asleep, not to prolong waking but because I could hear secret whisperings and plans going on between Andrew and the children. The ease in how he spoke with them, the joy in their conversations. I could feel my children's heart expand from the love Andrew gave them. I could feel my heart expand too. Here's my talk about roles again; the children needed us to be different. I would hear the whooping and roaring as they jumped and dived onto Andrew, and for a brief second a jealous pang would hit because I would never be that to them. Yet I knew that was how it should be. My love was different, they needed me when they fell or something crumpled them up inside; I was the one they ran away from when I was nagging, but ran to when they hurt. After Henry was born, I looked into his eyes for the first time and I knew right then, he would break my heart because one day he would leave me. I didn't feel that way about Sophie. A daughter never really leaves her mother, even if she wants to.

The discovery of Andrew's adultery changed me. It differed from the loss of Adam. Adam's death was incomparable, way worse than anything else that could ever happen. The betrayal made me see Andrew differently. He was no longer the person I knew because *that* Andrew, the man I thought I knew, his priority was to keep me safe and never hurt me. The person who, without thinking, pushed me onto the inside of the pavement out of harm's way, the one who opened doors and shouldered the coffin of my child to take the pain from me. How could that Andrew do this?

On the day meant to celebrate his birthday, I didn't offer the usual cake, didn't wake him up to breakfast in bed. I let the kids make it. Let them take it up to him. Let them bring a home-made card. I sat in the kitchen and drank a coffee. The minute we were alone, I decided I would confront and roar at him. I wanted to claw him, rip at him, tear his heart out like he had done to me. My heart burned.

When he entered the kitchen, he flashed me an accusatory look, which annoyed me more. How dare he after what he did. How dare he act upset, as if I was the wrongdoer. It thrilled me a little too, because he did not know what was coming; he had no idea of the fury he was about to unleash.

'What's up with you?' He said.

'Mum's got a headache,' Sophie said as she wrapped her arms around Andrew's waist. I closed my eyes to her sweetness. Even though she was eleven, the embarrassment of hugging had yet to come. Before that day, we were a family of huggers.

Henry entered the kitchen then, in a ball of excitement. 'Dad said we can go to the beach and then eat at the Kings.'

'I've a headache,' I said.

'It's Dad's day. You know that means we have to do whatever he wants.'

'I'd say in fairness, Henry, he's doing what you want with that plan.'

'It is what I want actually,' Andrew said. He walked over to the medicine cabinet, took out some painkillers, brought them over, put his hand on my shoulder. I flinched and moved my shoulder away. His hand hovered in the space above. My unspoken action clear. My way to show him without words in front of the children. My way of telling him all was not OK.

'Take them,' he said. 'The sooner they work, the quicker your mood will go away.'

He dropped the pills onto the table. I left them there.

'Go on without me, I'm going to lie down,' I said as I walked out of the room.

I knew with that action, I'd decided. I knew my doing that on his birthday was the beginning of the end, but I didn't care. With Andrew, I could never conceal my feelings or my sadness. With him I didn't want to hide it, I wanted him to feel my coldness, feel when my love withered away from him; to notice my withdrawal and wonder what he had done. As I scaled the stairs, I decided I would let Andrew tackle me. I would wait until that day to confront him. That day had yet to come.

Elephant

Andrew was waiting on the balcony. I could tell by the straight back and the crossed arms he wasn't in nice Andrew mode. I took a deep breath and thought about dear Edward and knew he was right. It was time to kick the elephant out.

I took the bottle of wine I had ordered from downstairs and pulled out two glasses from the kitchenette and walked out to join him. The night was windy, the view just as stunning. As I spoke, my words washed away with the ocean.

'What did you say?' he said.

'Can I join you?'

'Well, since I've been sitting here waiting for you, I would say that question's pretty redundant.'

Don't rise, Adaline.

'I met a man a while ago.'

Andrew's jaw clenched.

'An old man. He gave me some advice. He was scattering his wife's ashes. Edward said if we don't love each other, we should let each other go.'

'That's nice of him to presume he knows me. Nice of you to talk behind my back.'

I opened the bottle of wine. Poured us both a glass and sat by his side and handed him my offering without resentment or annoyance.

'Andrew, you couldn't answer me in the restaurant. You couldn't admit you still love me because you know in your heart you don't anymore. It's time we stop fooling ourselves, we are no longer good for each other. When you love someone you should want them to be happy, do anything to help them be happy. I stopped doing that. You are not a bad person and I know I have made mistakes. I should have talked. I should have confronted instead of the silence I gave. You're a decent man. Just not always to me.'

Andrew expected something else. He looked at the sea and then at me like he was trying to figure out what to say. He let out a long breath, the sound like a balloon deflating.

'I know. I'm sorry. We've both done such horrible things. This place, though. We could start over. It's reminded me of what we had, of what we *can* have.'

I shook my head. 'It's just an illusion. Us on our best behaviour. Us at our best. Who couldn't work here? We always worked well on holidays. It's when we're not at our best, when we're tired or feeling unwell or stressed, that we'll go for the jugular. It's when a couple are at their worst that truly tests the relationship. That's when you see if the person picks you up and keeps you balanced or sticks the foot out and keeps you under. You chose the latter. I chose it too. At least now we can walk away from this remembering the love that was once there. When I booked this trip, I thought I needed us to come back to each other, but now I see what I really needed was to come back to myself. I'm not going home with you, not as a couple.'

'So, what? What was this Adaline? You brought me out here to remember?'

'Deep down I hoped we could save us, I wanted to find a way for it to work. Out here, today I sat in St. Paul's Pillar watching so much love around me and I realised it needed to be a last goodbye. We have been so unhappy. Neither of us knows our way anymore. We have to find it separately, otherwise we will go home and become miserable together again. I can't do that, go back to being that.'

'But this is the happiest we've been in years. How can you walk away from that? I felt something change between us, didn't you?'

'I did, I felt it. But it's false. I can't do that anymore, I won't.'

He sighed, this time in relief. He expected an argument and I threw him with my words, with my tone, with my niceness. The thing was, I meant every word. For once it wasn't said in anticipation for his reaction. I did not calculate it to sidestep or hurt or placate. I meant it; I wanted us both to be happy. Andrew deserved as much happiness as me. I took a drink of my wine, pleased with myself for the way I'd handled it, and could see he'd accepted what I said. All so very grown up. All genuinely nice and civilised; an amicable split like I hoped for. Then I remembered my promise on the plane. I remembered how hurt I was when I saw them together outside the hotel. I remembered what Edward said and decided to follow his advice and fire all the niceness out the window. I wouldn't stay quiet any longer. For courage, I took a large gulp of wine. I was about to derail the lovely tracks underneath Andrew.

'One more thing. I know about Maria. That you slept with her. I saw you going into a hotel with your arm around her. There I was in the city getting you a present for your birthday and you were going in to a hotel. You, the person who told me you were away in Dublin with work and there you were sleeping with the clichéd assistant.'

Andrew's head shot up in alarm, his eyes quizzical at first, then glazed over with the realisation. There it was, the confirmation. It hurt as much as I feared it would. More actually, it felt like a blow. The pain was more than I could have imagined. For such a long time all my thoughts were about leaving Andrew, yet here we were on the verge and all I felt was sadness. Instantly, I regretted the confrontation. There wouldn't be closure in knowledge. Hearing the details of his dirty affair wouldn't help me. Why couldn't I leave it where it was? Why couldn't I leave it as a nice splitting of ways? Lovely and ignorant.

'I didn't. You saw wrong, Adaline.'

'You're seriously going with denial? Andrew, come on, you at least owe me honesty.'

'Is this what broke us? You've kept that in, this whole time. Why didn't you confront me, Adaline? Why didn't you shout and roar at me like you would have done when we first met? I know why. Because you didn't love me enough anymore to get angry.'

'Stop trying to turn it on me. I couldn't say anything Andrew, even after knowing, I loved you too much to say a word because I knew if I did, that would be it. If I talked about it, there would be no going back.'

'So why now then?'

'Because there is no going back, anyway. I can't go back to the way things were.'

'Me neither.'

'I guess I'm telling you so we can move on, so we both understand the other's actions. Now you know why I went cold. After I saw that, I couldn't. I couldn't sleep with you knowing you slept with her. The infidelity tore through me. Sickened me. I carried it around in my stomach like a sickness. The only way to survive was to shrivel it and distract myself with the kids.'

'I didn't sleep with her Adaline.'

'Don't lie to me, Andrew. You owe me this, you owe me the truth. Just tell me, if you value me for who I have been to you, so we can try to be friends in the future. Don't you see it is the only way I can move on? If you lay it all out here now, maybe, just maybe we can salvage this.'

He stood and walked to the door.

'So what, you're going to run off now?'

He unplugged his phone from the socket by the door. That phone.

Of course he would take that. But instead of walking out the door, or going to the bedroom, he walked back to me, while scrolling. He handed me the phone open on a message. The sender was Donald. I read.

I appreciate you helping me out with this, Andrew. Please explain to Maria that I love her and I hope the procedure went as well as can be expected. Let me know if she needs anything. I hope she is recovering and isn't too distraught. Thank you for staying with her, I didn't think she should be left alone after. She isn't taking my calls. I would have given anything to be there, but Regina was too weak and needed to stay in the hospital. I had no choice. I'm sorry for taking you away from Adaline and the kids for the weekend. I've put you in an awkward situation but I beg you, please don't tell Regina yet. I'm afraid it would kill her. My actions lately haven't been something I'm proud of. Thank you for your kindness and understanding.

The truth smacked me full force. Everything I believed was real hit me with its falseness. Every action I took since was in reaction to something untrue. It hurt to understand. It hurt more than the untruth did.

'Why didn't you tell me, Andrew? You told me everything. We never had secrets before.'

'It wasn't my secret to tell,' he said, wiping at his eyes.

'But it changed everything. It changed us.'

'I didn't know that's what did it. If I'd known you knew, I would have told you everything. I knew how you'd feel about Donald if you found out, how you would have to carry the burden of keeping it from Regina. I didn't want you to have to do that. You can't lie, Adaline. You've always been a terrible liar. That's how I knew we were in trouble, you couldn't ever hide how you felt. I felt your disgust and I hated you for it. And now I see why, I thought you blamed me for Adam. Yet you thought I'd done this terrible thing. I never. Even after, when we didn't. I still didn't. With anyone. Even through the loneliness of seeing you happy with the kids, knowing you didn't show me the same affection.'

I took a massive gulp of wine. 'I don't know what to say. What to do now. I thought I knew our relationship and its failures, and I've been wrong. All this time I've looked at us through a distorted mirror. Andrew, I didn't even blame you for the affair. I hated you for it, but I didn't blame you. It destroyed me to know you would do that, that you would betray me. Even after Adam, you were the strong one. I knew I detached from you, knew the hole sucked me under, that it made sense why you would have an affair. I thought it was your way to cope, and that made me angrier to think you used the excuse of grieving for your son to cheat. All this time I thought you let me down. That felt like another death. I mourned you, Andrew, mourned us. I thought this trip would end my grief for us but now it was for nothing. All this time wasted.'

'You were mourning Adaline. I knew that, I understood that, and I hoped one day we would find a way back. Now I know everything.'

We sat in silence. Different to the noiseless space between us before; that had been condensed with resentment, passion even. Now that existed was immense sadness.

'I feel tired Andrew, I can't even process this, my brain is whirring. This holiday has been exhausting.'

It was Andrew's turn to take a big gulp of wine. 'Give me one day. If you still feel like walking away, I promise I will not say a word.'

'I don't have the energy, Andrew. Aren't you tired from it all?'

'Please Ad. One day.'

I shrugged. He hadn't called me Ad for a long time. His phone caught my eye on the table, the screensaver a picture of my face. From that day at the castle when he called me *my queen*, the day we became intimate again. I picked it up and examined it. The woman in the picture tanned, with a slight smile, dared me to take a chance. 'OK.

One day.'

Instead of feeling relieved, I drained my glass and stood for bed. My body was heavy from exhaustion, so tired that I could barely carry myself to the room. I heard the clink of Andrew's glass, the glug of the bottle as he poured some more. The pat of his fingers on his phone. As I closed my eyes, I laid my arm outstretched on the empty side of the bed. It wasn't the first occasion I'd touched the place he should have been, yet that time I never felt the space as much; I never felt more alone.

I woke in the night, at the hour when time seemed to stretch and desist. The hour that was the loneliest and the longest and the darkest. When the possibility of staying up was no longer wished for, when the morning light was not yet upon the day. The time when a place was at its quietest and eeriest and everyone else away in another life, dreaming their dreams. It was always when the ghosts came for me. I could never ignore the horrors of the past that I could bat off throughout the day. All my mistakes ran over me.

Edward's words were playing on my mind. About how I punished Andrew. About gratitude. How many times did I tell Andrew I thought he was a good father? Or that I loved him? When was the last time I thought of him with love? It had been a long time for any of that, for any compliment. I stopped seeing him that way. There was no appreciation for the little things; how hard he worked; how kind he could be; how funny. I saw him as a succession of roles instead of a person. A caricature that would share responsibility of the children. How he felt ceased in importance. His happiness hadn't been my concern.

Even in the good years before our life imploded and after the first few years with declarations of love, I stopped telling him the little things. I stopped showing him or telling him I still saw them. Still noticed them. I took it for granted that he knew how I felt. All my stupid assumptions. Why didn't I ask him about the affair? Being innocent wasn't a consideration. I didn't once doubt his guilt. What did that say about me?

I touched the shortest, widest scar on my stomach. The place that man killed our son. The skin had knotted together. I rubbed it for comfort because it was where our blood mixed.

That was why I was so sure of Andrew's guilt. Because I was disgusting. It made perfect sense he would want to be with someone else. Someone like Maria. Pretty and sweet and scar less and undamaged. I rubbed that scar and whispered to Adam:

'Help me, baby. Please help me.'

One Day

Andrew woke me early before the sun rose. My eyes were puffy and sore. Weary was the only word that summed me up.

'It's not even morning, Andrew.'

'If I only have one day, I need as much of it as I can get.'

I got dressed half asleep. I lassoed on a swimsuit and hoisted a loose cotton dress over it, patted cream to soothe my tired eyes. Slipped wedge sandals on that would be easy to walk in, then threw in two towels, flip-flops and sunscreen into a travel bag. That way I'd covered everything.

There was no time for breakfast. Andrew waited at the open door. I walked past. In the lift I avoided him, I couldn't meet his expectant, hopeful gaze, I couldn't promise him what I knew he wanted. I followed him out to the entrance of the hotel. He gestured at a parked car, a black flashy car with an open top. The bonnet dipped down until it almost touched the ground. Its headlights were like eyes, daring me.

'It's a Shelby Cobra. Do you know how much I've wanted to drive one of these?' He shrugged at my raised eyebrow. 'One day Ad.'

We got in and he drove, the engine purring like a cat and revving like it was meant to. The wind came at me from all directions, filling my lungs, whipping my hair, and even though I wouldn't admit it, excitement bubbled for what was to come. As he continued along the coast road, I pulled my tossed hair back from my face and secured it with a hairband. I knew where he was taking me; to Coral Bay beach, a place we went to all those years ago. Where we walked along the sand and needed nothing in the world but each other. How I loved him then. It hurt to remember that; it hurt to remember all the hurt that came after.

Again, I was wrong. Andrew turned right where we should have continued straight on for Coral Bay. We drove up a hill. The car made the ascent easily, but it was steep enough to make me wonder if I could tip out of it or how an older, slower car would manage. We were almost vertical. That hill would be a nightmare to walk, a killer on the spine, going upwards as far as my eye could see, far away to the bend. Andrew took a sharp turn into a driveway. The pebbles scurried underneath the tyres. The wall on Andrew's side was dangerously close, I grimaced in anticipation of the door scraping but Andrew counteracted it by swerving left. He pulled into an empty driveway. The entrance was all glass doors and windows. Hidden from the road by the surrounding bushes and wall of the drive, it tucked in like a secret, as if it didn't want to be found. It felt like we were disturbing the building, and I wondered why we had pulled into someone's private home or business. Andrew turned off the engine and looked at me, his eyes wide in apology.

'Sorry bit of a close one, I'm not used to a car like this and I didn't think there would be that much of a bend. Couldn't tell in this light.'

The darkness had shifted to a light grey, the sunrise soon upon us. My eyes landed on a sign by the door. Cyclamen. Each letter a metal piece on the wall. A bearded man stood at the doorway, his hands in his pockets, waiting. Andrew smiled with a goofy grin. 'Wait here a second.'

Andrew ran up to the man and spoke to him. They shifted as they talked. Andrew bounced on his heels; always done when he was excited. The man went back inside. Andrew ran to me, opened my door. Held out his hand.

'Please join me for breakfast?'

'Sure,' I said, taking his hand. He didn't let go, leading me through the open glass doors. The room was dark and empty, but I gathered by the tables laid out it was a restaurant.

'What's going on?'

'Shush,' Andrew said, squeezing my hand.

The room was shaped in a semi-circle with a straight wall on one side with a bar, and two doors I guessed were the entrance to the bathroom and the kitchen. The opposite side was wall to wall, ceiling to floor, curved glass. The dark obscured any view. Andrew continued walking. He led me to the end of the room where he brought me outside to an area covered in hundreds of pink and white flowers leading up to steps. I stopped for a moment to touch one, an unusual type I'd never seen before. The petal was smooth against my finger. The top petals stood up, reminding me of a cute fox's pointy ears, with a tip of pink where the snout would be. Andrew leaned close. Whispered in my ear. His breath tickled.

'That's why it's called cyclamen. The restaurant takes its name from those flowers.'

He led me on until there were steps in front of us. The steps led to a single small table with candles lit. Andrew pulled out a chair for me and I sat down. He took the seat by my side rather than opposite.

The man followed us out.

'Hello Adaline, how are you? I'm George.'

'Hi George. I'm good, a bit confused though.'

'We never open for breakfast, but I understand this is a special day. When your husband rang me I took a bit of convincing, but I'm a sucker for love, what can I say? I'm going to bring you out a nice breakfast now. You hungry?'

'Starving.' I grinned at Andrew.

'Good. Breakfast coming up. Just enjoy.'

'Why are we here, Andrew?' I said when George disappeared back inside humming my song.

'Just wait, Adaline.'

I didn't have to wait long before George came out with a tray.

'Mimosa's, and a starter while you're waiting,' he said.

He handed me a champagne glass with orange liquid inside. Andrew held his glass up.

'To watching the sunrise and sunset together.'

We clinked and then drank. The bubbles tap-danced on my tongue.

The darkness shifted. In the distance, the allude of a horizon appeared; an outline of orange. We sipped our drinks. And there it was, at first a curve, then a dome of brighter orange, the line framing the horizon now with pink. It unleashed all that was in front of us. We overlooked Paphos. With the sea far down below and the coast. The green patches of olive trees and houses with blue private pools. It was a view of dreams; it was a hold your breath for, etch in your mind forever view. I was glad Andrew didn't fill the silence, glad that George didn't walk out in front of that first glimpse. I wanted that moment. To act like a queen overlooking her kingdom. By letting me be alone, by allowing me that time, I felt closer to Andrew.

He knew me.

He remembered me.

As the sun rose, the area revealed more. The terracotta rooftops, the patches of green next to tan fields, the shrubs and grey roads and that turquoise sea.

'Thank you for this,' I whispered.

'We didn't have enough time left to book a hot-air balloon, but this comes close.'

I didn't take my eyes away from the view. 'I never wanted that again. No, this is much better.'

George brought us piled plates of colour with green and black olives and grilled halloumi stacked on top of each other in a puzzle of cheese. Sliced tomatoes lay next to poached eggs beside the pink of the lountza.

Afterwards we ate melon drizzled with honey and Greek yoghurt and drank coffee and I just let myself be, I allowed Adaline to just be with Andrew.

The sun became hot, but the breeze from the hills cooled me. Andrew looked at his watch and stood up.

'It's time to go.'

We said our goodbyes to George with the promise to come back if we ever visited Cyprus again. Andrew ran to the car and opened the door.

'I remember you used to do things like this for me all the time.'

'We stopped doing so many things Ad.'

'I know.'

He drove back the way we came and after some time he turned left instead of going back to the hotel, along a dirt road with no barriers or railings. With rocks and hill on one side and a sheer drop on the other. The car shook and rattled from the bumps. The road became so narrow it threatened to lurch us over the side of the cliff edge. There was a tour bus ahead, leaving a trail of dust behind. The horror of how we would manage if a bus came towards us hit me.

'Andrew slow down.'

Andrew burst out laughing, loving my terror.

'Glad I could amuse you. I thought you were trying to impress, not give me a heart attack.'

He suppressed a scowl, then chuckled. 'Just wait.'

A sign on the side of the road read: *Waterfall.*

We pulled up at what looked like a shed with an open window. The man didn't say a word, didn't look up from what he was reading, just pointed to a wooded area. The sun was scorching now and the heaviness of the food sat on me. I was lightheaded from the mimosas.

There was a multitude of steps. We walked up and up, the steps unending until we reached a worn trail. We ducked and avoided branches and bushes and then we stood in front of water. There was only a small piece of ground, which meant we stood side by side. The lake was small; it looked man made. There was a waterfall with a small amount of water trickling out. Trees surrounded us, the leaves blocked the sun, making the area dark. Instead of cooling, it brought a closeted feel. It amplified the heat. Coupled with the restricted space for a walkway, I felt locked in. Stifled. Andrew scratched his jaw.

'This is where Adonis died in Aphrodite's arms.'

'Is that why you brought me here? Am I meeting the same fate?'

He cocked his head and grinned.

'Aphrodite didn't kill him. She loved him. She tried to bring him back.'

The water looked stagnant. A green film floated on top. I wasn't sure if my vision was off or whether it was the alcohol in the mimosa, or the early rise, or the heat, or the scary road, or the unused to gestures, but something became too much. I felt shaky and off balance.

'Andrew, I don't feel that great.'

He caught my arm, balanced me. 'Let's get you back to the car.'

I couldn't breathe. I needed a breeze. My legs buckled. Andrew didn't question me. He lifted me into his arms and carried me as if I were a child. I nuzzled into him, into the smell of him, into the familiar feel of his skin, into his safety. Instead of calming me, it felt worse. It was all too different. The change was too much. Andrew lay me softly in the passenger seat of the car. He ran to the driver's seat and turned the ignition on. He drove off; he knew I needed to go.

On the drive back I saw the sheer drop, closer to me this time, on my side. The lack of roof made it seem easier to fall off the edge. My chest tightened and closed. My heart rate quickened so much it jumped and felt like it touched against bone. Breath left me. A pressure pressed down from outside of me, onto my breastbone and moved up my throat. Blood whooshed to my head. The pressure filled inside my brain and I knew I would pass out. Yet I knew I wasn't fainting. It was more than that. The pressure built, expanded until there was no more room in my skull. I was going to die. I couldn't. I wasn't ready. I didn't want to leave the kids. I didn't want to leave Andrew.

I grabbed his hand then, needing him and his quiet reassurances, looking for that steadfastness. Andrew could always talk me down when life got too much, when panic took over. This was much worse. Something more was going on. It was not lost on me that at the moment I thought I was dying, the only person I looked for was Andrew. He knew by my grasp I was in trouble; I saw his concern, I tried to talk, but the words I needed to say wouldn't come, because I zoned out, became wordless. It didn't matter because I could see Andrew didn't need the words, he already knew everything that needed to be said. The world became fuzzy, nothing made sense. He stopped the car, not caring about any cars in front or behind, I understood the urgency because I felt it too. My head was off kilter, my balance shifted, sounds were tinny, my view brighter, clearer, so clear I could almost see through things, could feel them. Clarity brought the truth. For so long, I believed I would only be happy when I joined Adam in death. Now I understood I wasn't ready. I wasn't ready to join him.

'Look at me, Adaline. You are OK.'

'I can't breathe,' I said, between gasps.

'Look at me, we'll breathe together.' He closed his eyes and took an exaggerated breath. I couldn't, I struggled to maintain an order to my breathing. He continued in and out. I broke it down to just focusing on the shape of his mouth, timing it until I fell in line with him. It helped. Breathing to his beat calmed me enough to let the panic attack find a rhythm. Each time I thought of it as an actual thing, it grabbed hold of me again. My chest rose again. I was a caged animal, I had to escape, I had to get out of there. Andrew placed his hands on the side of my face.

'You are safe. Keep looking in my eyes. Believe me. We will get through this together.'

I tried to twitch away, to break myself lose so I could run. He held me there.

'Believe me. You are safe. Nothing will happen to you now. I didn't stop him. I should have been able to stop him, but I couldn't. I wasn't there. I'm sorry for not being there. I'm here now.'

My hands went over his. We breathed in unison. We did not look away. We stayed that way until my gasps subdued. My hands were still shaky, but the brightness shifted. Colours slipped to normal. I saw the world again. Trees and sky and road and Andrew. And cars behind us.

'We need to move.'

'Shush,' Andrew said. He wiped a strand of my hair away. 'Let them wait, Ad.'

'That will panic me more. Go on, I'll be OK now.'

Andrew reluctantly drove on to the relief of the drivers behind. Their politeness surprised me for not beeping. They had seen our interaction, the lack of roof had given them plenty of entertainment. I avoided looking over the drop, frightened it would spark another onset of fear.

'I haven't had an attack in a long time. You always knew how to calm me.'

Andrew shrugged, a sadness over him. Remembering Adam. The panic attacks were synonymous with our baby's death. I closed my eyes for the rest of the windy road. Andrew drove for a good ten minutes and it's what I needed. Time to slow my rapid heart and overthinking brain. I opened them when we stopped. He had pulled in, overlooking the water of Coral Bay.

'Do you want me to stay quiet?' he asked.

'No, talk. It'll distract me.'

'I think I went overboard here. I was so desperate to convince you to give us another chance, I slapped ten years of romance into the one day. I just wanted you to know how much I want this, how much I want you. But I overwhelmed you.'

I didn't talk for a while, as I tried to gather the words correctly, to order them in my jumbled brain. Andrew waited, I always marvelled at his patience.

'Do you know what I feel most, Andrew? Grateful. It was the shock I needed. Because thinking I might die made me see how it would feel. How empty it would feel to turn away from you. From your love. I was so caught up in thinking of all your wrongdoings, I forgot all the good. That man I met the other day, Edward, he said something that stuck with me, about how the things you fall in love with in a person can become the very things you hate. But then, when they are gone, they are the traits you miss the most. I get it. Your calmness drew me to you and how rock solid you always were. After the children, your calmness felt more like disinterest sometimes and it bugged me. I forgot how I needed you to be calm, to help balance me. The times you held me after Adam. The sadness you must have felt too. How you shielded me from your hurt to protect me. How strong you tried to be, even though your heart was breaking, when you picked out the little coffin because I couldn't bear it. The silence it brought between us. The wedge that formed. Then Maria. Or what I thought happened with Maria. Your betrayal took over me, the hurt I thought you put me through replaced my love. Resentment wrapped around me and I felt broken, like a part of me died inside. If I'm honest, I think a part of me did die with Adam.'

Andrew's breath caught. In his suppression of his tears, his voice came out disjointed. 'I think a part of me did too. I think of him all the time, of what he would have looked like, what he would do now.'

'I thought you just got on with it. Your days went on whereas I couldn't function, couldn't breathe. The only reason I carried on in the end was because of the kids.'

'My days went on because someone had to keep it together and I don't mean that as a dig. I needed to be the rock Adaline because that gave me a role. It gave me something I could make sense of while hoping it was helping you. I was trying to be strong even though inside I wanted to die too. He was my son too.'

The tears came. 'Adam *was* your son too. I'm sorry for not protecting him, I'm sorry I walked down that corridor. My instincts told me something was off. I shouldn't have put myself in that situation. I would have blamed me.'

'Never Adaline, never. I blamed me. I should have listened to you when you suggested going on early maternity leave, I knew you were tired, I knew you could have done with a rest, but I wanted you to keep as much holidays until after. If you had taken it early, you wouldn't have been at the hospital. I should have protected you. It was me that failed you.'

It was Andrew's turn to let go. He cried then, sobs that tore into me, the pain raw and unleashed. I leant over and clasped onto him. We held each other. I held my Andrew. He hadn't changed. He was the same Andrew I met and fell in love with, the man I said my vows with, the man I gave my body to and the man I had grown to despise.

Andrew never changed. The way I saw him had.

My ingratitude had changed the picture of who the man holding me was. That was the truth; I stopped being grateful for being loved by him. I had taken love as a given, like it was compulsory instead of a choice.

Years of grief and anger and sexual frustration and annoyance liquified into a gush of tears.

'What have I done? What did I do to us? All this time I blamed you, but how could you be interested when I was so ungrateful, so cold to you?'

'Adaline, let's not forget I was an arsehole.'

We both laughed.

'I knew you were grieving, and I still acted that way. It was down to me to fix it, and I didn't. I don't blame you.'

'Well, even if you don't, I'm sorry.'

'I'm sorry too.'

We kissed each other with open eyes. It seemed to me we were looking at the other like it was that first time on the beach again.

'I had the rest of the day planned but I can see you're spent. Do you want to go home to the hotel?'

'What was the plan?'

'I was going to drive to the rock of Aphrodite. Supposedly, if you swim around the rock, it makes you a year younger. Then I was going to take you for a boat trip, followed by watching the sun rise in a house I rented in Tala.'

I laughed. 'Overkill all right, I would have keeled over. A swim around a rock could be nice, though. It might erase some wrinkles.'

* * *

I was coy getting undressed in front of him, like a teenager, as I discarded my clothes onto the sand. Even though he had seen me naked a million times, even though he had kissed every millimetre of my body. Even though he had seen my scars and stroked them and still loved me. This was different. I was shy like the first time he saw me take off my clothes because there was something new to that day. You can know someone all your life and still discover things, you can still have sides that need to be uncovered.

Cyclamen flowers covered the hills leading down to the beach. I saw it as a sign. We held hands as we stepped into the water. Cold and welcome after the claustrophobic heat that gripped me by the waterfall; I let the water engulf me. Let the self-inflicted baptism cleanse away the hurt and resentment I held onto for far too long. We swam towards the rock and as Andrew made symmetrical strokes by my side, I realised I didn't care less about the legend. All I cared about was I could see my husband again. My Andrew.

I stopped and tread water, then called to him, 'I don't want to swim around the rock, Andrew.'

He swam back to me. 'What's wrong? Are you feeling panicky again?'

I shook my head. 'I don't want to swim around it. I don't want to be a year younger. Doing that would mean I have to lose one of my years. I don't want to lose any that have you in it.'

Andrew held me then and kissed me. As I dipped under with the weight of his embrace, my toes tipped sand. With the safety of shallowness underneath, I kissed Andrew back. We kissed like teenagers and for once I didn't care who saw me. There were no more words between us, there were no more untruths. I wrapped my legs and arms around him, and our laughter swam away with the waves.

After, we sat on the sand and watched the other people, the water and the sunlight as it glistened on the top. We just took in the day.

We skipped the boat trip, my head still a little woozy for a stay on the water. Andrew drove us to Tala, up in the hills, where we went to a food market and bought food to BBQ. Andrew knew my preferences well; the house was all marble and leather. With a view that rivalled the one I saw that morning. We went out to the back and saw the infinity pool that seemed to drop into the ocean miles away. A hot tub tucked discreetly to the side. Andrew fired up the BBQ. I poured us both a drink of white wine and alternated between watching him and the view in front of me. Something healed in me sitting there. For the first time since Adam, I felt fully content. As we watched the sunset, the lights from the houses below turned on one by one like fireflies dancing in the air.

'It won't get better than this, will it?' I asked.

'No, I'm afraid it's downhill after this place. But I never cared where I lived as long as we were happy.'

I remembered our wedding day, and how the thought had struck me then, that I'd reached the pinnacle of happiness. I had been so wrong. There had been so many happy memories since then. And there would be so many more to come.

We found our way back to each other through our bodies, exploring as if we were new lovers. In a way we were, our bodies had changed so much over the years, but instead of feeling self-conscious of my lumps and scars and stretch mark's, I felt proud, because every mark bore a story, every scar was proof of my survival. Of our survival. He kissed the scar that took our baby's life for the longest amount of time. The raised, thinner skin now a connection for us both to him. We had faced the tatters of our relationship and pieced it together like a fragile jigsaw. We could stand back now and see no pieces missing. Some were a little bent, some definitely with frayed corners, but there, all the same.

I believed when the initial, intense love petered out, it left for good. Once it faded, it disappeared and that was your lot. Now I see if you want it enough, you can retrieve love, you can get it back, and when it comes, it's deeper because now you have years and years of experience and memories to back it up. And the pain you've experienced, the hurt and regret, can be a stepping stone to lift you higher. Instead of staying down and wallowing, you can stand on the ground of forgiveness, only cementing the relationship more.

I think we come back to ourselves. Our loves, our likes and the things we've once wanted. We forget our dreams for a while; we need to sift through pain and crap so when the good happens again we'll appreciate them. When we find ourselves again, we realise the importance of those dreams, and this time we are unwilling to cast them aside. Or ignore them any longer. And when we get a taste for that discarded dream, it tastes even sweeter than before.

As we made love for the hundredth time that holiday, Andrew sang into my belly button.

'Oh Ad-da-line.

Why d'you look so fine?

What can I do to make you mine?

You know she don't mean a dime?

I'll give her up if you give me some time.

Let me prove that I'll walk you down the line.'

I kissed him. We sang the chorus together.

'Cos there's a fire in you,

That lights a fire in me,

Oh can't you let it be,

give into your destiny,

take me out of this agony.'

Last Day

The next morning, our last, I asked Andrew to wait for me as I made my last walk through Paphos. The church doors were open. There was no priest, or anyone else in sight. I sat in a chair in the first row and spoke out loud to the altar, to the painted faces, to the church and whoever was up there.

'I want you to know I blamed you. For letting my child die. I'm still angry. You took him from us. Before he could feel our love. You never gave us a chance to show him how much he meant. You never let me see him grow up. I understand I have to let go a little. I have to leave some of the pain. That's why I'm here, to mark this. To say I am going to do things differently. We are going to do things differently. I have another chance, but it will only work if I try to live. Living without the blame. Without blaming myself all the time.'

There was a noise, the sound of the door swinging slightly in the wind. It continued to swing then bang, swing then bang. I waited. No one was there.

I let the silence and the pain in. In that church, I let my tears come because I wanted to empty. I let out a groan that turned into a wail and with that sound, with that expulsion, something left and I hollowed out. It whooshed from me, and instead of gaining energy, it drained me and left me exhausted. Even though the tears stopped, I was unsure how I would make the journey back to the hotel.

I heard birdsong then. From above. I looked up at the dome of the arched church. There, on a wire above me, was a solitary bird. A swallow. It craned its head. As if it looked down on me.

'Hello Adam,' I whispered.

The swallow flew in a circle and then landed again on its wiry perch.

This was my sign.

Adam felt my love. Adam knew my grief, and he was here now to tell me he wanted me to stop crying. That it was time to be happy. Time to forgive myself. Other people could say I was crazy, that it was just a bird that flew into a cool space away from the heat, but they weren't beside me. They didn't feel what I felt. They didn't see the way the swallow looked down on me. I believed. That was what mattered.

I walked to the altar. Touched the smooth wood. Looked at the images on the wall. Spoke to them.

'It wasn't you, was it? You didn't do these things to me. That man done it. That sick man done it. You've been here all along trying to pick up my pieces. Whoever you are. You are the one who sent the robin. Who sent this swallow.'

The swallow flew away. My chest puffed with gratitude. I took one last look around that church.

'Thank you. For looking after my Adam.'

I walked out of that church, and although I would always have pain from the loss, I now felt Adam around me. My body was a dead child lighter.

We filled up the car with our luggage ready for the airport and waved at Nicholas and Marina as they stood at the doorway to the hotel. There was an excitement between us, between Andrew and I. The excitement replaced our secrets. Replaced the truths we couldn't bear to face. But facing those fears, allowing the truth in, had brought us together at the same time.

There was still so much of that country I wanted to see: Limassol, the eerie silent village of Famagusta, the crossing of borders into Kyrenia. I wanted to buy lace in Nicosia and count the flowers at the Akamas Peninsula. To drive over the volcanic Troodos and see the sights from Mount Olympus. Or travel to the village of Chlorakas and find the Adonis Baths and let my hair get wet under the huge waterfall. I wanted to dance in Bar street until the sun rose. To retire in Tala. On that trip, sights and excursions weren't the objective. I'd seen enough. Because I uncovered my husband again and he revealed myself to me.

I was thankful for that trip. For saying the words we needed to. To live on with the proof life wasn't a certainty. I was grateful for the peace that came over me, for the forgiveness I allowed to come. Most of all, I was thankful for that vow I made in fear on the plane because I'd kept my promise to decide. We had an answer, one that I didn't dream was possible. One I didn't dare to dream about.

I made another promise as I sat in the car. A vow to book a visit back the following year, the minute I got home. The kids would love Paphos. The car was hot. I rolled down the window, put my arm on the sill. Let my skin feel the last rays of the beautiful sun in that beautiful country. I said a silent, regretful goodbye to the rays; I was not ready for the Irish winter. What I was ready for was to get back home, to our children, to our life. A life I could look forward to. To home, *our* home again. Cyprus had again worked its magic.

Andrew sat in the car and smiled at me. There was no vein in sight.

'Ready?' he said.

'Ready,' I said.

As the car drove off, I splayed my fingers out to admire the diamonds in my engagement and wedding ring. They glistened as the sun hit the facets. I would never take them off again.

Enjoy this book? You can make a difference.

Honest reviews of my books help bring them to the attention of other readers. If you enjoyed The Truth Between Us, I would really appreciate if you could spend a few minutes leaving your feedback. Reviews help the buyer understand the 'feel' of the book so your review could be the difference in whether someone picks it up.

My deepest thanks,
Natasha Karis.

Special thanks to Linda O' Neill for her nursing expertise and encouragement and Norma McElligott for her eagle eye.

About the Author

Natasha Karis is the author of The Truth Between Us, The Initiates, The Initiation of Alayne Adams and The Happiness Initiative. She is currently writing her third fiction novel. She lives in Cork, Ireland.

Want another story?

If you subscribe to the Natasha Karis newsletter, you will get:
The Initiation of Alayne Adams. (an uplifting prequel novella)
Exclusive cover reveals.
Giveaways.

Get it today at: https://www.subscribepage.com/initiation

You can connect with me on:

https://natashakaris.com
https://www.facebook.com/natashakarisbooks
https://www.bookbub.com/authors/natasha-karis
https://www.instagram.com/natashakarisbooks

Subscribe to my newsletter:

https://www.subscribepage.com/initiation

Also by Natasha Karis

The Initiates
A suicide note. Five lost students. One teacher who will stop at nothing to help them.

Teacher Alayne Adams loves nothing more than to help. So when the Principal of her school in Knockfarraig, a small town in Cork, Ireland, suggests a series of detentions for some wayward sixth year students, she volunteers. But the discovery of a note reveals one student intends to end their life. When she questions who wrote it, there is silence. Alayne has no choice but to take action. Taking inspiration from a book based on ancient teachings, Alayne embarks on a series of life lessons that encourages each of them to discover ways to heal their pain. Can she steer them onto a path that will change all their lives?

Includes a link to the free eBook The Happiness Initiative, a practical exercise book based on Alayne's teachings.

The Initiation of Alayne Adams
Torn between partying with her friends and doing the right thing, Alayne's life lacks any direction. Until an altercation leaves her spiralling.

Left with nowhere to turn, Alayne tries to find her way. But an encounter in a library opens up new possibilities and a chance to learn. Can Alayne change or will old habits prove too strong?

Read the prequel novella for free at www.natashakaris.com

The Happiness Initiative
TIRED OF BEING CONTROLLED BY YOUR EMOTIONS? ARE
YOU UNSATISFIED WITH THE LIFE YOUR LIVING?

Discover ways to shift a negative emotion. Learn how to work up the
emotional poles. Figure out what it is you really want. This book uses
practical exercises to help you get to the heart of what makes YOU
happy.

These are Alayne Adams, from The Initiates further teachings.

JOIN THE HAPPINESS INITIATIVE TODAY!

The Breaking of Dawn
**Dawn Moloney cannot say no. But life is about to step in and
force her to.**

Dependable Dawn spends her life doing what others tell her to. Taken
for granted by her work and friends, she can never find the words to
stand up to them. Nobody takes Dawn seriously, including herself.
She yearns for more meaning but hasn't a clue how to find it. Until a
series of events causes Dawn to lose everything. Forced to move back
to her childhood home, Dawn tries to work out what to do with her
life.

Can she start again, or even better, find the strength to discover who
she is?

Due to be released in early 2022. Available for preorder now.